The Shimmering – ka 'olili

The Shimmering - ka 'olili

island stories
by Keola Beamer

843 Waine'e Street, F5 # 685
Lahaina, HI 96761-1685

843 Waine'e Street, F5 # 685
Lahaina, HI 96761-1685
(808) 661 0090

This book is a work of fiction. Names, characters, places and incidents either are products of the author's imagination or are used fictitiously. Any resemblance to actual events or locales or persons, living or dead, is entirely coincidental.

© 2002 Keola Beamer

All rights reserved, including the right of reproduction in whole or in part in any form.

Printed in the United States of America

ISBN 0-9713877-0-2

Library of Congress Control Number: 2002111073

Edited by Betty Santos and Kaliko Beamer-Trapp

'Ohe Books are printed on acid-free paper and meet the guidelines for permanence and durability of the Council on Library Resources.

Cover Design by Sueann Carter / Photograph by Tom Pfeiffer
Book Design by Sueann Carter / Keola Beamer Photograph by Matt Thayer

Glossary by Kaliko Beamer-Trapp

For information regarding special discounts for bulk purchases, please contact 1 800 945-5651 or orders@kbeamer.com

In memory of my grandparents,
Pono and Louise Beamer

Contents

Acknowledgments	ix
The Shimmering – ka ʻolili	1
Pōhaku	27
Our Ticket to Cannes	43
It Swims When You Sleep	53
Nā Iwi	81
My Beautiful Puka	109
Hānau Hope	141
Stalking Haunani	157
Glossary	179
About The Author	201
Selected Works	205

Acknowledgments

I live in a world enriched by love, friendship, and the sweet sounds of *kī hōʻalu*. I have no idea how I got to be this lucky, and I am truly grateful. In my heart, I try to begin every day with the simple word, *mahalo*.

I would like to acknowledge the help and contributions of the following people:

My wife - Moanalani Beamer, Betty Santos, George Vincent, Nona Beamer, James D. Houston, Dr. Sam Gon III - Director of Science - The Nature Conservancy, Keaumiki Akui, Sueann Carter, Keola Donaghy, Eileen Adams, Maile Meyer.

A special *mahalo* is due my brother, Kaliko Beamer–Trapp for the excellent glossary he prepared at the end of this book.

The Shimmering - ka ʻolili

I breathe raggedly, my sides heaving from the exertion of running through the dense underbrush. I have run so far and so hard that I can taste the metallic flavor of my own blood. It wells up in my lungs and foams at the edge of my mouth. Behind me, the ravenous wailing shifts upward in pitch. Soon they will be upon me.

Ahead there is a change in the scent-pattern of the forest. The fragrance of the *ʻōhiʻa* bark is undercut by the dark and musky smell of damp earth. It is my beloved. She offers her own body to shield me from the pursuing beasts. As tendrils of thick gray fog reach down through the high branches of the *ʻōhiʻa lehua* trees, I chant her name. I sniff the air and move cautiously towards the hidden entrance of the cave.

The fog parts for my passage and swirls down the embankment, moving among the dark red blossoms of *lehua*. In the upland forest, the first stars appear through the high canopy of leaves. Seeing the points of light, I am lost in the reverie of my thoughts. Perhaps when one is close to death, memories of life unfold to ease the passage. I recall the curve of her neck, and the way I pressed her to the earth, her hair flowing around her body like a soft, black wave. I breathe more evenly and I smile. She has taught me to appreciate the mysterious beauty of the forest and even in the destruction I have caused, the beauty persists. A cold wind descends from the mountain, and as the mist swirls amongst the uprooted *hāpuʻu*, their grotesque and fallen stumps sail gently beneath the soft glow of a crescent moon.

The howling pack of canines approach, tearing through the shrubbery. I can almost feel the gnashing of their serrated and deadly teeth. The hair on my back bristles. I have only moments left. I flee to the cave and penetrate her warm darkness. Praying that the wind will blow my scent further into the depths and away from the pursuing beasts, I kneel beneath the dripping ceiling.

There will be another time, another life. I have reached the end of my journey. Holding her name just once more on my tongue, I settle in the darkness and begin *ka ʻolili* – the shimmering.

When the hunters come crashing through the undergrowth, their weapons become entangled in the *ʻamaʻumaʻu* and the *ʻuhaloa*. It is as I wish, but in the swirling mist, the lead dog of the pack breaks free of the stubborn weeds and runs snarling into the dark entrance of the cave. He is a devil dog, that one, and somehow he has found me. When his jaws open and he lunges for the soft flesh of my side, I chant to my beloved—

Kekē hoʻi ka niho	The teeth are exposed
ʻAneʻane nanahu mai	Ready to bite
Moku au lā	I am bitten,
Moku au lā.	I am bitten.

I scream in agony.

Her voice, like no other, responds in haste. I hear the deep rumbling beneath the earth, the swift tremor of her anger moving down the flanks of *Kīlauea*, towards the sea. In the closeness of the cave, the devil dog is frightened. He loosens his jaws and backs away.

* * * * * * * * * *

"Eh Manny, you not going believe dis," the hunter says, shining the big flashlight in my face. My hair is entangled with dry twigs and *honohono* grass. Saliva hangs from the side of my mouth.

"Why one big *haole* hippie wen come insai hea?" the other one says, sheathing the knife. He kneels beside me and raises my head. "Mus' be mushroom or something. Da guy naked, he stay stone out of his mind." The beam from the flashlight moves down my body. "Eh… shit, da buggah bleeding." The light illuminates the pool of blood next to my side. The other hunter reaches for his pack. There are two beams of light now, both men aiming their flashlights at the glistening pool of my blood. The beams of light move erratically, reflections glowing on the far wall of the cave. The reflected light paints the cave red.

"Call the KMC ambulance fo' come quick, Derek."

"Stupid mutt," Derek says, dragging the animal out by the loose folds of skin on his neck. He gives it a hard kick with his boot. The big dog growls and scurries away. The hunter straightens up from the entrance of the dripping cave and lifts the walkie-talkie to his mouth.

Strapped to the gurney, I roll slowly towards the ambulance. The wheels lurch in the loose gravel and the bright red emergency light flashes repeatedly on my face. Through the drizzling rain, I can see a fine mist hovering in the moonlight. The shining red beacon reflects from the wet boughs and the tangle of *'ōhi'a* trees surrounding the parking lot. Engines 12 and 17 idle on the wet asphalt, their exhausts misting in the cool air. The men are tired and cold, their muscles aching from the long haul down the trail. They stand beside the fire trucks, smoking cigarettes, putting away ropes and emergency gear. I blink as the *ua li'ili'i,* the light rain, clings to my beard and the lashes of my eyes. The emergency medics slide the gurney into the back of the ambulance and close the door. I do not resist. I lie exhausted beneath the sheets. When we are bloodied, it takes longer for the *'olili* to complete.

The ambulance moves across the parking lot in the light rain. The vehicle picks up speed and crosses the centerline of the wet pavement. I hear the tires drumming on the lane dividers of Volcano Highway. In the confines of the ambulance, the scent of the Emergency Medical Technician next to me reaches my nostrils. A sour aroma emanates from the perspiration in the hollow beneath his left arm. I suspect that he has an undiagnosed form of lymphatic cancer. He will be dead soon. The uniformed medic works quickly to attach the intravenous line into the thick vein of my left arm. When the solution drips slowly, he seems satisfied.

He asks slowly and clearly, "Who are you?" He looks closely at my face. "What is your name?"

I raise my head and struggle to respond: "***Ka haole nui maka 'ālohilohi***," I growl softly. I cannot speak. After the *'olili* there is a period of alignment, a period of silence and fog. It is in this space that the shadow of the *kino lau* is released. I will wait to speak again.

The medic puts his gloved hand on my forehead and says, "Easy now. It's O.K., take it easy."

I lay my head back down on the gurney and close my eyes. I am *ka haole nui maka 'ālohilohi*, I am the large foreigner with the bright eyes. It is my blood that seeps through the white gauze. As the ambulance speeds down the incline, I listen to the rain and the swoosh of tires on the wet pavement. I begin to remember who I am. The content of my thoughts, at first expressed in the Hawaiian language, metamorphoses into English as the *'olili* finally solidifies.

My name is Kenneth Weir. I was born in the winter of 1964 in Socorro, New Mexico. I am unmarried. I have no siblings. My parents were killed in an automobile accident when I was 17 years old. I am six feet two inches tall. I have brown hair and I weigh 217 pounds. I am a volcanologist; I undertake the classification of volcanic activity and study the nature and causes of volcanic eruptions.

I served a brief internship at Stromboli, an active volcano that lies on an island off the coast of Italy. I came to the Hawaii Volcanoes National Park Observatory in 1994 as a research associate. I am currently employed in seismic data correlation for the National Park Service.

I was working at the observatory and writing my dissertation in volcanology when Nicholas Granger, one of the Park's senior scientists, invited me to his home for dinner. Nicholas had a fondness for me and took me under his guidance at the Observatory. Over a glass of merlot, he intimated that it might be good idea for me to "broaden the base of my understanding." I wasn't quite following him at first. Nicholas was something of a radical in our field in that he believed that a life based solely on intellectual acquisition was incomplete. He was a proponent of contextual learning. As Nicholas described it, this was learning that occurs in close relationship with actual experience. Since the study of Hawaiian volcanology could not conceivably be separated from the word "Hawaiian," Nicholas was suggesting that I might be missing part of the equation. I was listening intently when he suggested that it might be good for me to learn the Hawaiian language, implying that what I learned would aid in the development of the historical references outlined in my dissertation. When he discovered that I was generally receptive to this idea, he further recommended that I join one of the *hālau hula* on the Island. He saw this as a way to gain a more balanced perspective of my work "from within a cultural context." Since I respected Nicholas a great deal, I gave these ideas considerable deliberation. Both suggestions intrigued me. The University of Hawaii at Hilo was widely recognized as having the best Hawaiian language department in the state and I had heard that there were several *hālau* of merit located nearby.

After a period of investigation and earnest inquiry, I was invited to join a *hālau hula* in Hilo town. In a few short months, I was studying the basics of the art form called *hula*. At approximately the same time, I enrolled at the University and began my studies of *'ōlelo Hawai'i* - the Hawaiian language. My studies and work at the observatory continued without interruption. I experienced a true love for the things I was learning. I began to understand that all around us, the unique aspects of things Hawaiian were diminishing in the hurried pace of the 21st century. These sad contemplations came to me at night when I was alone in my cabin.

At the end of the next year, the men in the *hālau* moved towards the study of *kahiko*. *Kahiko* was the ancient form of Hawaiian dance and we met to chant and dance for several days of each week. I was a good student; I worked hard, I listened to the *kumu hula*, and I learned the rudiments of fixed movement in time that comprise the basic elements of *kahiko*. It took a while for my big *haole* body to understand and feel the rhythm. At first, I was *hemahema*, awkward and unskilled, but I kept at it. Perhaps someday, I hoped, I could become a decent practitioner of the art of *hula kahiko*.

I matriculated into third year Hawaiian language as the *hālau* focused on a series of chants honoring the Fire Goddess Pele. As soon as this endeavor commenced, I experienced an integral sense of peace, a quiet grounding of my spirit. I felt at my best with these chants. My complete acceptance of them and, it seems, of them to me, was a mysterious epiphany. In a manner of speaking, I experienced a religious conversion. A feeling of warmth and completeness washed over me each time *Kumu* raised his voice to chant—

Aia lā ʻo Pele i Hawaiʻi ʻeā, ke haʻa maila i Maukele ʻeā

ʻŪhī, ʻūhā mai ana ʻeā, ke nome aʻela i nā Puna ʻeā

Ka mea nani ka i Paliuli ʻeā, ke pulelo aʻela i nā pali ʻeā

As the months went by, I made slow progress in the completion of my dissertation. I continued my study of the Pele chants and I continued dancing with the *hālau*. Except for the occasional bout of loneliness, I felt that I had a good life. I enjoyed the rich cultural tapestry of the Hawaiian people and on a professional level, my work at the Observatory was interesting and intellectually rewarding. In short, I was content.

But this contentment was an illusion.

One afternoon, I was sitting at my desk at the Observatory, adjusting the calibration of a tiltometer, when suddenly a Hawaiian hawk, an ʻio, landed on the ledge of the window and raked its sharp claws across the thick pane of glass. The noise of those brittle claws against the glass startled me. I snapped my head up and looked at the window. It was eerie. The dark bird stared in at me intensely as the seismograph in the corner plotted a long upward arc. On the monitor of my computer screen, a message coalesced from the vaporous, green phosphors. It said:

Come, my beloved

The skin on my arm turned to gooseflesh. The ʻio shrieked and flew from the window ledge. A few seconds later, the message was gone and the screen returned to the data I was running. How odd, I thought, rubbing my tingling arm and logging into the system administrator files. I was checking to see who had tapped into my computer. Willard Drakes, the new supervisor, was a difficult, irritating man. Maybe he had suddenly developed a sense of humor. More likely, this was a hacker trying to break in to our network from outside. I ran a complete access check and found no other users logged on to the system. I walked around the lab, peeking into the partially opened door of the administration office. Drakes wasn't even in the building. I ran a complete virus scan, checked the firewall and again found nothing. This was extremely odd, I thought. Extremely odd. I backed up the data, executed a low level re-formatting of the main drive and went to lunch.

In the small dining room that day, the lasagna seemed unappetizing. The fresh avocados that someone had bought from home and placed on the counter seemed much more appealing. The texture of the avocados felt good in my mouth and the flavor was exquisite. I felt guilty, eating several of them, piling the green skins high on my plastic tray.

That night, I lay in my bed reading Martha Beckwith's "Hawaiian

Mythology." I drifted off. Instead of sleeping soundly, as I usually did, I experienced a disturbing dream. In the vivid mental imagery, I scurried through the caliginous growth of the forest floor. I was moving swiftly, down low to the ground, as the forest around me exploded in fascinating colors and smells.

At the observatory the next day, we had a small celebration in honor of Nicholas, who was leaving for a year's sabbatical. Some of the staff had bought cake and ice cream. I had constructed a *lei haku*, made of *laua'e* fern and *liko lehua*. I placed the *lei* on his shoulders, shook his hand heartily and wished him luck. I was sad that Nicholas was leaving. I had wanted more time with him to discuss my mystifying computer problems. After the festivities, Supervisor Drakes approached my desk with his hands in his pockets and a tight smile. He said, "Weir, clean up this crap before you leave. This is a professional institution, not a high school prom." He was referring to the small leaves and bits of *liko* that had fallen on the floor from the *lei haku*. It was Drake's way of warning me that now that Nicholas was gone, I had better watch my step.

During my studies with the *hālau*, I met an attractive woman named Cassandra. She was a divorcee, in her third year at UH Hilo. Sometimes I'd pick her up and take her to see a movie in town. We seemed to enjoy each other's company. I was hoping that our relationship would lead to something more substantial, but I wasn't quite sure if she felt the same way. Cassandra and her roommate had three large dogs. Often, when I went to pick her up, I brought a pull-toy or a rubber ball. I'd play with the dogs in the driveway while I waited for her to get ready. As I played with them that day, I detected a strange metallic scent emanating from inside the house. It was the smell of blood and something else. Cassandra came to the porch and said that she was not feeling well. She said she would prefer to stay home and rest.

"Are you feeling all right?" I asked.

"Just female trouble," she mentioned, somewhat embarrassed, "I'm having my period."

We have an alternating schedule at the Observatory. I was working the night shift again, correlating seismic data. The wind picked up suddenly from the crater, howling along the ridgeline and the under the eves of the building. It was two o'clock in the morning when another terrifying missive appeared on my screen. This time, the green phosphors telegraphed:

I chant from deep within - your name so sweet

Kama - my own

The lateness of the hour and the fact that I was alone in the building increased my apprehension. The message really scared me. I ran all the computer checks I could think of and came up, again, with nothing. I was not a computer novice. I had worked around the damn things my entire professional life, but something very strange was happening here and it was infuriating. I emailed Drakes and requested that a qualified technician examine the operating system of every single computer in the system. Feeling tired and wired at the same time, I logged out from my machine and left the premises.

The sky was pink that early morning and the caustic smell of vog lingered along the highway. I opened the window of the jeep and felt the cold air engulf me. I inhaled the fumes deeply, smiling at the acrid smell. I was glad to be away from New Mexico and the dry expanse of red desert soil. I liked it here in the mist and the rain; I felt good in these Islands. I had my work. I had the *hālau*. I had my dissertation. Lost in these thoughts, I barely noticed the dark wings of a *pueo*, trailing effortlessly in the rear view mirror.

I drove to my small cabin in *Kīlauea*. My needs there were simple. A small wood-burning fireplace, a kitchen table, a few chairs, a desk, a bed. I took off my muddy boots and walked into the kitchen to make myself breakfast. I began by arranging the ingredients on the counter: mushrooms, onion, cheese. I pulled a dozen eggs out of the refrigerator and opened the cover of the container. The raw eggs looked so beautiful. I studied each one of them, lined up and nestled in the gray cardboard box. I felt my pulse quicken as I took a single egg from the carton, cupped it in my hand and bought it up to my nostrils, sniffing inquisitively. I placed the egg at eye level and studied its shape closely, admiring the porous, white surface of the shell. I rolled it gently in my fingers, feeling its weight. So round and smooth. So perfect. I extended my tongue and licked it softly. I licked it again, moving my tongue along the cool circumference. The egg had a clean taste, suggesting a deliciousness within. I placed the whole egg in between my teeth. I bit down slowly, cracking the shell and spilling the yolk and whites into my warm mouth. I cradled the yolk in my tongue, rolling it from side to side. Unable to contain my hunger any longer, I bit down abruptly. When the yolk burst and ran between my teeth, I swallowed greedily. It was an incredibly luscious taste. The flavor of the raw egg caused me to salivate uncontrollably. Bending over the small stainless steel sink, I consumed eight more eggs, gulping them down, shell and all. My thick saliva, the yolks and the whites, dripped from both sides of my mouth, splattering down the front of my flannel shirt.

At the observatory, Drakes came angrily up to my desk and threw the tech requisition on my desk.

"What the hell is this, Weir? We are not examining every damn computer in the building. Are you out of your mind?"

"Drakes," I tried to explain, "there's a real possibility of data corruption, if we can't…"

Drakes wouldn't let me finish, he put his hands on his hips and bellowed, "Then why don't you and your *lei* making friends wave some *ti* leaves around and voodoo the damn things. We are NOT spending any money on this ridiculous request. Jesus H. Christ, Weir, get a goddamn grip!" He stomped away, fuming.

I called Cassandra. She was feeling better, so I went over to pick her up. I honked the horn and opened the door of the jeep, taking the rubber ball from my jacket pocket. The canines refused to engage in any activity with me at all, no matter how many times I entreated them. They waited apprehensively on the porch and sniffed cautiously as I came near. When I went up the stairs, one of the big Alsatians began whining and crawling on his belly. He lowered his head, flattened his ears back and urinated like a puppy.

A few days later, I was studying the printouts of seismic activity along the northern rift zone. A *nēnē* goose, disrupted by the flow of hot air upwards from the crater, crashed heavily into the main observatory window. The big bird screamed, leaving a trail of blood smeared across the thick glass. I felt a sense of deja vu and deep dread. I turned my head slowly to the right and looked at the seismograph readings. The reading that was coming in was very specific. The chart was displaying precise movements in time, as though there was a form of intelligence at work. My hands trembled as I held the printout. I looked at the baseline and the peaks and translated the reading into a rhythm felt somewhere in the center of my chest. The seismograph had produced the definitive *kahiko* beat of the *pahu* drum; **U U – U TE TE / U U – U TE TE**

Another message appeared, at my computer monitor, this time in *'ōlelo Hawai'i*:

> O Kama hoi paha oe,
>
> Kanaka o ka pali ku
>
> O ka pali moe
>
> O ka pali kuhoho
>
> O ka pali ka'a o ka pohaku.

I understood these words.

Thou art indeed Kama,

The man of the high cliffs,

Of the low lying cliffs,

Of the steep cliffs,

Of the cliffs of the rolling stones.

I stared at the monitor with an ashen face. Then I pulled the jacket close to my body and shivered uncontrollably. My limbs were very cold. I read it again. My flesh began to crawl. I wondered if I was losing my mind.

At *hālau* that week, our *kumu* demonstrated a form of low crouching style called *'ai ha'a*. He said that it was very difficult and required considerable muscular strength in the upper thighs and calves. Though he was a master dancer, he appeared to strain a bit in demonstrating the low squatting movements of this style. In simple choreography accompanied by the large *pahu* drum, we each took turns, knees bent, squatting, moving. I was the last to attempt this exercise. To my surprise, the movement came easily. The strength in my lower body seemed formidable. Somehow, without my even noticing, the muscles in my stomach, thighs and calves had strengthened. It seemed natural to me, to move along the ground, down close to the earth. As the *pahu* beats continued, I expanded the movements of my body in concentric circles radiating outward and moved lower … and lower, closer to the wooden floor of the old gymnasium. I was moving very fast and very low, the *pahu* thundering. As I danced, I began to lose myself and I felt as though I was parting a veil, reentering the enigmatic forest world of the dream. As I closed my eyes and began to move *'ai ha'a* through the low undergrowth, the *pahu* drumming suddenly stopped.

I slowed my movement and closed. I straightened out uncomfortably and stood, turning to face the assembled students. The entire class was staring at me, their faces completely drained of color. I was sweating and breathing heavily in short, staccato, *uh- uh –uh* noises. At first, no other sound could be heard. Then, in the damp silence, I heard the shuffling of their bare feet. Almost as one, they backed away from me. I looked cautiously around the big gymnasium as the smell of fear permeated the air.

On the way back up the hill, the rain came down heavily on Volcano Highway, splashing in big, fat drops on the windshield of the jeep. I pulled over at Hirano Store to buy something for dinner. When I saw the salad bags of *hō'i'o* fern tips, I paused, feeling intense hunger pangs. I held the bag, sniffing, and moving my nostrils up and down the outside of it. I paid for the bag at the small counter, but before I even got back to the car, I tore through the plastic with my teeth, snorting with joy as I reached the small, delicious shoots within. I stood outside the store, near a cluster of swaying, green bamboo and ate greedily.

I ran back inside the store and bought five more bags. I would consume each one of those bags as I sat, hunched over in the front seat of the jeep. An elderly Japanese woman in a Camry pulled in to the space next to me. When the small terrier in the back seat saw me, he howled maniacally, lunging with his small, bared teeth at the inside of the window. I wiped my mouth with the back of my hand, still relishing the taste of the fern shoots. The woman seemed unable to control the animal, her bewildered and frightened face blurred by the heavy drip of rain on the glass. I reversed the jeep quickly. The clamoring of the little dog faded as lightening zigzagged across the black sky.

That night, there was a terrible thunderstorm. The power to the Observatory stalled, then re-energized, the battery back-ups kicking in and out. From the Volcano House, all the way down to the coast, the storm unleashed its fury. It pummeled the trees, tremendous bolts of lightening tearing through the *'ōhi'a* leaves. In the crater, the mist swirled and swirled, spinning counter-clockwise in the ghostly cauldron of Halemaʻumaʻu. As the worst of the storm stalled overhead, the security system of the building short-circuited, sending sparks flying across the room. The alarm system wailed and screamed in the building. One of the tiltometers on the southern flank illustrated a grotesque bulge in the earth. My stomach turned. This is impossible, I thought, struggling with my own sanity. In the horrible cacophony of the wind, rain and screaming alarms, my monitor flickered insanely and the streaking cursor messaged:

My beloved kane - more beautiful with each passing day

Trembling, almost useless, my fingers stabbed forcefully at the keyboard:

Who areYoU

Suddenly, the electrical power died in the lab and the computers crashed, their back-up circuits beeping intolerably. The shrieking alarms continued to wail until I could stand it no longer. I grabbed an emergency flashlight and left as quickly as I could, running through the puddles of the flooded parking lot. As I opened the door of the jeep, I could see lightning bursting in great sheets above the caldera. The world had gone insane. I was witnessing Nature, seized by dementia and wondering if perhaps, I too, was so afflicted. I shifted the jeep into gear and stomped on the accelerator.

I sped along the highway then pulled into the driveway of my small cabin. The branches of the *ʻōhiʻa lehua* were rubbing together, screeching and making sounds I had never heard. The trees swayed and shuddered in the onslaught of the howling wind. When I stepped out of the jeep, my boots sunk into the thick mud and I stood there in the pouring rain feeling lost and afraid. I took off my boots and my socks and I felt my bare feet sink into the cool, thick *lepo* of the driveway. The mud felt so good, so soothing. I walked slowly towards the steps of the porch, feeling the delicious wet earth beneath the arches of my feet. I looked towards the house. What I felt was inexplicable. The old house just didn't seem to suit me anymore. I thought of the small, uncomfortable chair at the kitchen table and the stiff bed in the back room. The house seemed unwelcoming, its furnishings awkward and unpleasant. Instead of going up the steps to the front door, I turned and walked to the small gate securing the crawl space beneath the house. I bent over and pushed it with my hand. The gate opened on screeching hinges.

I inhaled deeply. A musty, damp smell came from under the house. Hanging from the floor joists were long, ghostly wisps of spider webs, swinging in the blustering wind. I stared into the space, my eyes adjusting to the deep blackness. I found the low space comforting. I would be safe here, I knew. I removed my clothing, feeling the drops of rain on my bare chest. Then, I lowered myself *'ai ha'a* style into the sweet darkness. As I entered, the suspended cobwebs caught on my brow. Shredded bits of *liko lehua* and pieces of *'a'ali'i* drifted in with the storm to tangle in my hair. I raised my arms slowly and placed them in front of me, clasping both hands.

I pronounced the *kāhea*, **"Aia lā 'o Pele i Hawai'i 'eā,"** and paused. I didn't hold for long. The clouds cleared and the moon rose up magnificently from behind the ridge. Fingers of bluish-white moonlight reached for me through the latticework skirting the house. Above me, the striking thunder of the heavens synchronized into a distinct rhythmic pattern. **U U - U TE TE / U U - U TE TE.** It was the same fixed pattern of the seismograph reading. Inconceivably, the thunderclaps expressed the *pahu* beats of ancient *kahiko*.

I leapt into movement, dancing vigorously beneath the joists of the old floor. I circled in the damp earth, turning forward, turning back, the muscles in my thighs flexing and extending. I had never experienced this level of control over my own body before. It was as if my limbs were obeying my thoughts, not approximately, but exactly and precisely as I commanded. In raiment of spider-silk and the small shreds of leaves, I danced savagely in ʻai haʻa style. Though my body seemed capable of an incredible range of expression, the actual choreography or movement positions were telegraphed to me by a consciousness outside of my own. It was *hula* that was coming, not from me, but through me. The rhythmic cadences I enjoined were so powerful, so compelling that I felt inwardly changed. I was no longer afraid. I was no longer alone. I danced for those who had come before me and for those who follow. I danced for those who were born and those who would die. I danced with the inspired abandonment of human reason. In that dank small space beneath the old house, I felt connected to a life force much greater than my own. As it was power, then powerful I had become. The heavy beats of the celestial *pahu* thundered mightily in the dark night and for the first time ever in my life, I danced *kahiko* from the very depths of my being.

When the dance ended, my body was covered with a thin sheen of perspiration that glistened in the soft glow of moonlight. I felt an admiration in the tender fingers of that moonlight reaching towards me through the diamond spaces of the latticework. I felt it caress my shoulders, my chest, the engorged muscles in my thighs. Exhausted, I moved into the far corner of the low space, towards the rear of the old house. In the soft, soothing mud, I lay down on my side, breathing *uh-uh-uh* contentedly, as the rain dripped down the outside of the house.

I slept soundly through the night.

The next evening I went over to Cassandra's. I wanted her help in trying to understand what was happening to me. As I approached in the jeep, the three big dogs roared off of the porch, barking and snarling. They attacked the tires of the vehicle ferociously, snapping with their bare teeth at the door handle and window. The Akita jumped from the ground and up to the partly opened passenger window of the jeep. He hung partially through the window, snarling and snapping, his fangs bared and muzzle frothing. The thick hair on the back of my neck stood on end and I snarled in return, spraying the dashboard with saliva. I struck at him mightily with my right fist, crashing against the top of his skull and hammering his neck into the edge of the raised glass. The glass shattered. The dog was immediately silenced, shards of broken glass cutting into his jugular vein and vocal chords. Thick blood pulsed from his neck, running in rivulets down the inside of the door. He was still scrabbling with his rear legs, trying to gain purchase, when I yanked the steering wheel to the left and he fell heavily from the window. I felt the rear tire hit solidly, as it rolled completely over him. Beneath the surge of the engine, I heard the crunch of his ribcage. I quickly sped away.

I called Cassandra later from a pay phone at the village.

"Cassandra, I'm sorry," I said.

"Don't come back here anymore, EVER!" she screamed. "Stay away. You stay away!"

She slammed the phone down. In the drizzling rain, I listened to the dial tone and wondered what had become of my life.

It was unusually cold that evening. I turned on the light and looked at myself in the mirror. I used to think of myself as an attractive man, but I could no longer hold this belief. My beard was thick and bristly. My lateral incisors and canine teeth had elongated. The shape of my head was somehow protracted and my nose - well I'm not sure what that looked like, I couldn't see it anymore, my eyes were filled with tears. "Dear God," I thought. "What is happening to me?"

I lit a fire in the small fireplace and watched the sparking embers snap from the damp ʻōhiʻa logs. I lay on my side on the floor and struggled to understand the feelings that tormented me. Was it love that I feared the most? The unequivocal devotion of one being to another? I remembered the feeling of moonlight glistening on the pectoral muscles of my chest. Was this the love of an entity outside of my own world? Something more powerful than I could possibly imagine? I chewed on a piece of *'awa* root, enjoying the gritty taste of dirt on the small roots. The *'awa* numbed my gums and lips. I held the pulp on my tongue savoring the dry, wooden taste. I was losing hold of all that I had ever been, I thought, staring into the embers of the crackling fire.

Magically, the burning sparks rose in the wall of flames and spelled out:

You are loved by me, my Kama

Beautiful as the lehua blossom

That night, I chanted in the soft moonlight and smacked my thin, black lips. I danced, *'ai ha'a*, beneath the wooden floor of the small cottage until my legs were leaden and my ankles were weak from exertion. Again, I felt her embrace in the deep darkness, as she favored me with silk, shreds of *lehua*, and tiny fragments of fresh, white ginger. These tender ministrations of sweet *aloha* eased the loneliness in my heart. The ache that had haunted me for so many years was finally gone. For the first time since the death of my parents did I again feel loved. I closed and ended the *kahiko* and my tears fell, streaming through the coarse, black hair of my face. The world I had believed in for so many years, a world of rational thought, governed by the rules of scientific logic, was finally proven to be an illusion. It became clear to me that I had created my life from a false and vain intellectualism. The antiseptic world I fashioned was never able to fill even the smallest vacancy in my heart. My useless paradigm had failed. I felt relieved to let it go. I felt joy in its release. I felt it leave my chest and fly upward through the old wooden floor. I knew that a door to the past had closed, and that a new and mysterious one had to some extent, opened. I could see it in my mind as clearly as I could see my own hands, the fierce red light streaming from within. I lowered my head and placed my palms on the outside of that door. I squared my shoulders, dug my feet into the thick *lepo* and grunted forcefully into the waning starlight. The strength that flowed through my spine seemed inhuman. I pushed mightily and prepared my heart for a new beginning.

I awoke to the sound of crunching gravel. Through the lattice, I could see the National Park Emblem on the door of the gray pickup truck coming down the driveway. I noticed at the end of the clearing that several *'apapane* birds had flown out of the green forest and had gathered on the telephone wire. The truck was coming closer. More and more of the *'apapane* arrived. The truck braked in front of the house. The little birds began to chirp, to squawk and flutter their wings, trilling in the cool morning air. There were several dozen of them and more arriving as the truck door opened. Disembodied legs in pressed khaki pants swung down and marched towards the steps. It could only be Drakes, his fancy leather shoes moving towards my hiding place beneath the house. I could barely repress a deep, almost unconscious snarl as I heard him come up the mossy wooden steps of the porch. The *'apapane* were quite agitated now. They had completely filled the telephone wire. They landed in large numbers on the roofline of the house and flew over to the rafters of the small open garage. They squawked in the adjacent trees, trilling louder and louder. Drakes pounded on the wooden door, nervously noticing the birds all around him.

"Weir!" he hollered. "Weir!"

I struggled not to make a sound. All of a sudden, the *'apapane* became very quiet, hundreds of them tilting their heads and leaning forward from their perches, looking menacingly down at Drakes. In their enormous numbers, the sight was intimidating.

"Damn!" he muttered, backing up and looking around at them. He proceeded to walk very slowly back to the truck. He quietly opened the door. When he felt he was safe from the birds, he slammed the door of the truck and started the engine, revving it and spraying dirt and gravel from the rear wheels of the vehicle. The *'apapane* exploded from their perches, screaming insanely. A dark cloud of angry birds swirled around the departing vehicle, their small, black wings furiously beating the air. The sound of their exclamations carried through the forest, shattering the quiet calm of the morning.

At work, a few days later, Drakes abruptly pulled up a chair to face me across from my desk.

"Look, Weir, I'll tell you right now, you are in serious trouble. I'm fed up with your irregular hours and your damned disrespectful attitude. I'm simply not going to put up with it anymore." He laced his fingers together and leaned forward on my desk. I was snacking on whole macadamias from a paper bag. I had discovered that I could crush the hard outside shell with my teeth. I spat the broken pieces into the bag and relished the sweet, oily nut. I chewed the raw nut and swallowed slowly, looking silently at Drake.

"Weir, how many volcanologists would give their gonads to have your job? Do you have any idea?" he raised his voice sharply. "Your productivity is down and your illusory problems with the computers are wasting time. Nicholas can't protect you anymore, Weir, he's gone. Maybe we should get a volcanologist who wouldn't waste time with moronic cultural pap and actually accomplish some real science. I'm seriously thinking about letting you go, Weir. Perhaps selling *lei*s down at the airport would be more suited to your temperament."

There was silence between us that thickened like the mist in the adjacent crater. I spit more sharp pieces into the bag and looked at Drakes' self-satisfied, sadistic smile. I noticed the message displayed on my computer monitor. I smiled back at Drakes. The screen said simply:

Bring him to me, my beloved

I felt a quiver run down my spine and looked down at my left forearm on the support of the chair. The hair was thick and coarse, extending from the back of my hand up beneath the sleeve of my shirt.

"Look Drakes," I said hesitantly, "I apologize for the irregularities." I put the paper bag down on the desk. "I'm struggling with my dissertation and having some difficulties finishing up. I'd appreciate one more chance. Come with me to take a look at Halemaʻumaʻu later this afternoon. It will explain everything."

Drakes looked at me and considered this. "What's in it for me, Weir? You going to make me a nice *lei* too?"

He smiled thinly. I pushed my chair back. Drakes' arrogant cynicism was disturbing but not as disturbing as the scent emanating from his body. The man smelled awful.

"This discovery will make an impressive addition to the field data in your monthly administration reports. You can have all the credit. You'll be lauded for this finding, Drakes ... could be they'd even consider better funding for your position."

He considered this new angle for another moment. "You'd better be right, Weir," Drakes said sullenly, "and clean this damn crap off your desk."

He pushed his arm across the desk, knocking the paper bag of macadamia shells to the floor. He rose stiffly and returned to his office.

I picked up the phone a minute later and called him. "Drakes, we should be as discreet as possible. You know how competitive it can get around here, we don't want to tip our hand. Let's wait until everybody else has left, then we can go out to the crater together. I'd like the credit to go exclusively to you Drakes, not Marshals or Lane. Perhaps you could sign out when we leave, and I'll come back up and sign out later. It might be less suspicious if I wasn't officially with you when you log the finding."

"Weir, if this is a waste of my time, it will mean your termination," he said ominously and hung up.

I typed into the system:

WHO ARE YOU?

After a few seconds, the swirling green phosphors came to life.

It is I, ke ahi, who loves you

I looked out the window of the observatory. The sun was setting over Mauna Loa, deep streaks of crimson giving way to the cool turquoise blues of an early twilight. I removed a small bottle of gin from the bottom drawer of my filing cabinet. I joined Drakes in the parking lot and looked around to be sure that we were not observed. We drove down the Chain Of Craters road, then I parked the jeep off to the side, near a thick jumble of ferns. We began to walk. On our way out to the crater, I went over to one of the steam vents and knelt over the sparkling yellow crystals that coated the rocks of the opening. I inhaled deeply. The sulfur felt so good in my nostrils.

"Can you hear that?" I asked Drakes, as he approached curiously.

"Hear what?" Drakes replied.

"The chanting," I said, studying the vent. "It's coming from below, beneath the molten lava."

"What?" Drakes said. He couldn't hear me, as the vent began to hiss. His eyes narrowed and he looked at me suspiciously.

We hiked a little further in the gathering darkness.

"This way, Drakes, we're almost there," I said. We lay on our bellies, inching forward. I leaned over carefully to observe the inconceivable vista of the fiery pit beneath us. The crater was beautiful in the fading light, bubbling and boiling, roiling in phosphorescent pinks, reds and oranges. Drakes was coming up beside me, very afraid; I could smell the stink on him. "She's down there," I whispered in veneration, feeling the hardness of my *kano* digging into the earth. Drakes' trembling hand reached for the edge of the crater rim. Slowly he pulled himself towards the edge. I reached into my back pocket for the fifth of gin, unscrewed the cap and took a long swig.

"Drakes," I said, looking down into a sea of molten lava. "I don't think I'd enjoy selling *lei*s at the airport. I like it here, engaged in my work. In fact, I've recently discovered a completely new aspect to volcanology. It's the radically transformative idea that nothing is really what we think it is, Drakes.... Nothing."

I extended my arm and released the bottle down into the deep abyss. There was a tinkling sound, way, way down there as the glass shattered.

I stood evenly on the crater rim and began *ka 'olili* – the shimmering. Drakes jumped to his feet and started to run, but he moved awkwardly in his leather shoes. Mine were already off, the nails of my toes, joining, as if hoofed. Drakes had run about thirty yards, but I cut off his escape easily. I moved in towards him relishing the smell of his fear. He stumbled backwards, holding up his hands and pleading with me. His voice was small and timid. I ran my tongue across my lips. He backed up to the edge of the crater where he could go no further.

I dropped down to all fours.

"My God," he whimpered, releasing the smell of urine into the air.

I bellowed joyously, flying over the rocks to slam my face into the soft flesh of his pelvis. The muscles in my neck strained mightily as I flung him upwards with my head. Drakes went over the cliff backwards, screaming all the way down to the fiery bottom.

When he hit the molten pond, the upward splash of lava threw shimmering strands of liquefied fire into the cool night air. She was indeed a goddess. In her own incredible *'olili*, her glorious red eyes burned in the darkness. Pele smiled, beckoning, her radiant splendor without comparison. Above the seething caldera, the smell of burnt flesh rose. Sniffing at the twisting smoke and dancing *'ai ha'a* along the rim, I was fulfilled to the center of my being.

When the full moon came out from behind the clouds, the *'olili* finally solidified. I chanted vibrantly into the heavenly darkness—

He miki, he miki

A i hānau mai 'oe e Hina

Ka maka o ka pua'a

E lele ana i ka lani

E lele ana i ke kuahiwi

'Ewalu maka o ke keiki pua'a a Hina

I ran like the wind: powerful, low. My beastly hooves struck the ground, pulverizing and smashing the *pāhoehoe* into dirt. In the cold breath of the *'ena makani*, dust from my swift passage floated upwards and away beneath the purple starlight. I inhaled the volcanic spores of her essence, her beauty flooding my senses. Cloaked in the dark cape of night, I raced forward to the promise of her womanhood.

Behold **Kamapua'a**, lover of the Fire Goddess.

* * * * * * * * * *

When the ambulance stops, they transport me on the gurney to the operating table. The nurses attach electrodes to my chest. I can see the monitor off to the side of the surgeon. Beep, beep, beep. The data dissolves and the dancing blue cathode rays declare her sweet epistle:

Return to me soon, beloved

Her message is visible only for an instant, for a single heart beat, then the screen returns to the normal output of the cardiac display.

It seems quite fitting, that the woman I love so passionately speaks within the beating of my own heart. The anesthesiologist frowns above his mask and raps gently on the side of the screen. I am smiling, my eyes shining in the bright lights of the operating theater.

It is so good to be loved. The anesthetic begins to take effect. I close my eyes as the surgeon leans forward to irrigate and repair the wound. As he enters and tugs at my flesh, I recall her gentle caress. The smell of her hair. The incredible taste of her warm mouth. The way I parted her thighs with the movement of my dark snout. This was not the love I had hoped for in my life. It was more. So much more.

The next morning, I look in the mirror of the bathroom and see my face. Miraculously, I am handsome again and I feel good. I raise the hospital gown and examine the wound. There is no pain. The stitches are secure. The healing has commenced.

In a few days, I will wear my flannel shirt and drink a cup of *mamaki* tea. I will read the Hilo Tribune and back up the seismic data on the big drives. I open the hospital window and inhale the soft, sweet scent of vog. It is the most delicate of perfumes.

For now, I am hungry. I roam the kitchen early, before any of the staff arrive. I find a carton of eggs.

One by one, I place them in my mouth.

Author's Note:

The demi-god Kamapua'a had two principle forms: human being and that of a hog. According to the Kumulipo creation chant, he was born in the fifth era. I was engaged in the production research for the show "'Ulalena" on Maui, when I came upon a reference in the Fornander Collection of Hawaiian Antiquities and Folklore first published in 1918-1919 by The Bishop Museum Press in Honolulu as "Memoirs of Bernice Pauahi Bishop Museum of Polynesian Ethnology and Natural History, Vol. V, Parts I, II and III." What stunned me was a mysterious reference in the text, a description of Kamapua'a as "ka haole nui maka 'ālohilohi - the large foreigner with the bright eyes." I had to put down my pen and think about this. Then I began to wonder what would happen, if after all this time, Pele longed for her old lover?

All chant references in this story except for "Aia Lā 'O Pele" are from the Fornander Collection of Hawaiian Antiquities and Folklore, Volume V, Part II pg. 314-363. The facsimile edition (text pages) was published in 1999 by 'Ai Pohaku Press, 1244 North School Street, Honolulu, HI 96817. "Aia Lā 'O Pele" is from the Beamer family collection.

Pōhaku

For a painter, there is nothing quite like natural light. Perhaps that is why I do my best work in the afternoons. In lower Manhattan at this time of the year, the light is just about perfect at 2 p.m. That is when the sun rises above even the tallest buildings of the city. It streams down through the big windows of the loft and scatters across the yellowing finish of the wooden floor.

In that profuse light, my palette awakens and I dip my brushes into the colors, not just seeing them, but seeing through them. I savor the sweet trace of turpentine in the air and study the empty space ahead of me. I step forward to the easel, mixing the paint to reveal what the canvas is to become, what it yearns to be.

I chose the medium of oil because I loved, and still love, the textures that oils create. Sometimes when the work is dry, I trace my fingers across the canvas. I can feel the shapes of the oils rising and falling beneath the tips of my fingers. Slowly, I close my eyes and journey into the painting.

Tonight, I have agreed to attend a reception. I put on a suit and tie. I grab the keys to the car. On my way to the parking garage, the keys jingle in my pocket. It's a quarter to nine. I am already late.

For artists, attending receptions is a regular part of what we do. It's where we meet with patrons who support our work. At these gatherings are gallery owners, fine art collectors, wholesale distributors and usually a couple of hangers-on, who nobody can quite remember inviting. I step out of my car, hand the keys to the valet and greet my business manager, who has arrived ahead of me. I suspect he has been waiting for a while. He extends his hand, smiles and nods his approval. I am wearing the only suit I own; still it is better than the smock he is used to seeing me in. "Don't let my glamour blind you, Carl," I tell him as we enter the building.

I feel a bit ill at ease. I'm uncomfortable at social events because it's something I've never been any good at. While the patrons think they know me from my work, they don't know that my sense of humor lacks sophistication or that my conversational skills are weak. So I simply stumble from one small group to the next, winging it as best I can. I shrug my shoulders as Carl presses the elevator button for the penthouse. They'll find out soon enough, I think to myself. "One hour," I tell him. "One hour and that's it."

It could be that I've had to show my face at too many of these things. I don't look forward them anymore. I am tired and cranky, because I have been painting non-stop for three full weeks in preparation for the new show. I want to go to back to my apartment on West 39th, lay my head down on the pillow and sleep. The elevator door opens and we exit cautiously. It is too late. Carl, my Armani-clad keeper, would never let me escape. A few of the patrons take pictures. Carl eases away as I become the living equivalent of a series of bad photographs. One after another my awkward moments are captured. Here with the eyes squeezed shut and there lurching for the chair. Here I am with a canapé bulging my cheeks. Look at me. I'm a Native Hawaiian man in an ill-fitting suit. Watch me "make a good impression" as Carl puts it. My shoes scuff across the thick carpet of the penthouse, leaving a trail of insipid remarks and flimsy witticisms.

Through the windows, there is a magnificent view of the city and something tells me that I should try and be more appreciative of the Florences' generous hospitality. These must be important clients. Edward Florence has several galleries on the East side where he could have done this, but this is his home. I help myself to the *foie gras* from a mirrored tray and I will myself to relax, to calm down and to stop feeling so awkward.

My style of painting is impressionistic, descended from the French *plein air* (open air) methods. Over the years, I have grown accustomed to compliments of my work. I have learned to pretend that each utterance from a patron is valuable and interesting, yet in truth, I don't understand why people say these things about my work. Deep down inside of me, I feel like a fraud. I seriously doubt that I deserve the accolades I receive. But the art world is not about the truth; it is only about the perception of the truth. These are two completely different things.

An hors d'oeuvre toast round topped with salmon roe accidentally slips from my fingers and drops to the floor. Carl looks in my direction and gasps. As the oily redness seeps into the creamy carpet, he winces. The maid is ushered in, quickly working to clean up the mess. Mrs. Florence then guides me to a safer part of the living room, where I have less of a chance of embarrassing myself. I don't think this is going so well.

"Don't worry about it," she giggles, as I attempt to apologize. "So you've been painting and painting! Edward is thrilled! We love your work, you know. It's so contemporary, yet bolstered by a kind of primitivism that one finds refreshing."

"Thank you so much... well..." I blink nervously and look at the carpet.

"Anything, sort of... new?" she asks sweetly. It is my turn to wince.

Below us, the urban landscape of New York twinkles in the distance, magnificent in the cool night air. Soon, the liquor is flowing and the voices in the room are blending together. My business manager confers with Edward, undoubtedly making deals that will affect my income for the next several years. It seems, all in all, strangely pointless. It occurs to me that I am barely capable of understanding the chaos in this room, let alone relating to it, and I yearn for a hearing impairment. The alcohol reaches my blood stream and I begin to feel mentally adrift: floating, smiling, feigning interest, not really listening to anybody at all. Native peoples and booze, what a sorry association that has been. The alcohol burns like acid through the tethers of my inhibitions. Like a child's helium balloon, I rise slowly upward.

"Thank you so very much... well... please... excuse me," I say, sprinkling this ingenious verbal fairy dust from my position high on the ceiling.

I can't take it anymore, I am tired of the art world and for the first time in my life, I am desperately tired of my own work. I find little comfort in it anymore. I trace my fingers along the center of the canvas, but I can no longer enter. My work is empty; there is no light within it. I am not an artist. I am a mechanic. I manufacture impressionist paintings.

I ease open the iron door to the balcony and the sounds of conversation from the party retreat to the more distant assault of noise from the streets below. I hear honking horns, police sirens and auto alarms; a vague jumble of discord being born into the smoggy night. Why did I ever decide to come to New York, I ask myself. It is so far away from the place of my birth, I must have been out of my mind to even consider it. I know it is every artist's dream to live and work in this city, but one must be careful of what one wishes for. I have achieved success, but not happiness. I have assets but lack fulfillment. I live alone. Utterly alone. There is only the work.

I look in the direction of what used to be the World Trade Center, but the landscape has changed. The two tall buildings are missing, and in their place is an enormous hole in the ground, still emitting smoke, months after the destruction of September 11. Floodlights illuminate the rectangular area. From this distance, the entire scene could be a halogen-lit painting on a dark gallery wall. The ghastly canvas depicts the hatred entrenched in the hearts of a few human beings. My god, I think to myself, what is happening to the world? One could paint every moment of every hour until the end of time and would that body of work really change anything? Would it change a heart so filled with hatred? Does what I do with my life make a difference? Does anything I create matter at all?

The lights from thousands of vehicles trail down through the streets below. There are so many cars, so many people. Wisps of steam float upwards from subway grates and the homeless congregate around them in an oily darkness. I am grateful that we are high up in the air, so that it all seems rather far away. I feel like jumping. How easy it would be. I'd put the drink down, climb over the railing and let go. I imagine myself plunging downward at great speed. Flippity flap is the sound my trousers make as they whack against my legs. Whoosh goes my tie, as I descend, plummeting through the night sky. I lean over precariously, then I jerk back from the railing and almost spill the whisky on my polished shoes. Carl would probably like it if I died, I think bitterly. The value of my paintings would skyrocket.

I move from the balcony and walk towards the garden of the penthouse, and notice an unusual rock wall. I don't think I've ever seen anything quite like it in this part of the world. It is the labor of a dedicated craftsman, a work of art. I bend down to examine the wall more closely. For a moment I am lost in the simple beauty of the rocks. I study them closely. These smooth stones, where did they come from? How did they come to be so perfectly placed, high above the city of New York?

A light rain begins to fall, enshrouding the city. The stones in the wall begin to darken from the drops of rain. The rain falls harder now, and the city lights below begin to disappear. I place the fingers of my right hand against the smooth surface of the wall and close my eyes.

I begin to think about an earlier time in my life. A time when I was a young boy growing up in Hawai'i. It was a time of innocence, a time before suicidal men flew airplanes into buildings. I slowly trace my fingertips across the surface of one of the stones. Immediately I remembered an old fisherman who loved a massive *pōhaku* beneath the murmuring currents of a moonlit bay...

* * * * * * * * *

I was raised with my cousin on the Island of Hawai'i. My cousin was a gregarious kid, full of laughter and an inadvertent kind of mischief. He was cursed with a natural clumsiness. He broke a lot of things. In his peculiar world of faux pas, accident, misfortune and miscue, my cousin had a certain star status, a stunning stage presence. His were memorable performances underlined with a heart of gold. It was his special gift.

After he would break something, I'd scowl at him and start to get angry. Then by some quirk of the imagination, I'd see his last funny exploit flash in my memory. It was always enough to forgive him.

Because he was a kind and genuinely wonderful kid, I never wanted to hurt his feelings. I'd chew on my lip, barely managing to turn away and strangle my own laughter as with elbows and knees whirling, he would descend yet another staircase on his backside. "Careful going down the stairs dear," grandmother would say sweetly as he'd take a header at the bottom of the stairway and slam directly into the wall.

We were living with our grandparents in the little ranching town of Waimea, Hawai'i, when early one morning, our grandfather began to think about his favorite fishing grounds and his old *koa* canoe. "Eh deah," grandfather said over his coffee and Saloon-Pilot crackers, "Let's take these boys fishing." So we went to live for the summer in the tiny fishing village of Miloli'i on the southern coast of the island of Hawai'i.

Sitting in the back seat of the car with the wind whistling through the open windows, my cousin and I smiled at each other. As we headed to our family beach house down on the rocky coast, the Nureyev of the pratfall somehow got the draw-string of his surf shorts tangled up in the chrome window crank.

"Papa, I stuck," he said after about an hour of yanking on the cord of his shorts. Muttering in Hawaiian under his breath, my grandfather pulled over to the side of the road, took out his buck knife and quickly freed him.

"Careful you don't get tangled up dear," said my grandmother, sweetly.

Those were special days in my growing awareness of the incredible beauty of Hawai'i. I can still see the pale salt mist rising up slowly in the air and stunning bolts of sunlight streaking through the *kiawe* trees. Yellow sprays of *pili* grass angled upward through the sharp cracks of an endless *'a'ā* field. Everywhere, the fierce, massive permanence of black lava reigned over the island like an immense *ali'i*. Looking down the mountain, you could see the *ali'i*'s powerful hand as it reached out to hold the tiny village. Churning between those tremendous volcanic fingers, bright splashes of the cerulean blue Pacific danced off to a thousand far away places.

In that abundant light, children and pigs ran together along the only dirt road leading down to the village. What was this with the pigs? In our town, pigs were kept in pens. Playing with them - well, nobody did that. Seeing the smile on my cousin's face as we approached this happy parade of pork, I sensed catastrophe. The local kids drove the pigs off to the side of the road with their guava sticks, and waved to us as our old car wheezed by. Kicking up a huge cloud of dust, the car slowed to a crawl and Grandfather gave a great big smile and an easy wave of his hand. As the engine of the old Valiant labored slowly through the gears, we looked out the back window. The kids shrank in size until they were finally swallowed up by the shimmering blur of heat waves rising up silently from the dusty road. My cousin and I looked at each other curiously. What kind of a place was this?

The bay of the little fishing village was protected by a reef formation that acted as a natural barrier. In the center of the bay was a very large rock. On the ride down the hill, grandfather said that it was not just an ordinary rock, but a special *Pōhaku*. Hawaiians had discovered that it had very special powers. They had known this for centuries.

We pulled into the front yard trailed by a cloud of dust. Papa turned the engine off and we stared at the small house that we would be staying in for the summer. The paint was peeling from the sides and part of the porch looked like it was going to fall down. The little house beneath the rusting tin roof was weather-beaten and old. We noticed that there was a small outhouse off the side. Papa smiled at us and said it was a "two holer," meaning that if you were afraid of the dark at night, you could wake up your cousin and get him to sit in there with you.

The next day, we unpacked most of our boxes and spent the afternoon swimming from the small dock. In the evening, we helped an old fisherman push his canoe up on the sand. He smiled at us, his long, dark hair encrusted with salt. Then he rewarded us with a big handful of *'ōpelu*.

"Da canoe almost wen bang da big rock," I told him as he handed me the fish.

"Rock?" he asked, seeming puzzled.

Because we were the new kids in Miloli'i and because we had just helped him as best as we could, he gathered his patience. It had been a long day in the canoe and now the sun was descending into the sea. He told us to come with him down the beach and then motioned for us to sit with him in the sand.

He pointed to the large stone protruding from the middle of the bay and explained that in the night, the reflection of moonlight from the surface of the stone guided many a lost canoe into the safe haven of the harbor. For those desperate men —he looked straight at me when he said this— the *Pōhaku* was not just a rock. It was a savior.

The old fisherman really loved the *Pōhaku*. As he spoke his simple words and gestured with his thin hands, I could hear his love for the great stone singing in his voice. He told us that the *Pōhaku* was as old as time itself. It was there when his father's father was born and the generations before him. He said that he had felt the stone's *mana*, its power and presence, for every single day of his life.

He spoke of a time when he was a boy, when a group of *haole* sailors arrived. They were drinking beer on the beach and went for a swim in the bay. When they encountered the large stone rising out of the water, they perceived it as an insult to their recreation. Using a powerful truck winch and a steel cable, the men rolled and tumbled the *Pōhaku*. They tied a chain around it and dragged it off to the side of the bay.

Those same men camped out on the beach that night and were inundated by a huge wave. All nine of them drowned. After a few days, the swirling currents brought their broken bodies back to the surface. The authorities came over from Kona and Hilo and eventually found them driven against the outside reef, partially covered with sand and seaweed and hungry crabs, their small, sharp pincers digging into waterlogged flesh.

Inexplicably, the huge brooding stone had somehow moved back to exactly the same place, swimming slowly in the moonlight to stand again on the horizon, its reflected light slicing through the darkness like a jewel on fire.

The old fisherman stopped in mid sentence, staring intently out at the bay. Had he seen some movement beneath the water? Some vague undertow approaching the old stone? I followed his eyes with mine, trying in vain to see beneath the reflection of the watery surface.

Before the *kupuna* could speak again my cousin stumbled precariously to his feet and, looking out over the water at the giant stone, stammered, "But... uhh... what wen really happen to da sailors?" The old fisherman looked at him, incredulous, raised his voice, and said:

"Dey all dead boy! *Make loa!* No one move da *Pōhaku!*"

I felt a chill go down my spine and got chicken skin on my arms. My hand, still holding the *'ōpelu*, started to tremble. It was as if the fish were trembling too, as if they had been somehow miraculously resurrected. Far away in the distance, I heard the sound of a wave crashing against the *Pōhaku*; then the sea became eerily quiet.

The old fisherman stood up and disgustedly shook his head. "You boys too young," he said. "You no can understand." As he walked back to the canoe, I could hear him muttering in Hawaiian, bitterly deriding our youthful lack of intelligence as his voice trailed off into the freshening wind.

My cousin looked at me with wide eyes. "Whew..." he said, exhaling a small, scared breath.

"Yeah," I said, nervously dropping the *'ōpelu* in the sand and clasping my knees. We stared long and hard at the *Pōhaku* and thought of the sailors that had drowned in the bay. The wind was increasing in strength and the waves again began to form. As the big blue waves began crashing around it, the *Pōhaku* remained unmoved. We walked slowly back along the beach as the giant stone stood firmly amidst the churning whitewater.

Almost every day that summer, we went out in the canoe to fish with our grandfather. The fish were plentiful. I had never seen so many of them. Many a night, after a dinner of aku and poi served by my grandmother on the big wooden table, my cousin and I would set out with our fishing poles and an old gas lantern. We'd hike out along the lava to fish, play cards and listen to some very odd music on our short-wave radio. We heard the far away voices of strange people singing strange songs. When my cousin hooked a fish, he'd holler, "Shine da light!" with a furious trilling sound emanating from the gap where he'd lost a tooth. I watched him fighting a fish, tumbling around, flailing and whistling like a broken teakettle. I came perilously close to laughing and hurting his feelings as the Baryshnikov of Bumbledom broke his little *mākoi* almost completely in two. "WHAPAAK!" went the pole echoing amongst the rocks. Still trying not to laugh, I snorted and fell to my knees. Then we both started laughing until our stomachs were sore.

Back at the beach house, grandmother made us some cocoa, and after tucking us in to *moe*, arranged the mosquito nets surrounding our beds. One night, I had almost fallen asleep when I heard a slight ripping sound and a loud "whump." My cousin had somehow torn the mosquito net from its fastening and had fallen to the floor. "Careful you don't fall off the bed dear," my grandmother said sweetly from somewhere down the hallway.

During those nights as I lay beneath the mosquito netting, I began to notice a kind of ethereal flow to the passage of time. There was a mysterious rhythm to it. I was certain that the days passed by more slowly here than they did anywhere else in the world. What was the passage of time? Did some colossal *aliʻi* take a hold of the *kapa* on his bed and with both hands, slowly send a ripple across the fabric of space? Did that giant wave flood through the darkness, arriving at last to whirl at the base of the old *Pōhaku*?

I kicked the covers from my skinny legs and took a deep breath. The sweet smell of the sea was aloft in the air, drifting in the wind that blew through the white netting. I thought about the old *Pōhaku* swimming alone in the moonlight and my young heart filled with awe.

As the days passed by, we got browner and browner and the calluses on the bottoms of our feet grew bigger and tougher. The concept of shoes didn't really fit in too well with our life style. In those days I'd bet that my cousin and I could have easily outrun a billy goat on the jagged, bare surface of the lava. And speaking of bare, clothes weren't too popular an item either. We'd splash and swim all day naked and happy. Nobody really seemed to mind.

One day we just swam right up to the *Pōhaku*. I am sure that we remembered what the old fisherman had said, but in the bright reason of sunlight, we were not afraid. The *Pōhaku* wasn't evil or frightening. It was simply a magnificent old stone weathered by the passage of a million tides. Climbing on it and hanging from it, and sliding bare bottomed down its massive sides, we laughed and shouted and played for the rest of the summer. Over time, the sun set later on the little fishing village and the water grew colder. The end of our stay approached. Each evening it became harder and harder to say good-bye to the smooth, beautiful stone.

When I went down to the beach that last night, I saw him again: the old fisherman. He was alone on the sand as the tide came in to embrace the giant stone. Around him, the wind rattled in the leaves of a *hau* tree and the moonlight wandered delicately on the surface of the water. He was getting old. He seemed thinner, and more fragile than when I first met him. His shoulders were hunched. I listened quietly under the *hau* tree as the old man prayed earnestly in Hawaiian.

* * * * * * * * *

It is getting late and the reception is winding down. I go back into the apartment.

"Oh, goodness!" cries Julia, "you're soaking wet!" She has her maid fetch a small towel.

"Sorry, Julia, it's just such a beautiful view," I say, toweling my hair and face. "I didn't realize I was getting so wet."

Carl looks at Edward and shrugs his shoulders, "Artists…" he says, letting the word dangle in the air.

I toss back the rest of my drink, give the towel back to the maid and mumble my good-byes to our hosts. The Florences are gracious people, bidding me farewell and ringing the attendant to bring my car around to the front.

As the night flashes by, the rain continues to fall in New York. I flick the wiper button and bear down on the accelerator, slicing though the city, snarling across the black asphalt. In the rear view mirror my features appear exaggerated. I feel older than I am tonight, disconnected from this space.

I drive very fast.

Everywhere there is rain. On the pavement, slick tendrils reach towards me in the darkness. The world is melting, dribbling down the windows in the dark.

By way of the eastern coast of the Atlantic, and by the circuitous route of my own tangled navigation, I have somehow arrived to stand on the same shore as that old fisherman. I begin to see the lines that connect us, traced in the rivulets of rain on the windshield. There are other connections that I begin to notice. The men before him. And the men before them. We are a tribe, a brotherhood of tattooed arms and legs, a battalion of boys and men, revealed in the muted flash of a passing street lamp. We are the earthly guardians of the old *Pōhaku*, conscripted by the power of that extraordinary stone.

As I accelerate in the wet blackness, I wonder if I have come all this way in my life to become a man like him. A man like those before him.

Careening across the Brooklyn Bridge in the heavy downpour, I further depress the accelerator. The car streaks through the rain, the spans and girders of the bridge whipping by in a blur. I remember when I held on to the *Pōhaku*, when the wind sang a lullaby across the water and the face of the old stone seemed as soft as a caress. I had never known that happiness later in life, because I had lost my connection to my culture, to myself, to the meaning of my work. I remembered sobbing into my grandfather's shoulder, as he lifted me and carried me towards the old car, "Please Papa, please. Can we please, just stay here? Here with the *Pōhaku*?"

So I had finally come to understand why the *Pōhaku* had been cherished for thousands of years and why the savior of lost men waits at the opening of a small, beautiful bay. The great stone was a portal, connecting the generations of the future to the generations of antiquity. The *Pōhaku* withstood the powerful tides of time and change, to connect us to each other.

And I am not a fraud. I am Hawaiian.

Tomorrow in the loft, I will consider those in the world who find through art the luminous light of meaning. When the sun streams through the windows, I will step forward. I will compose the textures a man can trace to quiet his soul and begin his own journey. A journey towards the light of the old *Pōhaku*.

The clouds begin to clear above the city and a slight blush of moonlight glows through the wires and support columns of the bridge. I ease my foot off the accelerator. As the car slows, I lower the windows and feel the nearness of the ocean. I take it in my lungs, breathing deeply, no longer feeling so lost or alone.

He is with me now. The old fisherman and I swim together. From the darkness, the giant stone had come to ignite the horizon.

Author's Note;

We all lose our way sometimes.

To Pōhaku, *our lifetimes pass in the blink of an eye. Perhaps that is why they are so wise and so cherished.*

Our Ticket to Cannes

My *hānai* younger brother teaches science at the Hawaiian language immersion school on the Big Island. He is also a frustrated filmmaker whose next project is to make a movie about the Hawaiian *'a'ama* crab. Besides the somewhat unusual subject, his first attempt at cinema will have the distinction of a novel use of camera angles. This inspiring vision has led him to join a model aircraft-flying club, where he's currently learning to fly a remote-controlled, gasoline-powered, model-helicopter with an attached camera platform. My little brother will, in the words of Joseph Campbell, "follow his bliss." He told me that he plans to guide his baby helicopter in from the sea and cinematically capture for all time, *for all the world to see*, a close up view of life from the *'a'ama* crab perspective.

Whew! I thought, completely stunned by the implications. This could be our ticket to Cannes!

Then I had a few more cautious thoughts, like... why would anybody buy a ticket to see a movie about a crab? And where is that big bag of *arare* that was in my office? Then I got to thinking about the whole model aircraft cinematography concept. A small gasoline engine makes one hell of a racket. Did it ever occur to my dear brother that the *'a'ama* crab might not sit still for filming? *'A'ama* are notoriously skittish, especially when one is trying to capture them for dinner or introduce them to a helicopter. I wonder if my young brother might end up with a documentary on *'opihi*, whose movement skills are less than transcendent.

I exhale deeply and reconsider what may be in itself a brilliant idea. *'Opihi* are truly interesting and tolerant of just about anything. I think a movie about *'opihi* would be wonderful! I know this, because small kid time, I had an *'opihi* for a pet. "Blaize" was my black, round, steadfast and sticky friend. He was never too busy to listen to my boyhood problems, of which there were quite a few. Although his repertoire of tricks was limited, Blaize exhibited total and complete mastery of the command, "STAY." No other family pet has ever obeyed me with such certitude or conviction, and in thinking about it, I am positive that Blaize would not have even flinched if a small helicopter furiously beat in the air a few inches above his pointy little head.

"Count me in!" I beamed to my little brother, pumping his small hand enthusiastically. I am now the only investor in our fledgling company. After we conclude our business arrangements, I pump his little hand again, but this time I squeeze REALLY HARD and his eyes pop out a little. I want him to know that the money is important to me, and I will kick his little *'ōkole* if we don't get it back.

Unfortunately, the progress of the film has been hampered by an unfortunate crash that resulted in the total loss of our midget aircraft. While soaring in at a high rate of speed, brother's little skid caught hold of a stray pandanus leaf, veered left and shredded the top layer of a really nice *kukui* nut tree. In a final gut-wrenching moment, the 'copter plunged to the earth and beat a hellaceous tattoo into the dirt. The rising cloud of dust and rain of *kukui* nuts resulted in spectacular footage.

Unfortunately, the brand new digital camera I had financed was a total loss. Since it was still under warranty, the young director asked me to return it to Sony. I did, stating briefly the reason for return as: "Makes a funny noise and dirt comes out."

Lucky for us the film was preserved and no flying club members were injured or maimed. What a relief! In fact, according to my brother, the members must carry a million dollars worth of liability insurance, just in case a pilot bending over his plane on the runway gets rammed in the *'ōkole* by a giant model B52. Imagine the indignity, being admitted to Hilo Hospital, smelling of aviation fuel, with a huge, smoking hole in the back of your shorts.

The flying club was now asking for proof of insurance and brother was more nervous than a cockroach on a hot rice cooker. The young director seemed to think that the insurance premiums should come out of the budget for the *'a'ama* movie and wanted more money. My eyes began to bulge and my face got very red. I made a sort of a "why...you...liddle...@$#@!" sound, at the back of my throat. I found myself reaching with both hands for his neck and stumbling forward towards him, like... well... Frankenstein after a couple of triple lattes. When brother realized the extent of my impassioned objection, he disappeared in a little puff of red dirt. Gee, I had no idea he could move so swiftly. I doubt that any film director present or past, successful or poverty stricken, demented or sane, could outrun him in the 100 meter dash. His little slippers were smokin'. I lumbered after him, still really pissed off, but gave up shortly after I stepped on a ripe guava. It's that toe squish thing that really gets to you.

Someday in the future when we are interviewed about the "Making of..." (music swells here) "The 'A'ama Crab," Barbara Walters will remember this incident to film fans, as the deepest, darkest moment of tribulation: when financial losses and petty disagreements nearly wrecked the project, when the executive producer — now Barbara would lean in for her close-up and elucidate with her clipped and elegant accent— "NO CAN HANDLE."

Three days later, I called my dear *hānai* brother and apologized eloquently. Into the mouthpiece of my cell phone, I blurted, "Uhhh... I neva mean fo' Hulk out. Sorry eh, I dunno what wen happen." There was a long pause on the other end. Then the young director finally spoke to me. We are, after all... brothers. He helped me to understand the situation from his point of view. I agreed that being chased through the bushes in fear of his life was not conducive to artistic inspiration.

One day we journeyed to the Kamehameha Statue in front of Hilo Bay and he explained the remote controls of a small airplane he was learning to fly. My *hānai* brother was born on the Isle of Wight, a small island off the southern coast of England. He speaks fluent Hawaiian. He has a natural gift, from *Ke Akua*, no doubt. When he would speak to my grandmother in *'ōlelo Hawai'i* she would cry tears of joy. She was so happy to hear the Hawaiian language alive and flourishing and coming from the mouth of such a young person. Now, little brother was trying to explain the complexity of the controls to me in a manner related to his camera work: "If you push this thing in, then the houses get mo big. If you pull on it, then they get mo' small." Hmm… some kind of film parlance, no doubt. "ZZZZZZ" the little plane sang, off in the distance in the gray sky. Watching brother's little plane crash into the roof of a liquor store on Kino'ole Street, brought our production meeting to a close. King Kamehameha seemed to encourage our swift departure, by signaling with his outstretched arm, "go that-a-way, you damn *lōlō*s!" We left quickly, in case somebody had called the cops.

Liability insurance in my little brother's case is probably a good idea. Dwarf aircraft, however, are not insured and one bids a poignant, though anonymous *adieu* when they *puka*-through somebody's tin roof. "Thank goodness for eBay," my brother said sadly, as we made tuna sandwiches in the front seat of a rental car in the drizzling rain of Mamo street. It was at this precise moment, I must confess, that I wavered in my commitment to our project. My dear brother, sensing my disappointment, started in with his love of film, of the great films of the 20th century, of period films, film noir, documentaries, adult DVD, and … WHOA NELLY! Back up the daikon truck. Adult what? "Uhh… Sorry," he said quietly.

My blood pressure was hulking up again. I found my hands reaching for his thin neck, but this time he closed his eyes tightly and pulled his head down into his chest. Except for the scrabbling sound of his right hand, desperately seeking the location of the power door lock, there was a tense moment of silence between us. Somehow, listening to the patter of the rain and staring at my little brother's tightly closed eyes and perspiring forehead, I experienced what we call in our *moke* psychotherapy/anger management class, a feeling of "kill fight." The bloodlust had completely drained from my soul.

"What the hell," I thought, lowering my hands. "I know a winner when I see one!" Then, I grabbed the sides of his head and planted a big *honi* on the top of his forehead. I think this is what they called conflict resolution, but I was not certain. I was hungry. I grabbed the white plastic spoon and eagerly lathered a giant gob of mayonnaise onto yet another piece of Love's white bread.

I decided to participate further in the project as a way of protecting my small investment. I offered to assist the young director on his first non-flying shoot. It was what he called a "screen test."

I am not sure, but this may be similar to what we in the music world call a "demo." As a music professional, I have a clear and unwavering understanding of the nature of demos. Here's how they work: when the record company executive first hears your demo, you as the producer, must remember to cough at exactly the right moment. One does this in order to camouflage the major flaws in the material. These flaws can include the singer singing flat, the guitar player drunkenly banging on the wrong chord, or a phrase that just goes off to lala land or— as often happened in my earlier days— all of the above.

Before playing the demo, I always begin with a little lecture, urging the executive to see through the demo to recognize the true potential of the material. Then, I sit almost in the person's lap and bray like a donkey during the really bad sections. I have learned over the years that if I cough just right, I get the good budget. If I cough poorly, freeze up, or chicken out, I get a lousy budget— or worse, they promise to take you to lunch. One time during a ferociously bad demo, I coughed so much I nearly gave myself an asthma attack. At the conclusion of that demo, I prayed that the meeting would end mercifully. Absolutely the last thing I wanted to hear was a bright and shiny, "Well, that was nice. Let's hear it again!"

It's a lucky thing that record executives are very busy. They are so busy in fact, that they rarely have time to actually listen to music. They have to continually run around doing extremely important things. Musicians have never actually understood what these things are, but some of the recoupable expenses detailed on our business statements suggest it has something to do with Starbucks and those little pissants... oops... I mean croissants.

On the day of the screen test, my brother picked me up at Hilo airport in his Land Rover. This sounds Hollywood-glamorous until you understand that this piece of shit vehicle is 36 years old. He starts it with a crank and I am not kidding. There is an actual crank, that is cranked, like a Charley Chaplin routine. He explains that I need to sit in the back because he is still waiting for a front passenger seat that he has won in yet another auction at eBay. Sitting in the back is an inaccurate description for what I am required to do. It's more like leaning backwards at a slight recline, like the sultan of a really poor country, while my luggage and other crap is piled in upon my lower extremities. "Eh. No worry," he says, "we not going drive too far."

The Land Rover has a remarkable propensity to suck its exhaust fumes into the back hatch where the executive producer of a really poor film company reclines, building up a terrific migraine. After an eternity on a red dirt road sucking on leaded exhaust fumes and enjoying light hallucinations, we arrive on location. Brother has selected a 50 foot cliff in Puna that plunges straight-away into the Pacific Ocean. "Wow," I think, a bit nauseated, "impressive!"

We begin to assemble our camera rig, which consists of several large sections of PVC piping, adhesive, a clothesline and of course the Sony TRV-900 digital camera. With the adhesive and the PVC couplings, we make a pole that is about 20 feet long. We pull the clothesline through it, then make a sort of basket for the camera. Since the clothesline is a wire coated in plastic, it is stiff, so the basket seems to work fairly well. The idea is to dangle the pole off the cliff and lower the camera by feeding more clothesline into the pipe. My brother is quite excited by his ingenuity. I, as executive producer, am more concerned that after feeding the line through the pole, I will hear the dreaded "kerplunk" sound and have to write another letter to Sony. I have already composed this missive in my mind: "Makes a funny noise and water comes out."

His enthusiasm is quite contagious and soon I am ramming wire up the pipe with a joyful sense of fulfillment, as brother, lying on his belly at the edge of the cliff and dangling the pole, gives me terse directions in the technical jargon of film-speak. "More. OK. More. Lil' bit more! OK! *Pau!*" That boy has *director* running through his veins.

After about a half-hour of this, I regret my existence on this planet. My hands are sore, my fingers are tired, and my entire universe seems to revolve around the half-inch opening of a PVC pipe. Could my life be any more ludicrous? Anxious for any small, blessed diversion, I read the back of my brother's t-shirt and it says "Hilo get Choke everything. Choke rain, Choke fish, Choke anthurium," and my mind riffs, "Choke whacko film director." How did the little bastard talk me into this?

I am thinking about the credits that roll by at the end of films. What is a "best boy?" Is he an extremely popular homosexual? Is it the guy who feeds the wire through the pipe? Am I a best boy? Note to self: Refuse Best Boy Credit. Where is that damn bag of *arare*? I am going freakin' nuts.

Finally, we pull the camera up and flick out the small, slightly moist screen. In living color we see the jiggly decent of the camera, the dizzying montage of rocks/water/rocks/water/rocks. The wind pushes our little camera forward and then back. The rocks get bigger, then smaller. Then the camera finally stabilizes and we see... a big *'a'ama* crab, high two-ing us, with one giant black claw raised high to the silver screen.

"Yeaah!" my Little brother cheers. "WE CAN DO IT. WE CAN MAKE A MOVIE!" Brother sings in Hawaiian now and does a happy little dance on the slopes of the steep embankment. We are somewhere in the wilds of Puna and my little *hānai* brother is happier than a pig in *kūkae*.

We disassemble the pole and put the pipe pieces and soggy camera back in the Land Rover. Brother is still so happy, I cannot help but rejoice with him. But not enough to let him drive. He has had enough excitement today, poor little fella. This time, I drive and little brother hallucinates.

On the drive back, I recall, several years ago, his *hānai* ceremony in Waipi'o. Mom bought us all together in a small *hale*, deep in the valley. Ho, *choke* the slippers on that small porch! With *tī* leaves, *'alaea* salt and rainwater, mama chanted for little brother to join our *'ohana*, our family. Brother was so proud on that day, his eyes were shining as he received the *makana* we prepared. He answered her in beautiful, perfect Hawaiian, albeit with a slight British lilt. Then we bought out the guitars and *'ukulele* and sang and danced and partied for three days.

Since then, in countless ways that we never expected, my *hānai* brother has enriched our lives: in our work, in our play, in our music, in our hearts. It is a complete mystery to me how mama found him and called him to us from such a tiny island, so very far away.

We finally get to Hilo in the middle of an incredible downpour. I hug my dear brother under the dripping eaves of the airport terminal.

I tell him that I love him and that I am very proud of him. "I have a feeling you're going to make a terrific director," he says as he looks at me with red, slightly watering eyes. This could mean that he is really going to miss me, or the inhalation of the exhaust fumes has caused him some slight brain damage.

As I step into the street, bending over to reach into the back of the Land Rover to retrieve my luggage, *Ke Akua* bids me fond farewell by pouring a cold bucket of rainwater down the crack of my ass. "This is exactly freakin' why I live in Lahaina," I mutter indignantly, as I squish my way over to the counter.

In first class on Aloha Airlines —an old friend from high school works at check-in— I contemplate the whole Hawaiian *hānai* thing. I think we have it so we can call people we truly love into the inner circle of our lives.

The rain streaks across my little plastic window as the big jet lifts into the sky. Ahead, Mauna Kea's mantle of white snow sparkles beneath the silver wing.

I imagine my red-eyed *hānai* brother, slowly heading back to his *hale*, wheezing in the Rover's toxic fumes. The Cannes thing would be pretty cool, but I don't think it matters much. In my soggy underwear, munching on a small, stale packet of macadamia nuts, life seems incredibly sweet.

Author's Note;

When I think of the words hānai *and* aloha, *I feel proud to be Hawaiian. I feel blessed to hold these meanings in my heart.*

It Swims When You Sleep

Referral Number: 1874

Date: 17 March, 2002

Case Number: 496

Patient Name: Blake Timmons

Social Security Number: 573-57-9184

Age: 27

Height: 6'

Weight: 145lbs

Allergies: None

Medical Record Locator Number 54 97 89

Physician Notes: Examined by Dr. Michael Thompson GP. Diagnosis: Hemoptysis, excoriation / avulsion injury, possible PTS disorder. BP at 134/84 Borderline systolic. Temp 100.2°F. Present weight indicates significant weight loss (41 lbs) since last examination on 12/17/01. Diag. Testing in progress: X-ray/blood/AFB smear/urine/lab results exp. 19 March.

Patient presented on March 14, 02 in near schizophrenic state with avulsion injury to right forearm. Complaints of sleep deprivation and blood in coughed-up sputum. Patient suffers from repeated nightmares. Stiffness in medial and lateral rotation of L tibia and older abrasions to L knee, R ankle, exterior of L & R gastrocnemius. Most troubling is a significant abrasion extending from L deltoid to lumbar region w/mild edema and infection.

According to patient, during a recreational outing on 18 Feb, 02, patient and diving partner were attacked by a shark. Diving partner was killed. Patient may suffer from undiagnosed PTS disorder from emotional trauma related to event. Patient refuses to explain the cause of avulsion injuries, some more recent than others. Unknown if abrasions are self-inflicted. Sleep deprivation and level of anxiety indicate deteriorating mental condition. Patient is presently not on medication and refuses any prescription for sleep, infection or pain. Patient referred to Dr. Hillman for psychological evaluation. Recommend treatment without delay.

For Internal Use Only

BILLING/HEALTH INSURANCE INFORMATION

PPO

HMO x

POS

Plan G / vision/ drug

CPT Code(s) 1009

Blake sat on the edge of his chair in the waiting room. His long blonde hair was dirty and stringy, matted across the side of his forehead. He wore a baggy wrinkled shirt, with shorts and scuffed brown sandals. Blake hadn't shaved or bathed in at least a week. There were white gauze bandages on his arm, and on his ankle, a large, cracking scab. There was another scab on his left knee, oozing yellow fluid. His legs were pale and thin, like the legs of an elderly man.

The door opened and he was led into the psychiatrist's office. The nurse tried to make him comfortable on the couch, but Blake refused to lie back. He chose instead to sit upright, his hands placed nervously on his thighs. Dr. Jules Hillman M.D. entered the room, then sat down at his desk. Hillman was in his mid-fifties, a pleasant, earnest man, with the slight paunch of middle age. His head was slightly balding and he wore a pair of wire-rimmed spectacles on a light cord around his neck.

"Hello, Mr. Timmons, thank you for coming in this afternoon. I hope you are comfortable?"

"Yes."

"Well… let's see…. I've been reviewing your medical records and thought we might spend a little time getting to know each other this afternoon. Dr. Thompson, the physician who examined you on Thursday is a good friend of mine… in fact we both attended Stanford together in the 80's. Dr. Thompson has always been a compassionate professional and except for the fact that he beats me constantly on the golf course, I like him very much. In fact, I was pleased when we both ended up in the same provider system. I was able to speak to him personally about your case —well, actually, let me re-phrase that Mr. Timmons: Michael called me at home and expressed his opinion that there was some urgency involved in your situation."

Dr. Hillman paused and looked over at Blake. He was trying to read Blake's body language, looking for any sign or clue that would help him understand the patient's condition.

"Mind if I smoke, doc?"

"Not at all. I want you to be comfortable, Mr. Timmons. Go right ahead."

He handed Blake a small white ashtray emblazoned with – *Wisconsin, home of the cheddar heads.* "I'm a pipe smoker myself," Hillman said. "The wife hates it, but I find it comforting and I won't tell her if you won't." Dr. Hillman smiled. He looked at Blake carefully. "I'd like you to be as comfortable as possible, Mr. Timmons. I know it's a bit strange being in here and all, but I can assure you that

I am here to help and we can speak with every confidence."

"And what exactly does that mean… 'every confidence'?"

"That means that anything you tell me will be kept confidential. Psychiatrists have a duty to keep their patients' confidences, Mr. Timmons. It's the underpinning of our practice. In essence, it is our duty to maintain this confidentiality. It means that a doctor may not disclose any information revealed by the patient or discovered in connection with his treatment of that patient. What you share with me in our conversations during the course of our patient-psychiatrist relationship is considered confidential to the utmost degree."

Blake lit a Marlboro and exhaled slowly. He waved the match in the air to extinguish it. Dr. Hillman could see the thin bones of Blake's hands. He wondered if it was a sign of anorexia.

"Oh goody," Blake said.

Dr. Hillman sighed. "Usually my patients appreciate knowing this. In fact I had to re-schedule several of them today, so I could see you without delay. Dr. Thompson was quite insistent about it."

"No need to get snippy. And I do appreciate your seeing me. It's just that I doubt that you can help me," Blake paused. "It could be that I am wasting my time and yours."

Hillman leaned back in his chair. "I don't know if I can honestly give you the assurance you seek, Mr. Timmons. By the way, would it be all right if I addressed you as Blake?"

Blake nodded and took another drag from his cigarette.

Dr. Hillman opened up his desk drawer and took out his tobacco pouch. He removed a few pinches of the brown tobacco and placed it in his wooden pipe. "First of all, please don't be concerned with my time. I assure you Mr. Timmons… Blake, that I am well compensated for it. As far as your own time is concerned, I don't really know. I mean, I am able to help the vast majority of my patients and I certainly hope that I can help you, but I would need to understand the nature of the problem, more or less, in order to know if I can truly help you. Unfortunately, psychiatry is an indefinite—"

Blake interrupted, "Do you ever prescribe medication to prevent a patient from falling asleep?"

Dr. Hillman caught the urgency in Blake's voice and considered this revealing. "Indeed, we occasionally use a class of stimulant called amphetamines. As there is the very real danger of addiction, we are most careful with its administration. I see a lot of substance abuse in my line of work, Blake. Unfortunately 17% of the population suffers from it." Dr. Hillman paused and lit his pipe. "Why is it that you are uncomfortable with the idea of sleep, Blake?"

Blake considered his response. "When one hears or reads of a person dying in his sleep, is it possible that something scared him so intensely that it caused his heart to stop?" Blake's voice wavered a little bit and rose in pitch. "Is it possible that because of a terrible dream, he died of fright?"

Dr. Hillman laced his fingers together and rested them on his soft stomach. "Hmm…. Well, I suppose that sort of thing is remotely possible, but highly unlikely. It is more often the case that a physical condition caused the death. Heart arrhythmia, myocardial infarction." He nodded and looked at Blake.

Blake sounded annoyed. "Do me a favor doc, and don't give me any of that medical jargon crap. I don't really have the time for it." He rubbed his index finger on the flapping adhesive tape on his arm, trying to stick it back into place. "I doubt you are going to find a medical definition that fits my case," Blake looked at Hillman straight in the eye. "Neither would I be surprised if before we were through today, you regarded me as just another nut job, which I am not."

"See here, Blake... please don't concern yourself with that. Just share with me what has been happening to you and rest assured that I have heard many unusual things after twenty years in the practice of psychiatry." Dr. Hillman placed his pipe in the glass ashtray. He hadn't even lit it yet. He reached for his pen and notepad. "Talk to me, Blake. Let me help you. Tell me about these unusual dreams you've been having."

"How did you know about the nightmares?"

"Dr. Thompson mentioned a few things in the discussion we had. He was also concerned about the abrasions and other trauma he'd noticed."

Blake sighed and stubbed his cigarette into the white ashtray. He looked into Dr. Hillman's eyes and seemed to make a decision. He spoke cautiously. "It's really quite simple, doctor.... I have very bad dreams about a shark. A specific shark."

Hillman nodded, signaling him to continue.

"It's a tiger shark about 18 feet long. He has a name... a Hawaiian name that I am sure I do not pronounce correctly. They call him *Kaʻaipoʻo*. I looked it up in the dictionary. I'm fairly certain that it means, *The head eater*." Blake swallowed uncomfortably and lowered his head. In that brief moment, Hillman thought that he looked like a lost, little boy. Correction: a lost, sick, little boy.

Hillman felt a prickling on his arm.

"Doctor?" Blake asked nervously, "Can dreams kill people?" His forehead was moist with perspiration.

"No Blake, they cannot. They can elevate our pulse rate, they can increase our respiration, but I assure you, most certainly, that our dreams cannot harm us physically."

Blake felt frustrated, like he *was* wasting his time. "Doctor, if you don't believe that dreams can harm us physically, how can you possibly sit there and profess to help me?" He stood up to leave.

"Hold on a second Mr. Timmons. Look, Blake. I don't think you understand. You have hardly given me a chance here. We need some more time together. I can already tell by the behavior you are exhibiting that you are in some kind of distress. Let me help you. I can't force you, but if you do stay I am sure it would be helpful. At the very worst, you might think of me as simply being a good listener. I am a good listener, Blake. It is my gift. And I would like to share my gift with you, to help us both understand what is troubling you. Give this process a chance. Stay awhile, Blake. Stay and let me help you with this."

Blake sat down again but he perched himself uncomfortably on the edge of the couch. He shoulders were hunched. He slowly dragged the long blonde hair from his face. Blake took a deep breath, and spoke quietly. "If I'm going to stay for a while, I'm going to need you to make a promise, doc. You must promise me something, even though you don't understand why."

Hillman frowned slightly, "What kind of a promise?"

"You must promise that during the entire time we are together, you'll not let me fall asleep. I repeat, you must promise not to let me fall asleep."

"I think I can offer you that assurance, ahh... promise."

Blake stood up again.

Dr. Hillman raised both of his hands in a gesture of surrender. "I promise, Mr. Timmons. I promise."

Blake slowly sat down again, his left hand lightly caressing the bandage on his right arm. He took a shallow breath. "He comes when I am sleeping."

"Tell me everything." Hillman said calmly. "Remember Blake, I am a good listener. Be honest and as straightforward as you can."

"The first time it happened, I was asleep in my bedroom. I'm single and I live alone. I had just put down the book I was reading, turned off the light at my nightstand and closed my eyes. I began to fall asleep. I felt —at the back of my mind— the drapes moving in front of the bedroom windows, like the wind was blowing through them. The room was getting cold. I breathed in the thick, salty odor of the Pacific Ocean. I have learned since then to hate that smell, doc. It makes me sick."

"Do you live near the water Blake?"

"No, not at all. I live up in the mountains near a golf course. I was happy up there until recently."

"So you smelled the ocean and then what happened?"

"Then I pulled the covers over me, because it was freezing. I began to see an illuminated swirling in the darkness, like a kind of phosphorescence. It seemed to be creating an opening in what I thought was the far wall above the dresser. There was a kind of an ethereal tunnel that formed, and it began swirling in a counter-clockwise direction. The walls were greenish-blue except for the center, which was dark, dark blue. I couldn't believe it. I discovered that by staring directly into the dark blue center, I could see into it for what seemed like miles. Then I noticed a kind of luminescent smear approaching. That's when I first saw the gray dorsal fin." Blake gestured with his fingers in the air, like he was trying to grasp something. "The dorsal fin was moving so rapidly through the water, it seemed I could hear a sizzling sound. Like oil on a hot skillet. I stared at the center of the tunnel in horror as an eighteen-foot tiger shark came charging through it like a torpedo. The shark's speed was incredible." Blake's hands were trembling. He reached for another Marlboro.

Dr. Hillman nodded. "It sounds absolutely terrifying, Blake.

What did you do?"

"I screamed and twisted my body. I ducked my head in and pulled up my knees. The creature streaked past. My knees had come out from under the blanket. As he went by, his sandpaper-skin barely touched the surface of my left knee. I mean *barely* touched it. Blood flowed from it immediately and seeped into the bed sheets. Then the creature turned to make another pass. The second pass was even more terrifying than the first one. He has what they call 'nictating membranes'; it's a second set of eyelids. And as he turned back towards me, they opened. I saw his red eyes tracking me, Dr. Hillman. They were like eyes from hell. Truly ghostly and horrifying. No words can describe the inhuman quality of the look in the creature's eyes."

Hillman was very quiet. Blake had stopped talking and was trying to fish a cigarette from the pack. Dr. Hillman wanted to say something comforting, but he wasn't sure of what to say. He decided that he wanted to keep Blake talking, so he asked a bit hesitantly, "What do you think might be the message of this dream?"

Blake looked at him, surprised by what he thought was a stupid question. "Die? Die now? Die and rot in hell? There was no message, doc. It just wanted me dead. It came in again at my head, extending the teeth outward from its jaws. I saw those rows upon rows of murderous teeth and imagined the horror of being eaten alive. That's when I bolted upright from the bed." Blake couldn't get the Marlboro out of the crumpled pack, so he threw it down on the couch next to him in frustration. Blake looked at the pack of cigarettes and spoke quietly, "I neglected to mention that I pissed all over myself too, doc. What's your fucking medical term for that?"

There was a pause in the psychiatrist's office as Dr. Hillman scribbled on his pad. He pushed his wire-rimmed glasses up to the top of his forehead and exhaled slowly from his pursed lips. "Sometimes our dreams can be very revealing. They can guide us in our lives, help us to choose a direction or path. For a psychiatrist, they can serve as useful analytical tools. I can tell by your description of your dream that you are an intelligent man, Blake. We may want to explore the symbolism you encountered in future sessions."

"I don't think I'm going to be around for any future sessions."

"Maybe that's where I can help," Dr. Hillman said softly. He pressed the tobacco down into the bowl of his pipe and lit it. He exhaled and the smoke rose upwards to be dissipated by the slowly spinning ceiling fan. "As you can probably understand Blake, this kind of lucid dream does not come, pardon the expression, 'out of the blue;' rather it is sometimes an expression of the changes we face in life. Tell me a little bit of what you were doing then… what was happening with you."

Blake started hesitantly. "I'd moved over from Northern California about two years ago. I started working in real estate again. I was doing well. My life eased into a comfortable routine. It was a routine that very much resembled the life I had left in California. Why did I move to Hawaiʻi to live the same life I wondered. I was tired of the numbing regularity of it. I was successful in business. I had a nice girlfriend. But I wanted something in my life that would challenge me, something that was different, something out of the norm. I thought of maybe trying windsurfing, or tennis, but that seemed too… normal. I was also looking for a more meaningful interaction with some of the local people."

Blake took a breath and licked his lips. "One day, this Hawaiian carpenter came over to do a deck installation at the house and he seemed like an interesting man. So after work one day, I popped open a beer for him and we got to talking. He started telling me about a kind of spear fishing called 'night diving.' I could sense the love he had for it and his genuine enthusiasm. I knew right then that I wanted to learn how to do it. It was different, it was even a little strange. Jesse was a bit of a storyteller. He described it as, 'diving in the complete darkness, when the constellation Scorpio swam through the night sky like a great twisting eel.' He said that the dark totality of the sea at night was beautiful. Sounds intriguing, doesn't it doc? Those words of Jesse's still haunt me."

Hillman nodded encouragingly.

"Jesse was an expert free diver. He taught me everything he could. Together we went down in between the coral heads, submerging into the dark, cloudy ravines. He taught me to spear what we needed and only what we needed. I learned to hyperventilate and to hold my breath for long periods of time. I learned to go along the ragged bottom, through the dark green seaweed. I stayed down there until my ears ached, until my lungs screamed for air. In return I hooked Jesse up with several good contracting jobs. Because of my real estate connections, I always knew when clients were considering a remodel or addition."

Dr. Hillman nodded and drew on his pipe.

"That Hawaiian was fearless in the water, because his ancestors considered the shark to be what they called an *'aumakua*: a guardian spirit. It had been that way amongst them for centuries. Ever since I had known Jesse, he was proud of his Hawaiian blood. He seemed grateful for his family's deep connection to the sea. '*Mālama i ke kai*,' he used to say to me. '*Cherish the sea*, Blake. *Take care of the sea.*' He told me that all the time.

It was dark out there, with one small exception: the three foot radius of the dive-light we each carried. The light illuminated a circle on the reef. It was my connection to reality. My mind projected the elements of that circle into the black that surrounded me."

Blake covered his mouth and coughed softly.

"I constructed entire belief systems based on that shining circle, doc, as if the ocean could ever be that simple for a single human being to predict."

Dr. Hillman nodded encouragingly.

"It was during the nights of the new moon or the waning moon that we did our best diving. Jesse told me that when the water was dark, the fish were the most tranquil. We angled down from the surface and we killed them. Nice and tidy. Bang. Right through the head. Easy. The fish didn't struggle; they didn't fight. They flopped against the steel shaft a few times, but that was about it. After we brought them to the surface, Jesse and I dropped them into a bucket. It was a big metal tub, mounted on an inner tube that floated on the surface of the water. Jesse towed it about thirty feet behind us. We were really careful with the bucket. No holes. No leaks. And as soon as we speared the fish, they went in there. No guts spilling out and especially, no blood in the water. That was really important. Jesse was real strict about it. *No blood in the water.*"

"Because of the sharks?" Hillman asked.

"Yes. We took our time and we looked around carefully before we decided to shoot. We aimed well. We didn't want guts and intestines flying everywhere. There were so many fish sleeping at night that we could have speared most any of them. But we didn't. Maybe we would circle around looking for them, go down real slow and easy. Then, we'd aim and shoot."

Dr. Hillman scribbled some notes and frowned. "Blake," he asked, "could you describe your feelings here? How did it feel to be spearing those fish?"

"Well... that was a little weird." Blake tensed. He exhaled slowly through clenched teeth. "The strange thing was, I developed... a sort of... attachment to it. I began to take a very real pleasure in the moment of their deaths. The *whump* of the spear entering their heads was like music to me." Blake paused. "Ever play golf or baseball, doctor?"

"Yes... both."

"Then you know that satisfaction that you feel when the shot is perfect. The perfect connection, that perfect sound? Like the *thock* of the sweet spot on the golf club, or the *thwack* of perfectly hit baseball?"

"Yes, I think I do."

"Well that's what it was like when the spear entered their heads, only more magnified and somehow, more... twisted. I didn't really understand it, but I felt warm inside when I killed them."

Hillman cleared his throat. "I see..." he said awkwardly.

"I began to see myself as a kind of angel, the kind of angel who floated down from the dark sky. I extended my arms to my sides, kicked my fins and came down for them, one by one. *Ulua, āholehole*, snappers, squirrelfish, *kūmū*, squid, *kala, weke*. I drifted down with the dark currents and killed them all. I'd find the big ones yawning under the ledges or the small ones resting in their holes. A brief moment in the shining light, then *whump*, in the head with the silver spear."

Hillman was still scribbling. "How long were you and Jesse out there in the water normally. And how often did you dive?"

"We'd go out once or maybe twice a week. We'd stay out there... maybe three or four hours at a crack. Jesse taught me to carry a five gallon jug of warm water in the back of my Explorer, because after three hours in the salt water, the cold got down deep inside of you. I could feel it drifting in the currents of my blood, settling down into my spine, into the muscles of my legs. I would start to slow down in the water and ache. The signal we had agreed upon was three quick flicks of the switch on the dive light. I would signal to Jesse: *flick, flick, flick.*

Then we made our way back to the surface, back to the beach."

Blake smiled. Dr. Hillman noted that this was the first time he saw Blake smile. Although Blake appeared haggard and psychotic, Dr. Hillman could imagine that Blake was once an attractive man.

"I never knew, doc, that a warm jug could feel like heaven. It was like being resurrected from the dead. You'd hold it up and pour it down on your head and feel like a new man. We'd look at the lobsters, the *kala* and the *weke* in the bucket and we'd talk about the dive. Those were some good times Jesse and I had. I remember many nights talking with him, sitting on the tailgate of the Explorer."

Blake, for a few moments, seemed to be lost in thought. He smiled again and then stopped.

"When I drove him home I noticed that Jesse lived with his elderly mother. I would catch a glimpse of her occasionally, her dark face and long white hair, moving fleetingly past a window at those very odd hours. When we cleaned the fish down at the shore, Jesse always took the heads home for the old lady. He told me it was a delicacy she'd enjoyed since childhood."

Blake looked steadily at Hillman.

"Except for your unhealthy predilection for the death of the creatures, this all sounds like it was rather idyllic."

"I suppose so. But then things started to change," Blake leaned forward a little bit more and paused. "It began when I killed an *uhu*." Blake looked at Hillman's puzzled expression. "It's the name of a fish, doc. *Uhu* feed on the coral, and they sleep in a saliva-ball that they spin for themselves. That night, I came upon a good-sized one, asleep in a hollow on the reef. I swam down close to him, and fired the spear. The instant before the steel went through his forehead, the creature's eyes blinked open. Wide open. It gave me the creeps. That *uhu* looked straight into me as I delivered it to oblivion. I hung there in the current a bit longer, inverted under the ledge, then I dumped him into the bucket. I retreated into the darkness, and shivered from head to toe. I thought about the look in the creature's eyes and I felt the warmth inside me again. Only this time it was better than before. It was a delicious feeling. I wondered what this feeling was and if there was some kind of thread that connected me and that *uhu*."

"Hold on for a minute, Mr. Timmons... Blake." Hillman pressed his intercom button. "Nurse, do I have a three o'clock today?"

The intercom squealed briefly: "Yes sir. Another patient is scheduled."

"Please cancel that appointment and clear the rest of the afternoon."

"Yes doctor."

Hillman lifted his pipe from the ashtray and lit it. "This is most interesting, Blake. Please go on."

Blake lit a cigarette with nervous, trembling hands. "Fucking things will kill you," he chuckled. He took a deep drag and looked around Hillman's white office. He saw the clock on the wall, with its temperature and barometer indicators. He looked at the ceiling fan spinning slowly around and the small orchid plant on Hillman's desk. Blake felt sad and truly miserable. If this didn't work, he was going to die. He wondered how long it would actually take him to die. He wondered if his own death would be like that of a big, spiny lobster he'd caught once. The creature had lain silently beneath the ice of the cooler all night long. In the morning when Blake pulled it out, he was astonished to feel a sharp kick in his hand. It startled him so badly that he almost dropped it on the floor. Things that are alive in this world don't want to die, Blake thought. Things that are alive in this world *don't ever want to die*. That's the reason he was here: so he could get the amphetamines from Dr. Hillman; so he could stay awake

Blake felt that his life depended on it.

"So you were telling me about the *uhu*," Hillman pronounced it "yoohoo" like the chocolate drink. Blake took another drag and exhaled.

"That's right. I knew that the strange warmth I felt was wrong, but I didn't want to admit it to myself. I felt powerless as that... ecstasy, like the cold, seeped down into me. It was tickling me on the inside, like the feeling you get looking down from a tall building. As I continued along in the darkness, I wondered if this was the foreplay, what was the orgasm going to be like?"

Hillman stiffened in his chair.

"Jesse used a Hawaiian sling, a three pronged spear about five feet long. I never felt like that little thing was much protection in the water, so I began to use a Riffe gun that I had special ordered and air freighted from the mainland. The stock was black anodized, heat-treated aircraft aluminum. It was lightweight. The threaded head shaft was propelled by 3 high-power bands. It was a beautiful weapon, doc."

Blake clasped his hands together and continued. "I worked during the day, but the only real fulfillment I could find was in the diving and in the small flame that burned when I heard the *whump*. The Riffe kept recoiling into my shoulder. '*Fuck it*,' I swore, as everything fell apart. Aiming for their heads, I pulled the trigger again and again."

"What fell apart Blake?" Hillman asked, quietly.

"My relationship with my girlfriend, my own admittedly shallow understanding of myself, my professional career. It was quite a list, doc. The real estate market was booming, but it just wasn't interesting me anymore. I was a professional in an escalating market, and against all odds, I was failing. My sales plummeted. I stopped going to the office. I became increasingly annoyed with clients and co-workers. I lost my temper. One day when my girlfriend complained to me about a very small thing, I turned around and slapped her across the face."

Blake raked his fingers through his greasy hair.

"But you know something. Dr. Hillman? I really didn't care. Because nothing was interesting me. Nothing except the eyes of that dead *uhu* and the sheer joy I felt when I drove the spear through his head."

Hillman didn't seem to be taking many notes anymore. He was smoking his pipe, his eyes following Blake's every nuance, each slight movement, every small gesture of his hands.

"One night, Jesse told me to take it easy. He said I needed to be more selective. 'Only take what we need,' he said. 'Damn it Blake, the bucket is too full. Stop killing so many of them.' I looked at him in the darkness on the beach, and I felt like telling him, 'Who the hell do you think you are, talking to me like that?' But I didn't say anything. On the drive home, my anger burned. I smoked a Marlboro and stared straight ahead. Neither of us said a word. When I dropped him off around 3 a.m., the house was dark, but as he was getting his gear from the back, I saw the old lady again, her eyes shining from the small kitchen window."

"Was this man, this Jesse… was he your diving partner who was killed by a shark attack on…" Hillman turned to the notes in the referral, "February 18, of this year?"

"Wow… impressive, doc. I see you read the newspaper." Blake stubbed out his cigarette. "Yup, that was him. Bit the big one. Dropped into the big bucket in the sky. Etcetera, etcetera. Couldn't have happened to a nicer guy too. Boo fucking hoo."

Hillman seemed confused. "Blake, I don't think I understand. Do I take it that you are not saddened by the death of your friend?"

Blake thought about his answer. "I think I was at one time, but I'm not anymore. I'm sadder about this." Blake stood up and turned his back to Hillman. He pulled off his shirt, revealing the huge, still seeping abrasion that ran from his left shoulder in a zigzag pattern down to the end of his tailbone. Dr. Hillman could see where the blood had seeped into the elastic of his under shorts.

"Oh my God," Hillman said softly.

Blake continued with his back turned: "After I got this one, I went to the kitchen and filled up a glass with whiskey. My hands were trembling so badly, I spilled most of it. I took a few mouthfuls of air, trying to catch my breath, and I found myself surprised that I was still alive. The shark had come so close, so damn close. I felt angry and persecuted. I leaned against the kitchen counter and listened to the patter of my own blood, as it dripped down to the floor." Blake exhaled and shook his head.

Hillman twisted the wooden pipe in his hands as Blake resumed his story:

"I hadn't cooked a meal or eaten in the house for weeks. All I did was make coffee. Gallons and gallons of coffee. Coffee to keep away the darkness. Coffee to keep the horrible creature away from my head. I could not afford to fall asleep, because I knew that to sleep would invite the demon back into the world. I did not want that. I definitely did not want that. When the attack happened, I was sitting in my living room on a very uncomfortable wooden stool. After I recovered, I made a mental note to myself to place a wooden block on the seat of that stool. Something to make it even more uncomfortable than it actually was. I had already removed every piece of furniture that could provide the least bit of physical comfort. I threw out my bed, the sofa, the recliner in the living room, the dining room chairs, the patio set. All of it, gone. I couldn't risk sitting on the floor, because I might curl up and fall asleep, so I bought an odd assortment of hard wooden stools. I needed the stools when I discovered that I simply could not stand for a full twenty-four hours a day, Dr. Hillman. I just couldn't do it."

"How long had you been having these... dreams?" Hillman asked hesitantly.

"Since a few days after Jesse was killed. First there is the smell of the ocean, then the temperature drops. It's around that time that the man-eater comes for me. Always in that sequence. Always. The shark lurks outside the reef of my own waking mind. He circles endlessly, waiting for just the right moment to find an opening, to swim in, and kill me."

Blake took a slow breath and coughed a few times, licking the small flecks of blood off his lips. "There's the Hemoptysis," Hillman observed quietly to himself, noting the coughing up of blood that Michael had mentioned in his referral.

"You are probably wondering if I am insane. I'm thinking that is what you are going to tell me today, doc. I'm wondering if you are going to flip open your note book and write down that Blake Timmons is a nut case." Blake held his shirt in his hands and twisted around towards Hillman. "Put aside your scientific jargon, doctor. Consider the remote possibility that Blake Timmons is the victim of some kind of perverse mind-rape, a sick behavior that creatures from hell inflict on the living."

"Mr. Timmons, you can go ahead and put your shirt back on."

Blake pulled the shirt painfully over his back and sat down slowly. He shook his head and enunciated very clearly, *"Maybe I am already dead and your office with the Wisconsin ashtray and the ticking ceiling fan is my own personal hell. Maybe the dendrobium orchid on your desk is more alive than I am."*

Hillman blinked and studied him silently.

"Doc, I am only twenty seven years old. I was —until a short time ago— a successful real estate agent. I don't want to die, but I cannot, for the life of me, figure out how to defend myself. What is that thing? The instant I fall asleep, the horrible shark comes after me. It allows no rest. The creature possesses some kind of inhuman power, the demonic power to tear through the fabric of my dreams. The power to extend its ghostly jaws and lunge for my head. The power to touch my skin and make me bleed. After weeks of sleep deprivation, I am still finding fresh abrasions. God help me!"

"Blake... Blake, please take it easy. I agree you are not well, but please try to find the strength to continue. Maybe I can help you get to the bottom of this. Now... concentrate, please Blake, and let's go back to the diving, after the you speared the yoohoo."

Blake started slowly. "I kept dumping the fish into the bucket, one by one." Blake stared blankly ahead. "Later on, I saw them in my dreams. They had miraculously resurrected. They struggled up the slick, bloody sides of the bucket, cranium-exploded, yet, somehow still lurching towards me. Things that are alive in this world don't want to die, Dr. Hillman."

Blake wiped the perspiration from his forehead with trembling fingers. "One night, I lifted my face out of the water and heard laughter coming from the bucket. Laughter! It was an insane, wicked voice. Evil was spawning, laying its jellified eggs to hatch and crawl into the world."

The flesh on Dr. Hillman's arm crawled and he knew that it was time. "Tell me about how Jesse died, Blake."

Blake sat back a little and swallowed. He looked evenly at Hillman. "Jesse wanted to try a new place to dive. So I drove us out there. It was a beautiful, moonless night, the water... incredibly dark." Blake hesitated. "There were great fields of coral out there and they stretched along the ocean floor for what seemed like miles. We were going along on that last night and it was getting very spooky. Very, very spooky. Because the coral began to sprout a gathering of eels. Soon, we were surrounded by hundreds of them. There were zebras and snowflakes and white ones and purple ones. Their snake-like bodies were protruding from every opening in the coral. We were out there in the deep, as they continued to congregate. Eels were swaying in the currents, opening their mouths as if trying to speak. I could feel the water around us begin to vibrate, as if the eels were singing at some frequency beneath the threshold of human hearing. As we continued in the water, the eels multiplied, and as far as we could see, there were eels everywhere. Their mouths were open, and their eyes were shining. They were dancing on their tails in the beams of our dive lights. My hand clamped down hard on the Riffe gun, because something spooky was happening all around us and I didn't know what the hell it was." Blake's hands were shaking.

"Take it easy, Blake," Dr. Hillman said softly.

"At first I thought it was our dive lights that fascinated them, or maybe the movement of the bucket as Jesse towed it. But as their voices spread through the water, I knew finally that we didn't have a damn thing to do with it. It wasn't about us humans anymore. Something else was going on, something stranger and more deadly than we had ever known. The strong currents kept pushing me and I began struggling over a teeming metropolis, a great coral city of eels. The creatures were all staring upwards, like they were waiting for something impossible to come down from heaven. Slowly, my mind began to scream…"

Blake took in a gulp of air.

"I knew that something monstrous was coming, gliding over thousands of eels, its shadow darkening their teeth, eyes and gills. The eels went into a frenzy, gyrating in an eerie, rippling dance." Blake paused, blinking his eyes. A tear had fallen on his cheek.

"What was it Blake, what was out there?"

Hillman knew that Blake was reliving the horror in his mind; the patient was near a nervous breakdown.

"*The eels had come to worship*, doctor," Blake said forcefully. "Fear gripped my heart and I could not for the life of me shake it loose. A feeling of dread poured into me, like water though the holes of a sinking ship. With my left hand, I swept the light faster and faster. With my right hand I followed the beam with the Riffe gun, clenching the trigger tighter and tighter. I turned towards Jesse, wanting to signal frantically to him. Three quick flicks of the switch, I thought, *three quick flicks of the switch!* I was horrified. The eels were screaming and the circle seemed so small. So pitifully small. Jesse was about twenty feet down. I swam down rapidly, headed forward of him. *Three quick flicks of the switch*, my mind boomed, but one quick flick was all I got to, because in my panic, I used the wrong hand."

Blake sobbed.

"I am not quite sure I'm following you, Blake," Hillman said.

Blake yelled at him, "I saw the eyes again, doctor. The eyes of that sleeping *uhu*. Eyes that blinked open and stared into my soul. I saw them in Jesse's face mask, the instant the big Riffe gun fired."

Hillman swallowed slowly, his Adam's apple bobbing. He blinked his eyes behind his spectacles. The chair squeaked as he leaned slowly backward, instinctively covering his mouth with his fingers.

"The spear entered his head above the mask. The barb went completely through his skull and stuck out the back. Jesse froze at first, letting go of his light and his spear, then the mask broke off his face and drifted down in the current," Blake gulped. "He jerked around and blew the snorkel from his mouth, red bubbles of blood escaped towards the surface. Finally, he just kind of… stopped moving. The blood was pouring from the hole in his head. It colored the water like an enormous red haze. I watched the blood-cloud moving with the current, drifting downwards towards the reef. God forgive me, but as I stared at Jesse, a tiny ember of ecstasy flared in my soul and grew to become orgasmic release. His lifeless body pulling heavily on the stock of the Riffe hung there, dangling from his speared head. I panicked and hit the quick release on the stainless steel cable and watched as Jesse was pulled by the currents towards a seething mass of eels."

"My God," Hillman uttered.

In the silence that followed, the small sounds of the room seemed amplified. Blake heard the slow ticking of the ceiling fan, the quiet hush of the air conditioning vents, the rasp of his and Hillman's breathing.

"The authorities searched for him at daybreak. I imagine they searched for a day or two after that. All they ever found was the empty bucket and Jesse's dive light. If there was anything left, I sure as hell hoped it wasn't the part with the stainless steel spear sticking out of it." Blake paused briefly. "Especially since I told them that we were attacked by a tiger shark."

Hillman's face was still white. He appeared to be partially frozen at his desk. He reached for his notebook, but merely pawed at it before seeming to give up.

Blake looked at Dr. Hillman. "But that's not quite the end of the story," Blake took a breath and continued. "I was really frightened, and because of that, the authorities believed me. But Jesse's family? No way. Jesse's guardian spirit *was a shark*. Jesse's spooky mother came over to the house. She leaned her cane against the lacquered coffee table. She sat very quietly in the chair. She looked in my eyes. It was eerie, doc. I could feel her. I could feel her slithering into me, an old *puhi*, looking for a small opening that would lead to my deceit. I lit a cigarette and smiled at her. The old bitch barely even spoke English," Blake said disgustedly, "yet she had somehow managed to figure it out."

One night I came home from the other side of the island and my front door was wide open. Wide fucking open. I would never, ever leave it that way. Ever. I went in and I knew right away that someone had been there. A strange, salty odor lingered in the house, an odor I would soon become familiar with. I searched around frantically. At first, I couldn't find anything missing. I asked myself, who the hell had been here and what did they want? I drank a whiskey soda and took a long, hot shower. As the water streamed down my back, I thought about it again. What did they want from the house? The steam rose in the bathroom. I ran the water through my hair and rinsed off the shampoo. I kept thinking about it. Turning it over in my mind."

Dr. Hillman could sense Blake's fear. He was becoming very concerned.

"I stepped out of the shower and I saw her. In the condensation of the mirror, the old woman sat with her head tilted towards me. In her lap was a little boy. The boy had on a pair of brown shorts and a white shirt with a blue bow tie. I recognized his face. It was Jesse when he was little. The old lady was brushing his dark, curly hair with a silver brush. It looked as though an old photograph had suddenly come to life. The old lady was embracing the child, whispering the same two lines, over and over again:

Kaʻaipoʻo, ʻau i ka pō

Kaʻaipoʻo, ʻau i ka pō

There was something familiar about the object in the old woman's hand but I couldn't put my finger on it. I looked down at the counter. I could see my hairspray, my cologne, but wait. My hairbrush was missing. I looked in the mirror again and the adrenaline exploded inside me. My hairbrush… it was there, it was there in her wrinkled hand."

Blake shivered and wiped the tears from his eyes. He was crying and rocking back and forth.

Dr. Hillman whispered to him softly. "It's OK Blake... it's OK. I'm going to help you now, Blake. I'm going to help you."

Hillman stood up and walked to the side of the room. From the medicine chest, he pulled out a vial and a hypodermic syringe. Poor man, he thought. Poor, poor man. He inserted the needle in the bottle and withdrew the medication. Hillman squirted some of it out the tip of the needle.

"This is what you need. It will help you Blake. Please roll up your sleeve."

"Thank God, doctor. Amphetamine to keep me awake. Thank God you understand. Thank God you understand!" Tears were coming from Blake's eyes and he wiped his cheeks with his trembling hands. He was so grateful, so very grateful. Then he rolled up his sleeve, revealing his thin, pale arm.

The doctor swabbed his arm and inserted the needle. He pressed down on the plunger and removed the needle from Blake's arm. Dr. Hillman rubbed the spot again with the alcohol pad and patted him gently on the shoulder. "You just take it easy now Blake. Everything is going to be better."

Dr. Hillman turned to place the needle on his desk. Blake's head slumped as he blurted out confusedly, "Whaa? Wait... the... no... NO! YOU PROMIS... you were suppos..."

Blake's eyes blinked twice, then he fell forward into the doctor's arms. Hillman eased him down gently to the couch. He would let the patient sleep for a few hours, then come back into the office that evening and check him into the mental ward. Poor Mr. Timmons needed serious anti-psychotic medication. He would need to be restrained until Hillman could understand the baffling mechanism behind his determined self-mutilation.

Dr. Hillman left strict instructions that Blake was not to be disturbed for any reason. Shortly after he pulled out of the driveway, Hillman picked up his cell phone. He knew that the law required him to immediately report the fact that Mr. Timmons had killed another man. The patient's right of confidentiality only extended so far. Hillman spoke urgently into the receiver.

* * * * * * * * * *

Back at the office, there was a very cold draft coming out from the door, which had been left ajar. The temperature indicator on the wall clock inside was plummeting. Noticing the draft, the nurse rubbed her arms, and closed the door quietly so as not to wake Mr. Timmons. Puzzled, she picked up the phone and called building maintenance. "Tony, it's the air-conditioning. It must be on the fritz. It's freezing cold up here."

Blake did not awaken. The blue-green tunnel swirled. From its ethereal center, a huge, luminescent streak raced unerringly for his head. The gray fin was sizzling. He would live long enough to wish for a much stronger sedative as the red eyes found him.

The instant before Ka'aipo'o crushed Blake's severed head within its jaws, Blake's eyes blinked wide open.

* * * * * * * * * *

A few days later, Dr. Hillman sat at the desk. His face was very pale and perspiration dotted his brow. He remembered the nurse's description of the strange smell in the hallway about the time that Mr. Timmons died. She said it smelled "like when she took the kids to the beach." Hillman looked at the maintenance request on his desk, noting the report on that same afternoon of a malfunctioning thermostat in his office. It was logged but never fixed. The service person was unable to find anything wrong with it.

Dr. Hillman's hands shook as he held Blake Timmons' death certificate. He wasn't quite sure of what had happened to Mr. Timmons, but he looked slowly around his office, and, for the first time in his adult life, he felt truly afraid. Something very, very, strange had happened in here, he thought. He stared in disbelief at the small, dead dendrobium on his desk, thinking about what to write on the certificate. Dr. Hillman shook his head. He was seriously thinking of relocating his practice. He wanted to work someplace where sharks don't swim around in people's offices; where the dendrobiums don't die of frostbite. "God forgive me, I am sorry, Mr. Timmons," Hillman whispered. His right hand trembled as he recorded the cause of death:

myocardial infarction

Author's Note:

I've spent many a night under the stars with my Hawaiian sling. Once, an acquaintance of ours wanted to join us, and my dive partner, Herbert, asked me what kind of spear he would use. I found out it was one of those new, high-tech ones. When I told Herbert about it, he said we should not take him with us. "Why?" I asked. "Too dangerous" he replied. I started to think about it and I realized that Herbert was right: out there in the dark was not the time to have a novice diver come up behind you with a very powerful weapon.

Nā Iwi

As recently as thirty years ago, people on the Island of Hawai'i were still burying their dead in lava tubes along the coast. The bones of our great chiefs were buried in this manner, stripped of their flesh and hidden away for centuries. Perhaps this practice explains why Hawai'i is such a powerful place. There are spirits that dwell within the earth here. On the southeastern flank of the island their wispy exhalations appear, rising from beneath the lava to twist slowly in the breeze.

Years ago, my friend Colin and I were exploring that area of the Big Island. We felt fortunate to get an early start, when a soft ocean breeze wandered amongst the leaves of the *pōhuehue*. Their green vines had blanketed long stretches of the olivine-flecked sand, and in the diffused light they blossomed, opening their purple flowers out along the dunes and downwards towards the sea.

I think I'll always remember the smell of the ocean and the wind as it swept in from the sea. The way it murmured, the way it hushed across the water and turned our footprints back into the sand.

During our years in high school, Colin was described by the teachers at St. Louis as being a "real underachiever." They would pronounce this diagnosis under their breaths, looking at Colin struggling at his desk and shaking their heads. Colin wasn't smart like the rest of the Japanese boys his age; he was different.

Since my family lived in Kaimukī, I had also wanted to go to St. Louis, but because I was Hawaiian, there was no choice in this matter. I would go to Kamehameha. My mother insisted on it. In those days, the Kamehameha School for Boys was a strict, military type school. We rode the bus standing up so we wouldn't wrinkle our neatly pressed khaki uniforms. At school I spent a lot of time spit-shining my shoes and studying military history. I had doubts about how this would prepare me for life in the real world, but my mother never wavered in her decision. She knew I had a quick temper, and hoped that the discipline would be good for me.

At the end of each day at Kamehameha, there was a sequence of three quick bursts of sound: there was the bell, the loud screech of our chairs pulling away from our desks, and the thunder of our shiny shoes running down the hallway.

Curiously, a couple of valleys over, at exactly the same time, the sequence repeated with the kids from St. Louis. Colin didn't quite run with the herd, though. After the afternoon stampede, he meandered down the hallway at his own speed, wearing his wrinkled white shirt of underachievement. Colin walked easily down the steps, sat on the grass and slowly removed his shoes. Then he placed them with their soles together, tucked them under his arm, and proceeded to walk up the hill to Mrs. Hiromi's house, where he took remedial reading. Colin's mom had bought him a plastic pocket protector and a lot of pencils and pens, but he didn't really know how to use them. He had always faced a difficult time in school and his grades were never good.

Colin and I had no plan, no map, and no compass. It was supposed to be two weeks of exploration and two weeks of fun before we went our separate ways. As we came up from the beach that day in Ka'ū, the lava fields stretched from sea level to the much higher, cloud visited elevations of Mauna Loa. As we ate canned corned beef beneath the branches of an old *kiawe* tree, those expansive lava fields seemed like an endless ocean of black, immutable and silent. They held many unknowable secrets buried beneath them. We strapped on our packs and began to walk.

Colin never spoke proper English. He spoke Pidgin, a kind of jumbled up mixture of the languages of Hawai'i's working class.

Pidgin had altered the DNA of the English language and plopped these happy mutations on our tongues. It wasn't beautiful or poetic, but our homegrown dialect had character and honesty. It spread through Hawai'i like a benevolent virus. Our educators, a few petri dishes removed from this concoction, thought that Pidgin was the bawdy language of indolent, brown buffoons. I could turn it on and off, but Colin, well… he never had an off switch.

As we traveled further down along the coast, Colin and I could sense the ocean in the warm air. The force of the waves exploding against the steep embankments would carry for some distance. The muffled "whump" of a huge breaker smashing into the sea-cliffs of Ka'ū was followed by the delicate haze of tiny particles tossed high in the air. Floating in the light trade winds, these droplets would ascend to form a small rainbow. Beneath this shimmering arc we felt like the richest men on earth as the sky filled with a million tiny jewels, each one glistening and more beautiful than the next.

For a while, I wondered if Colin was having some adjustment problems. Not that I'm a person to judge, but for a long time it was almost as if he resisted the idea of growing up. When he was nineteen years old, he would still ride his dinged, beat-up old skateboard on the narrow sidewalk outside of his mother's house in Kaimukī. In fact, that's how I first met Colin when we were just small kids. He must have been eight years old. He came flying down the sidewalk on his skateboard and ran right over the water hose I was holding. The wheels of the skateboard snagged and he crashed into the bushes near the glass jar that we kept on the lawn, so that Mrs. Hanapī's dog couldn't get comfortable enough to make a mess.

"Sorry eh?" I said, watering the weeds and trying not to laugh.

"Ah… shit," he mumbled, dusting himself off and emerging from the shrubbery with a big scrape on his knee.

"You used the S word."

"Sorry," he said bashfully. We stared at each other on the sidewalk, fidgeting.

"You know why I wen' use the S word?" he asked.

"No."

"It's deez fuckin wheels!" he said in exasperation, flipping the skateboard over and pointing them out to me.

I found out that the Fukino family were our neighbors a few streets up the hill. Except for when he ended up in a bruised heap near the stop sign on 13th Avenue, those hellacious turns and airborne jumps along the sidewalk were Colin's pride and joy. He was out there almost every day. It got to be where I could hear him coming down the hill and I'd quickly yank the hose off the sidewalk, so he wouldn't crash into the bushes again. "Shoots!" He'd give me a quick shaka and continue on his way, as the board made a whoosh sound and he rolled down the hill.

Many years later, when I was a student at the UH, we would meet to play pool. His elbows, knees, and ankles were still covered with scabs. One time his knee looked like the knob of a tree branch with some kind of lichen growing on it. It was like my neighbor was covered with a funky purple bark, as he sat struggling through his high school equivalency test. One day, I flat out asked him, "Gee, you goin ride skateboard till you old man, or what? People goin think you retarded."

"Ah… no can help," he said, laughing. "It's… you know… da... da one my foddah wen' give me."

Colin and I hunkered down near the cliffs and smoked a joint. We weren't addicted stoners, but it was kind of a special occasion, plus it was rare that we could find the good stuff, the Puna Butter, grade AAA, "for vacation/recreation use only." Rumor had it they were growing it in a hot house right above the Hilo Police Station.

Crouching as a big wave advanced, we could feel the pressure in our ears when it exploded violently against the outside ledge. The awesome force of the wave would make the earth tremble beneath our feet. The thing was, we couldn't stand there for too long because the mere act of being so close to that tremendous force seemed sacrilegious, a betrayal of the power of nature. We finished smoking the sweet smelling *pakalōlō* and departed quickly.

The local merchants behind the little storefronts in Kaimukī really didn't mind Colin's antics. He was mostly Japanese, with a drop or two of "whatevas" thrown in there. The district of Kaimukī had always been an easygoing place to live and the Fukino family fit right in. As long as Colin didn't steal anything or run over anybody on his skateboard, the kid with the torn St. Louis t-shirt could ride down the sidewalk to his heart's content.

Before we took off, we had spread the gear out on the beach and tried to plan carefully. It would be difficult to carry heavy supplies through the rough, rocky terrain, so Colin and I decided that we would only carry a minimum amount of water with us. We figured that we could easily find fresh water in the exposed volcanic chasms of the area.

When we did find water, we drank thirstily. Although the liquid wasn't entirely pure, at least its brackish taste was tolerable and when we knelt to drink, we cupped the cool, life giving liquid in our hands. I raised my head and looked around me. In the bright sunlight, those wild grottos were strangely beautiful, yellow *pili* grasses and bright green vines cascaded down the steep sides of the hollows. Limpid pools of water stirred in deep caverns of black and green. Magically, on the surface of the pond, tiny flying insects nestled in sparkling concentric circles.

Colin's mother ran a saimin shop in Kaimukī. It was a great place to hang out when we were kids. She wore a blue kerchief wrapped around her hair and her face was always damp and flushed from the long hours she spent boiling the noodles. She would greet me with a shy bow, then take both of my hands and look at me carefully, bowing and smiling. Colin had told her that I was his best friend and in her own way she wanted me to know that she appreciated this. Mrs. Fukino was very generous; she gave us free saimin. Not just any saimin, but "broke da mout" saimin. In the stuffy classrooms at Kamehameha, I'd stare out of the window and could almost taste those long white noodles and that delicious golden broth.

Many times I had watched Colin when he was around his mother. He was always very kind and very respectful of her. Over the years I began to understand that she was the only thing in the world that he really and truly loved.

By about the third day out, the volcanic surface beneath our feet seemed to grow warmer in the deliberate aggression of uninterrupted sunlight. The southeastern district of Kaʻū was arid and dry in the summertime. I took the joint from Colin and inhaling deeply, held the smoke in my lungs as I wiped the back of my neck with an old handkerchief. The white-hot ball of the sun continued its journey, marching on brilliant legs across those relentlessly black fields. We could both feel the heat coming up from the soles of our boots, burning and uncomfortable. As the day lengthened, we continued to hike, our dripping perspiration making dark splashes on the uneven surface. On contact with the heated face of the lava, the tiny beads of moisture evaporated instantly.

We made camp that night and rolled out our sleeping bags. Though very short on water, we still had plenty of dope. This was not too intelligent, but what the hell, the stuff was light. Colin exhaled slowly, coughed and began to sing boyishly, Japanese style. His voice sounded like it was coming from a short-wave radio station in Nagoya:

Momotaro-san, Momotaro-san	*Mr. Momotaro, Mr. Momotaro*
Okoshini tsuketa kibidango	*Carrying kibidango in your waist pouch*
Hitotsu watashini kudasai na	*Please give me one*
Age mashou, age mashou	*I shall give you one, I shall give you one*
Kore kara oni no seibatsu ni	*I'm on my way to destroy the ogres*
Tsuite yuku nara	*If you will come with me*
Age mashou	*I shall give you one*

I remember the time I heard him practicing the piano when he was about nine years old. it. He sat there, with his little shoulders slumped, playing the same single bass note, again and again, staring vacantly at the music in front of him. He tried hard because his mom had wanted him to learn so badly, but according to his frustrated piano teacher, Colin would never become proficient. It's not that there wasn't any feeling in his heart, she said. It's just that she could never teach him how to read the music.

We were pretty stoned. The stars were unusually bright and vivid. In the dense lava fields that night, it was very quiet. Not even a cricket chirped as several falling stars streaked across the heavens. Later as we closed our eyes, a soft wind crept down the southern flanks of Mauna Loa and swirled towards the sea.

At Mrs. Fukino's restaurant, the dilapidated door of the Saimin House sang a chorus of squeaks. This greeting would announce each customer as they arrived to sit on little benches in front of the yellowing Formica tables. "Irashaimase!" she would sing cheerfully, as she brought paper napkins and chopsticks. On the ceiling, brown strips of paper hung down from rusted thumbtacks, each one weighted with a small cardboard tube. This was Mrs. Fukino's front line in an undeclared war against fly-

ing insects - flypaper from Japan. When the squeaky door opened, all the little strips would wave in unison. A dusty fan hummed monotonously in the far corner of the room, as day after day the gleeful field of yellowing goop danced from the ceiling of the Saimin House.

The next day, we woke up early and spent a full two hours looking for fresh water. We found none and continued onward, feeling thirsty and tired. Cresting a hill, we passed slowly over a smooth area. The surface here felt different. It was thinner. Colin and I had come to the top of a lava tube. Lava tubes are made when the outside layer of volcanic rock first cools. There are several famous lava tubes in Hawai'i. Geologists have lectured about them and given them names. Further towards the Hilo side, beneath the thin mantle of camouflaged earth and moving swiftly through blue rock, there exists an incredible network of lava tubes that no human being completely understands. It is these, the ones without names, which are the most dangerous. They are 'ai kanaka - the eaters of men.

Once when I walked in to the Saimin House with my girlfriend Sheila, I stepped on a thick clump of white rice. It clung to the bottom of my slipper. "Colin, you gotta sweep this place up," I said in the direction of the kitchen, hoisting my foot up and scraping off the rice with my fingernail. Colin was getting tired, frustrated with the monotony of the dirty dishes and the sticky floors. He glared at me from the kitchen doorway with a tremendous "stink eye."

"Eh, whatchu talking..." he said, lifting his chin up defiantly, "you neva work one real job in yo whole life!"

This was true and because it was true, it hurt my feelings. Here I was trying to impress Sheila with my sense of humor, but thanks to Colin's shitty attitude I was failing miserably. My temper flared. I clenched my hands into fists and tightened the muscles in my arms. I turned slowly to face him. I was ready to —as we said at Kamehameha, attired in our dress blues— "beef." Sheila sensed that something was wrong and quickly intervened with some comment about how nice the place looked. She was new to the Islands. She pointed to the fat porcelain cat on the counter, with its raised paw, and murmured, "Oh, how cute!" Then I realized, that instead of being Colin's best friend, I had become an unhappy customer with a complaint. Maybe he wished he could be studying at the UH too, instead of working for his mom. Looking at Colin's puffing chest and his soiled apron, my anger faded quickly. He was still my friend, he was just bummed out with all the work he had to do. "Colin... you big dumbass." I muttered, exhaling slowly. I didn't want to fight anymore. I flicked the miniature rice ball towards him, then I grabbed Sheila's hand and we left, the flimsy wooden door squeaking goodbye as we walked out.

"You neva know how deep undaneat stay," Colin said, staring at the black surface and wiping the sweat from an eyebrow with his index finger. "Sometime... maybe hun'red feet." I looked around. It didn't seem like anybody had been this way for a long, long time. We both slowed to a very deliberate pace, the very careful placement of one foot after the other.

I had heard stories about the fragile surfaces of these tubes, about the huge Caterpillar D9 bulldozers that accidentally punctured them, about the men and machines that were swallowed up whole. A cousin of mine in the construction business in Mountain View explained it to me. The operator of the bulldozer extends the rear claw attempting to rip the surface of the field. Everything goes along normally as he begins clearing the lot. Then without warning, the driver hears an enormous crack from behind him as the thin top of the lava tube disintegrates, like a plate of glass. The D9 shrieks, its steel tank treads spitting dirt and clanking in the air. The bulldozer desperately claws for traction because it doesn't have the sense to know that it is already too late. In an instant, all fifty-two tons of Detroit iron plunges down a sharp black ravine. My cousin said that you'd want to die quickly then, and not with an arm or a leg crushed, bleeding to death beneath the bulldozer in the dark

We continued slowly walking along the surface, listening very carefully for any kind of cracking or slippage. All we heard was our own footsteps and the sound of the wind. We camped several miles away for the night, lighting a fire with some small *kiawe* branches. My back was aching and I took out a small flask of brandy. The brandy went down easily, quickly soothing the throat after the harsh bite of the weed. Without adequate water, our throats were getting parched and dry. Off in the distance, I could hear the waves pounding far below us on the coast. The wind was bringing the sound up from the south. The waves down there must have been huge.

"I never really did thank you for the Diamond Head thing, Colin. Not even once. I sorry, eh."

"Ah... nea mind... you would have done um fo' me."

"Yeah but, spooky. How you wen know we was going to make it in?"

"I neva know," he said exhaling the sweet smoke and looking at me.

After classes at UH one day, Colin begged his mom for the afternoon off and even though the weather was bad, we decided to go surfing. We walked down the narrow, winding Diamond Head trail with our 60 pound long-boards and slipped into the water. The waves were running about 10 feet that day, and the wind was fierce, blowing the tops off the crests. We were the only surfers that made it out that far. On my second or third takeoff, I pearled, the nose of my board plowing deeply into the water. The board rocketed back out of the water and went airborne, flipping and turning in the stiff wind. Sticking my head way out of the water to see where it would land was a foolish amateur mistake. The big green tanker fell heavily on my skull. I sank beneath the surface and then rallied. Blood from a deep gash in my scalp poured down my forehead and into my eyes. From a day that had started with the Heisenberg Principle in Physics class at the University, I had made a startling transition. In the frenzied waters off Diamond Head, I was suddenly faced with my own mortality.

Try as I might, I couldn't seem to catch my breath as the next big wave pushed me under. The white foam around me was turning pink from my own blood and the more I struggled, the more I realized that I was badly hurt. The undertow kept pulling me out and the big waves kept pounding me and pounding me.

That is when the panic began.

There is no deadlier place to panic than in the water; it doesn't get any deadlier than that. Exactly when the body needs to conserve its own precious resources in order to survive, panic bursts into the heart muscle and injects the awful adrenaline of all-consuming fear. Try to imagine the disciplined and moral structure of your own mind, in an instant, caved in by an irresistible and snarling schizophrenia. The result of this extraordinary terror is the expelling of what little breath remains in your lungs. You struggle even harder, consuming even more oxygen. Finally, when the oxygen is completely exhausted, a brilliant light streaks through the interior of your mind like a shard of glass falling from a tall building. Millions of years of human evolution are overturned instantaneously, almost as if a switch, deep inside your psyche, has been flicked off. You are no longer an air-breathing creature. Time ceases. You sink beneath the surface of the waves. The water welcomes you. You inhale it. By accepting it into your body you join with it, in a deep, almost spiritual way. The final release is comforting. There is no good, no bad. Your weak arms flail, as the bitter salt water pours into your body. You are not afraid anymore. You stop retching. You stop convulsing. There is still enough electrical activity in your brain for you to process visual information, so you open your eyes and see yourself inverted and slowly twirling downwards.

The sea became exquisite. Beneath the undulating surface it was silken and smooth, like the skin of a beautiful woman. I knew I was dying. It would take a few moments longer for the electrical activity in my brain to cease, but I was resigned to my fate. The beautiful blue woman seemed to come closer. I could almost make her out, the shape of her shoulders, the smooth curve of her neck. I was filled with a bittersweet love and I yearned for her embrace. That was when a small fin cut like a scalpel through her flesh. It was circling in towards me.

Colin skirted around the break, dived under the water and miraculously caught me by the ankle. He surfaced with my head in the crook of his arm and pulled me up to the board. I must have been semi-conscious, because I heard him cry out when he saw my purple face.

It seemed like a long way in, and to tell you the truth, I don't remember much of it. Colin closed my nostrils and blew into my lungs. He rolled me over and after awhile, I held on to the board by myself, expelling the seawater and vomiting as he worked his way back to the shore. On the beach, a tourist ran over to one of the houses and called an ambulance. I was fading in and out of consciousness from the near drowning, blood loss and concussion. Blood from my head smeared into the plastic padding of the gurney as I closed my eyes and was carried up the trail.

I spent a couple of days at Queen's Hospital. They stitched up my scalp and used a mechanical respirator to re-inflate a collapsed section of my lung. Then they gave me some drugs to prevent the spasms I was having. In a lucid dream one night, the blue woman looked down at me from the textured ceiling of the hospital room.

After I was released from the hospital. I never had the courage to tell Colin how lucky it was that he found me <u>after</u> the panic had subsided. Had he arrived only moments earlier, I know I would have dragged him under with me. Of this, I am absolutely certain.

About the fifth day out we came across a large glazed field of *pāhoehoe*. The smooth shiny surface of this type of lava ran along the coast for miles. Halfway across the field, in between tufts of wild yellow grasses, we found a profusion of *ki'i pōhaku* - Hawaiian petroglyphs. These were evocative stick figures of animals, fish, men and women, engraved in the hard surface of the lava. It is human nature to make known the journey of life, but I wondered, why here? Why here as opposed to five feet away? Colin and I knelt to examine the fascinating icons when the answer came to me.

I explained it to Colin as best as I could. *Mana*, found in all matter and all forms of life, is cosmic energy or life force. There is no denying its reality. *Mana* is. For us it is often a question of strength or amplitude, or in Western parlance, different degrees or "voltages." For *Kanaka Maoli*, the *kapu* chiefs of old Hawai'i had the most *mana*. They were Gods who walked the earth. The area where we now stood was thought by my ancestors to have a special concentration of the life force and as I stood there, soaking in the aura of the petroglyph field, I wondered if the ancient symbols were being broadcast into the vastness of the universe, amplified by the powerful *mana* beneath them. Knowing the hands that had created it had certainly turned to dust, I studied a gloriously beautiful, deeply incised petroglyph of the Sun.

At camp that night, we sat up listening to the wind and talking. I busted out the mescaline I had bought from a pony-tailed dealer on the steps of Hamilton Library. In that same library was a book where Aldous Huxley had said about Trimethoxyphenethylamine:

"If we could sniff or swallow something that would, for five or six hours each day, abolish our solitude as individuals, atone us with our fellows in a glowing exaltation of affection and make life in all its aspects seem not only worth living, but divinely beautiful and significant, and if this heavenly, world-transfiguring drug were of such a kind that we could wake up next morning with a clear head and an undamaged constitution—then, it seems to me, all our problems (and not merely the one small problem of discovering a novel pleasure) would be wholly solved and earth would become paradise."

Huxley was "da man." Colin didn't know who Huxley was, but I figured I could tell him later. Since Colin didn't hang out with the same radicals at the university that I did, he was very hesitant to take a psychedelic, but I talked him into it.

"Why no chance 'um, brah?" I said with a smile. I figured he'd probably have a good time, but I got the feeling he was taking the stuff just to keep me company. There were only four tabs, so we took one each. I settled back to wait for my ego to dissolve.

"So how's it going at the Saimin House?" I asked blinking.

"Da guy from da bank came by and made my moddah cry. We not doing too good."

"Ah, shit. You work hard over there. Your father would be proud of you, Colin, I know he would."

"I not smart, like you. I just me." I was feeling the warmth of the mescaline surging through my system and the sound of his voice trailed off, wavering. The moon skipped across the water and I was bathed in its soft green light. I laid my head down, thinking of Colin's father and wondering if his view of heaven looked anything like the moon did on this night.

It had happened very suddenly. Colin's father went to the doctor one day and discovered he had terminal lung cancer. Six weeks later, he was dead. I remembered the funeral for Roland Fukino. It was a simple service in Nu'uanu during a rainy afternoon when the newly mowed lawn was fresh and green. Colin and his mother stood off to the side. The rain made a slow hushing sound as it came down the valley. There were orchids and anthuriums and sprigs of cherry blossoms. Mr. Fukino's ashes lay in a small urn as the priest and monks burned incense and chanted. The sweet incense smell mingled with the fragrance of newly mowed grass. The rain continued for a while, then it stopped. The big clouds tumbled forward towards the ocean, leaving the sky, once again, a deep cobalt blue. As the sunlight played on the rock wall behind him, Colin stood gently supporting his mother. It was their belief that when the father died, the son became the head of the family.

The priest's chant came to a crescendo as beams of sunlight flickered down among the dark crevices of the rocks in the small garden. A fresh wind came down from the Pali, moving gently through the colorful sprays of orchids. When the petals of the little yellow flowers quivered, I had the distinct feeling that Mr. Fukino's soul was on its way to heaven.

I wondered if Colin considered himself fortunate to have had at least a basic understanding of his father. My own father had deserted us when I was only a year old. When the adze was removed from the smooth surface of my life, there was nothing there. Not even a scratch. How does a person do this to his own son?

During the last week of Roland's life, Mrs. Fukino came down to the bus stop and spoke to me. She said that Roland wanted to see me. She showed me past Colin's abandoned piano, into her husband's small room off the hallway. The old man coughed into a bloody rag, rose up in bed and pressed $50 into my hand. He whispered, "Please. Boy. I no can go out. You know these things that you boys do. Please help. My son, he not smart boy like you, but he good boy. He real good boy. Buy my son something for me, something he can love."

The next day I skipped school and went to Kaimukī Sporting Goods. I bought the best damn skateboard they had. I took it home and wrapped it up and everything. On the card, I wrote in big block letters:

To Colin with love, from your Dad.

I took it over to their house and gave it to Mrs. Fukino before Colin got home from school. "You one good boy," Mrs. Fukino said, cradling the package in her arms on the steps. There were tears in her eyes.

"You miss um, Colin?" I asked.

"Who?"

"Your father."

Colin stirred a little and leaned up on his elbows. A small white moth flew into the campfire. "Yeah, but, he wen' die, and as why I gotta tink harder about stuff. Maybe I gotta help my moddah too."

"I wish my father was dead," I proclaimed, my voice breaking

Colin cocked his head to the side and seemed genuinely puzzled. "Wassa mata you, bra? No talk li dat. Bumbye you only come sad. Maybe yo' foddah, he love you, but someting wen happen and he no can stay." Colin reached out to put his hand on my shoulder, "You no have to be around all da time fo' love somebody," he said quietly.

We awoke the next morning and moved forward, feeling thirsty and dehydrated. As time went by, we were really starting to struggle in the heat. "I gotta rest," I said, breathing raggedly as we approached the top of a lava mound. We rested for a few minutes, so I could catch my breath.

There was something very odd about the place where we had stopped. It didn't feel right. There was a peculiar kind of slope to the surface and a strange feeling in the patterns of swirls that had hardened in the rock. I was beginning to think that someone had already been here before us. "Do you feel funny about dis place?" I asked Colin, looking around uneasily. He seemed to be having some difficulty breathing, so he didn't answer. I knew the canteen on his belt was empty. "Jesus, Colin, take one sip...." I said quietly, and gave him what little remained in mine. We were too tired to move on. There were only two mescaline tabs left, and thinking it might help ease the pain, we sat down and each swallowed one, dry.

I remember it was raining in Kaimukī. Big heavy drops of rain that splashed down on the sidewalk. The alleyway behind the Saimin House was almost flooded, as the water swirled downwards towards the storm

drains on Waiʻalae Avenue. I came in the door and lightly brushed the water off my hair with my fingers. I sat down at a wooden table, telling Colin how frustrated I was at the university. I told him I was at the top of my class but I didn't feel appreciated by the faculty and I felt like I was going nowhere. I told him I was going to apply to another university. Maybe even Boston College.

"Boston?" *he said blinking,* "Bruddah, it's cold ova deah! You betta bring extra strength BBD's, cuz you goin freeze yo olos off."

"Ha… Ha…" *I laughed, as a gust of wind blew the rain against the outside window. The cars driving by had turned their lights on, making swishing sounds in the torrential downpour. Down the street, the stoplight had gone out and a lone cop dressed in a yellow raincoat was directing traffic with a flashlight.* "Howz about you?" *I asked,* "How you and Mom doing in dis place?"

Colin looked in my eyes and the laughter in his voice emptied right out onto the cold, stone floor, "We not doing good. Da old folks, dey all… dey all old, dey no come around like how used to be." *Colin hesitated,* "Too much money we lose, too hard on my moddah. We gotta get some moa money somehow…. So… I goin join up."

I looked at him, incredulous and replied hesitantly, "Wha… Colin, no man, … no! You can't be serious! You eva heard of Vietnam?"

"Yeah," *he said softly, slowly putting his head down to look at the floor. The rain was really coming down now, drumming on the rooftop and pouring into the little streets of Kaimukī*

This was the person who had saved my life. He had saved my life so I could grow up, so I could get an education, so I could have a chance to be somebody. I wondered if there was some way I could prevent this stupid thing from happening and maybe, just maybe, return the favor. Colin was my best friend. I had to help him think through this before he got in too deep. Before it was too late for him and his mom. I searched my mind frantically. My breathing quickened and I slammed the glass down hard on the table. "What the hell is wrong with you, Colin?" *I yelled.* "Are you are going go from riding skateboard in Kaimukī to killing people in rice paddies? Are you fuckin' out of your mind? You always were pretty dumb Colin, but this is the dumbest, stupidest plan you have ever thought up. You betta' fuckin wise up, you dumbass, before you get yourself killed!" *It didn't quite come out the way I had hoped. The customers at the other tables turned to look in our direction. Mrs. Fukino came quickly through the doorway. She didn't understand what was going on, so she just stood there, looking uncomfortable and twisting a dishrag in her hands. Colin stood up, shook his head sadly then walked past his mother into the kitchen. I stared at his retreating back in sheer disbelief. The anger exploded in my chest and I swept everything off the table with a lunge of my forearm. The plates and glasses and the beautiful saimin bowls that Mrs. Fukino had hand carried from Japan broke into a thousand little pieces on the hard concrete floor. Mrs. Fukino stared at me in horror, as I screamed:*

"*You're a stupid fuck Colin. A stupid, stupid fuck! Come home in a body bag you dumb shit and see how much fuckin help you are then.*"

I slammed open the door with my shoulder and ran down the wet sidewalk. I kept going, splashing through the muddy puddles along Wai'alae Avenue. I walked over to the playground and sat down heavily on a swing made from an old rubber tire. The chain creaked under my weight. I held on to the chains with both hands, and swung my legs up, feeling the rain pelt my face and drip down my arms. Another squall had come down from the mountains, misting and swirling into the lush green valley below. The little streets and houses in the valley gradually disappeared behind a veil of dark, gray rain. I stopped swinging and put my hands over my face. I couldn't see where he lived anymore.

My eyes were feeling gritty. There just didn't seem to be enough moisture in them. One eye in particular seemed sticky and slow, shriveling up in my head like a rotting plum. Tripped out and dehydrated, I noticed the puzzling orientation of a large rock straight ahead of us. Colin saw it too. The odd placement of that rock didn't seem to be a natural occurrence of the lava flow in this area. The hair on the back of my neck squirmed and I moved back cautiously. The mescaline was kicking in big-time and I bent over and vomited a sticky mass of something unrecognizable. I straightened up and looked at the rock again. It was entirely possible that the *pōhaku* had been placed there by hands from another time. I staggered briefly as the sun beat on the back of my head.

It wasn't too long before I packed my bags and headed for college in Boston, Massachusetts. Colin drove his father's old Buick down to the airport to say goodbye. At the gate, Colin gave me a beautiful lei 'awapuhi. Along with the radiant ginger lei, he gave me a few packages of pickled mango. "You goin miss da local grinds," he told me, as I gave him a hug.

When the big plane thundered down the runway, I felt comforted somehow in the fragrant embrace of my friend's lei. I wondered how Colin would handle basic training in the U.S. Army and I was hoping that he wouldn't have to go to Vietnam. There were other places they could send him, I thought. Then I realized that those concerns were behind me now, there was simply nothing I could do. Colin's life was his own. My shoulders slumped. "Take care of yourself Colin," I mouthed silently as I looked out the window. One by one, our beautiful islands disappeared like jewels into the thick, purple darkness of the Pacific night.

Colin and I began to understand why men on the earth had always worshipped the Sun. Across the black desert a rioting nuclear furnace unfurled its unimaginable power. It was without mercy. In the space of a couple of weeks, the Sun had gone from life-giving friend to a dangerous adversary. Colin and I had completely run out of water. As the hours went by, the overwhelming energy of that burning mass seemed intent on killing us. In the blasting heat, we sat there with our parched lips and our blistering skin, wondering what we were going to do next. We were hoping that the mescaline would make it easier, but we both had a sinking feeling in our stomachs when we considered the fact that we might not even make it back at all. Nervously, I began scratching at my forearm, the small pieces of dead peeling skin clogging my broken fingernails

Sitting around the dormitory with my new longhaired friends, we watched Richard Nixon on television. He was pulling slips of paper out of a jar. Those little bits of paper held tremendous significance for us. They were our birth dates and lottery numbers for the draft. Tricky Dickie, smiling at the cameras, seemed happy in this element. Although we booed him soundly, drunkenly throwing our beer cans at the squawking TV, he never once flinched. Nixon's concentration could not be disturbed. He was busy sending American boys off to war.

The sun blazed in from the sea and was burning in my face. "We need water," I said weakly as Colin looked at me, confused and exhausted. In the withering heat, every breath burned in our lungs and our reward for even the smallest physical exertion was torture. All across the horizon, the sky was on fire. Colin and I were descending into hell.

Getting off the MAC transport, Colin swung the A.L.I.C.E. Pack over his shoulder and marched with the other soldiers down a steep metal ramp. The M1919A4 Browning machine gun that he carried was so new, it smelled of plastic and machine oil from the manufacturing plant. Before the big jet had touched down, Colin kept his promise to his mother and slipped a small good luck charm over his head. He thought of how she had given it to him, how she had pressed it into his hand as they stood in the kitchen. "I always love you, son," she said softly, leaning her head against his chest.

When he signed the enlistment papers, Colin had imagined that his

mother would be proud of him. He was finally doing something responsible. He would send her his paychecks and maybe at last, they could pay off the mortgage on the Saimin House. When he announced what he had already done, there was not even a hint of pride in her delicate face. There was only sadness. It was a kind of sorrow Colin had never witnessed before. It was a sorrow like the low notes of a grand piano: haunting, aching, and flowing like a river across the distance between them. There was something else too that he noticed when he looked into her eyes. She felt a longing for the boy he used to be, the boy that sat on her lap, clinging stubbornly to her cloth apron. "You grow up too fast, Colin!" she cried, sobbing and angry.

On the last day he saw her, she wore the same blue kerchief she had always worn. With her thin hands she covered her face and leaned sobbing against the kitchen sink. It was that vision of her that he carried with him now, the back of her shoulders shivering in anguish, as the steam from the boiling noodles rose in the air.

Colin stared at the big stone with a strange expression on his face. Hallucinating, he somehow believed that there was water beneath it. He knelt down, grabbed hold of the large stone and motioned for to me to help him. Together we rolled back the rock cover that someone long ago had so meticulously placed. When the old stone gave way, a shaft of sunlight pierced the darkness below and a musty putrid odor escaped from deep within the hole.

I inhaled sharply when I saw them. *Nā iwi.* The bones. Bleached white, they stood out in stark contrast to the *kā'ai*, or plaited container that had originally held them. Shining in the deep darkness of the cavern, the bones were intensely hypnotic. Incredibly, the luminous architecture of the skull seemed to float above the black surface of the floor. The old bones were frighteningly real, but at the same time they seemed to exist in a dream. Colin and I could not turn away. My mind was exploding. I knew that *nā iwi* contain great *mana*. Long after the body crumbles to dust, the bones emanate a potent cosmic force

Amongst contemporaries of mine, there were those who whispered that when the spirit "crossed over," the *mana* actually emanated from some other time, perhaps even from some other dimension.

As the power of gravity can be strong enough to bend light, so the power of *nā iwi* can be strong enough to bend human reality. Anyone stupid enough to touch these bones could live the rest of their days with hands, useless and dying; their fingers deformed, slowly spreading a horrific blackness further and further into the human psyche.

As Colin and I stared down into the black cavern, I became petrified with fear. The *iwi* stared back at us with empty eye sockets, framed by several long bones that seemed to have torn through the crumbling *kā'ai*. When I saw the revealed bones of one hand pointing directly up at us, I reeled backward from the opening, gasping for air.

Colin was waiting for the Lieutenant. He sat up in the driver's seat of the Jeep, and reached for a reefer. He was jumpy. An M-16 lay across his lap, close and comforting. The ring finger of Colin's right hand began tapping on the scarred clip. Tap tap tap... tap tap... tap tap tap, went the finger. Unconsciously, he repeated the pattern, tapping again and yet again. SOS... SOS... SOS... Colin telegraphed in Morse code. Help me... help me... help me. Listening to the radio, he heard the early recon reports coming in from the field. No enemy contact. Three more months, he thought. Three more months and I can go home.

A heartbreaking sound echoed out across the lava. It was the unexpected and sickening whoop of dementia. It was a sound that didn't seem to come from Colin's throat. It emerged instead, from his *na'au* - from Colin's gut. If you had heard it, you would never, ever want to hear it again.

The delicate structure that we call sanity began to unravel in Colin's head. Zzzing it sang, like a reel of fishing line fluttering to the floor. The closer we got to the powerful *mana*, the more of our own life force it exacted. Me, I had my ancestors to guard me, but Colin was not so lucky. The price that he paid, no one could have anticipated. It was the reality of his existence, eclipsed by a darkening and terrifying hallucination. He lurched forward, blowing through the circuits of his wiring as if they were cobwebs. He turned into a cornered animal. Snarling. Screaming. Before I could move to stop him, Colin had hurled a fist-sized rock down through the opening. The missile was dead on, catching the skeleton directly in the center of the chest. There followed an ungodly sound as the rib cage of *nā iwi* smashed into a thousand sharp fragments. Colin screamed a last horrible shriek as a cloud of dust rose up violently from the floor of the cave.

The humidity in the jungle air was almost unbearable. Colin, still in the jeep, felt the moisture settle around his face like a suffocating plastic bag. When he turned his head, the thick foliage assaulted his nostrils with a strange, ripe smell, and the sounds, the furtive whisper of who knows what. For him, the sounds marked the passage of his every footstep in this god-forsaken country. They were the musical accompaniment to his sojourn in Vietnam, composed in two distinct movements. The first movement was entitled "tedium," the second, "terror." A metallic clink there, a hushed voice here. Was it a tree in the wind? Or was it the harbinger of some really "bad shit," like the extreme violence of a few days ago, when a deadly column of little men in black pajamas advanced relentlessly on his forward position. Colin melted into the earth as their weapons shredded the jungle canopy above him. He leveled the Browning on full-auto and pressed the trigger, screaming. He finally stopped when the belt was empty, the barrel red hot and sizzling. Colin stopped speaking Pidgin on that day. In fact, he rarely spoke at all anymore. There didn't seem to be a need for it.

Looking at the destroyed *iwi*, I fell to my knees. Colin's psychotic scream was still reverberating in the dark cave like some kind of an insane nightmare. You have no idea what you have done my friend, I thought, terrified.

"Colin," I said through parched lips. "You should neva mess with the bones! I can't explain it, but…." I couldn't finish. There were no more words to say. My forehead was on fire and I began to shake in little twitching spasms. Staring uncomprehendingly at Colin, I stiffened up and fell forward to the ground.

The fatigues he wore were mud-caked and fouled with sweat. He was nearing the end of the tour and it was about time for some new replacements to come in from Da Nang. Damn! he thought, there it was again, that uncomfortable feeling at the back of his neck. He was tired of waiting for the lieutenant. He started the engine of the jeep, revving the motor. Feeling a slight buzz from the shitty dope, he had the strangest feeling that someone was watching him. He should move very quickly now. "Now Colin!" the inner voice roared. "NOW."

Colin hung by his hands, swaying slowly from the ceiling of the small lava tube. He released his grip. With a thump, he landed on the stone floor of the dark mausoleum. The destroyed *iwi* no longer seemed to glow; instead they lay decaying, enshrouded in the slowly settling dust. Colin had never felt the way he felt now. He was in the burial cave but then he wasn't. He was at home with his mother. No, he was smiling and riding his skateboard, the bearings in the wheels singing as they turned round and round. The faces of his neighbors in Kaimukī were smiling, nodding. His mother poured a steaming cup of green tea into a ceramic cup, which had the most beautiful flowing Kanji. Kimono blurring, she moved in reverse, then she began pouring the tea all over again. Roland pressed a bloody rag to his lips, coughed and told him that now, he was the head of the family. Suddenly a sharp acid exploded in Colin's throat and the bitter bile flooding his mouth shocked him back into the present. The mescaline was making him vomit. In a bizarre way, the wretched fluid had risen up in his defense. Fortunately for Colin, the shock of his own body revolting was just strong enough to shield his psyche from the passage of something truly unearthly. As he stood there dry heaving, a yellow vomit foamed along the side of his mouth and dripped down to the dark lava floor. A frigid needle pierced him right down to the center of his being. He shuddered horribly. For the tiniest fraction of a second, Colin Fukino was as cold as he had ever been.

In the hills beyond the parked jeep, a large black bird took to the sky. Drawn towards him, the bird flew on to circle over his position. Colin watched it gracefully riding the currents of warm air, soaring, gliding, rising and turning. As the bird circled, a growing certainty settled over him. Somehow he understood that he would never make it home, that he would die in Vietnam. Colin considered stomping on the gas pedal, but he couldn't seem to move his foot. He was extremely tired, tired of slogging though the rice paddies and tired of the war. Colin put down the M-16. He leaned it forward against the metal dashboard. He turned off the ignition. As the quiet flooded his senses, he seemed at last to appreciate the great beauty of the dense, green jungle that surrounded him. He felt the warm air, the damp of the earth. He tipped his helmet back and lit a cigarette, inhaling the smoke deeply into his lungs. More peaceful than he had felt in a long, long time, Colin leaned back in the seat and looked up through a perfectly clear sky. Slowly, effortlessly, the beautiful dark creature rode the air.

After a time in the burial cave, the coldness finally dissipated. When his senses began to recalibrate, Colin heard the very faint sound of water dripping. Soon, he found the source. Resurrected by the sight of the cool, pure reservoir, he cupped the water in his hands and drank deeply. He filled the canteen. Climbing up to the surface, he placed the canteen to my lips.

I received his letter one rainy day in early November. During that time of year in Boston, the trees were like sticks. When a cold gust of wind blew in from the north, they gestured in vain against a gray sky. As I hurried from Gasson Hall to my room, the temperature was plummeting. All around the campus, wet brown leaves blew in stiff circles. The snow would be falling soon. I ran up the stairs and turned up the heater, pulling off my woolen gloves with my teeth.

I looked slowly out the window and down to the courtyard as the fallen maple leaves swept down along a cobblestone alley. They were swirling in the bitter-cold wind and gathering in small dark mounds along the bottom of a wrought-iron fence. I held Colin's rain-spattered envelope with my clumsy and still-stiff hands, but I was afraid to open it. I missed my friend and yet I couldn't help but wonder how the passage of time and the influences of the two different worlds we inhabited would affect our friendship. Would these separate journeys diminish or strengthen the bond between us?

I didn't know the answer to this question, and I didn't know where to even look for the answer, so for the first time in my life, I spoke to Ke Akua. *I sat back in the worn chair and closed my eyes. I prayed that despite the differences that had shaped our lives since we left home, the bond of friendship that had begun from small kid time would remain strong, even if Colin were a soldier. Even if I was actively protesting the war. It wasn't much of a prayer, but what it lacked in eloquence, it made up for in sincerity. It was the best I could do. Things had changed so much since I saw him last and, of course, Colin had no way of knowing that the SDS was headed into Washington D.C. that weekend. I had just been elected one of its leaders. Under my bed was a gas mask.*

Sitting quietly in the dusk by the window I saw my prayers turn into vapor, my simple words to God misting in the icy air of the small room. On the coldest November day I had ever known, I opened his letter and the tears finally came.

Colin wrote that he didn't want to be in the army anymore, that he hated the war. I still remember the last part of his letter, which he had underlined:

I like come home

Years later, I received a visit from the lieutenant whom Colin was driving on the day he died. Sipping a beer and nervously glancing around the bar, he told me the story of how Colin's life had ended. The first mortar round hit near the jeep, blowing him into a steep trench at the side of he road. The lieutenant thought he might have still been alive then, because it wasn't shrapnel that killed him. It was a fist-sized rock, blasted from the hillside by a second mortar round. The murderous stone ripped into the trench and struck him full on in the center of the chest. By the time the platoon had fought off the VC patrol and returned to find him, a third mortar had scored a direct hit on the jeep. Colin had been dead for over an hour. His remains lay at the bottom of the trench, his flesh and uniform burned away from the gasoline. When they saw him, some of the men lowered their weapons, bowed their heads and made the sign of the cross. He was just a skeleton by then, said the lieutenant, a skeleton with the bones of his chest caved in.

The hair on the back of my neck stood up and I looked down at my left arm, covered with chicken skin.

* * * * * * * * * *

The sun is coming up over Punchbowl, the National Memorial Cemetery Of The Pacific. I park the rental car and ask my wife to wait for me. Before closing the door, I reach into the back seat and take the yellow flowers in my hands. As I walk out along the path, I begin to feel the serenity of this beautiful place, this volcanic crater on the Island of Oʻahu. The scent of ginger blossoms breathes gently in the morning air. I remember that in old Hawaiʻi, this area was called Pūowaina - a hill for placing human sacrifices. All around me, the morning the sun casts little shadows on the grass.

Human sacrifices indeed. I rake my hands through my hair and try to remember my dear friend. The good times we had growing up together, Mrs. Fukino and her golden noodles, the rickety skateboard rolling along the sidewalk. My best friend who told me, "you no have to be around all da time fo' love somebody."

"It's O.K. Colin, you're home now," I whisper, placing the *lei 'awapuhi* on his grave.

Across vast green fields, headstones are lined up by the thousands, row after endless row.

Legions of *Nā Iwi*.

Author's Notes;

I graduated from the Kamehameha Schools in 1969 and went on to attend Goddard College in Plainfield, Vermont. This was during the height of the Vietnam War. Several friends of mine were killed during that conflict. "Nā Iwi" is based on an incident that really happened. We did find those precious bones hidden in a lava tube.

My Beautiful Puka

The sea made funky music. It was the thunder of big waves breaking and the warm slurp of currents moving gently up the pilings of the old dock. I stood there in the stinking hot sun and felt the powerful urge to give up my landlocked existence. Gazing into the deep blue of the channel, I wanted to get out there, out into the vast Pacific, where men are men and the big *'ahi* lift weights and mock us.

I was standing at Mala wharf in Lahaina, watching the mosquito fleet come in. The decrepit wooden dock reeked of fish scales and gasoline. I paced along its weathered, creaking boards, desperately yearning for my own boat. I could feel this desire put-putting within me, churning through my guts like the dented propeller of a small outboard motor. Then again, could be heat stroke, I thought, suddenly immersed in a cloud of exhaust from some dumb hippie's prehistoric outboard engine. It was mid-July and unbelievably hot. High overhead, the cruel Lahaina sun dragged its burning *'ōkole* across the sky.

As I made my way across the asphalt of the parking lot, I noticed that even the mynah birds were sweating. They hopped about frantically in their little black coats - not because they wanted to, it was just so frickin' hot, their little feet were burning.

Up from the boat ramp, my friend Bruddah Louie had one of those suction things attached to the motor on his homemade sampan. Bruddah was flushing the engine, smoking a reefer, blowing *hūpē* out of one nostril, and trying to pick up chicks, all at the same time. Gee, I was kind of impressed. In this modern age, even us Hawaiian guys were learning to multi-task. Bruddah had his shirt off and his big belly rolled over a pair of *puka* camouflage combat shorts. Now how could any woman in her right mind resist that, I thought. I was jealous that he had his own boat. His rusting Evinrude was so loud, I couldn't understand what the hell he was saying. It sounded like,

"*Hūi* Bruddah! Nice day for one PUT PUT PUT PUT eh?"

"Yeah, but hot like one PUTPUTPUTPUTPUT."

"As why get wata hose and PUTPUTPUT fan eh?"

"K'den RRRRRRRRRRPUTPUT."

I get mad at Bruddah Louie, mostly because he still owes me twenty bucks, but I would have given my left nut to trade places with him. Unfortunately, I'm pretty sure a lien was placed on it by the IRS. I slammed the door of my rusting piece of *kūkae* and rested my head wearily on the steering wheel. You see, I was suffering from some ... shall we say ... tax *pilikia*? Almost every other day, the Feds were hounding me with nasty phone calls. I answered my telephone now in the voice of an extremely elderly Japanese lady,

"Haaado..."

"Mr. Beemer please?"

"Hehehehhe," I snickered. I wasn't that dumb. "No missy Beaner."

"Please may I speak to Mr. Kohola Beemer?"

"Hai....dee...ku...ichy...kola fever?" At that point I'd usually mumble through the theme song to "Kikaida" which was the only Japanese song I had ever been able to learn.

"Uhh... never mind lady. We'll call back."

Thanks to my impersonation skills, and the fact that in a past life, I actually was an old Japanese woman, I hadn't actually talked to anybody from the IRS. There, in a macadamia nut shell, was my quandary: If I paid off my back taxes, how could I afford to buy a boat? I banged my fist in frustration against the hotter-than-hell steering wheel. Why was life was so unfair?

I have heard that great men in times of crisis listen to a wise and intuitive inner voice. My inner voice is different. He is neither wise nor intuitive. He may not even be intelligent. He is a little *menehune*. I suspect that the assistance he is providing is some kind of community service alternative to *menehune* hard time.

The sunlight streamed down from the sky and the thick windshield of the truck amplified it. It seemed like God was putting a magnifying glass on a very sinful ant. I could feel my hair begin to smoke. I heard the voice of my inner *menehune*. "It's your own damn money, bruddah," the tiny voice squeaked, "mo' better you spend 'um, than Uncle Sam spend 'um. And eh, dummy, you not going' live fo'eva eh? And when you die, goin' smell funnie kine, you know."

Then something wonderful happened. Gliding by on a silver trailer was a beautiful new Boston Whaler. The boat was exquisite. Watching her pass by with those graceful curved lines and the two shining Mercs mounted on the transom, I felt as if fate was guiding me forward. My wounded spirit began to rally. I gunned the engine of the old truck and popped the clutch. As the balding tires smoked on the pavement, the mynah birds exploded from the parking lot and flew into the arid sky. They gathered above the ramp and aligned in what mynah bird aficionados call, the "missing moron" formation.

Because the tires were still squealing, my inner *menehune* had to yell to be heard. He shouted out indignantly that if you are Hawaiian, then paying Federal taxes is actually screwing yourself twice. A satisfied smile came over my face. Thanks to his miniature reasoning, I had arrived at an important decision. **I not goin' pay**.

Several yellowish-white globs of goop splattered on the windshield and the mynah bird squadron, several pounds lighter, giggled happily above the roof of the old truck. They had scored a direct hit, but I didn't care. At last, some cool air was actually coming through the window. I turned on the windshield wipers and pressed the "wash" switch. Of course no water came out; the wiper-washer had been broken for the last 15 years. But what the hell, I am an optimist. I just keep hoping to get lucky. All my life I've had the same problem. I can't seem to separate optimism from stupidity. This is how I lost 20 bucks to a Coke machine in Wailuku. As I continually fed the machine quarters and pressed the same button, I had a mystical feeling that my luck would change. This same mystical feeling is what welled up in me as I drove away now. After a couple of minutes, the wipers had smeared the mess evenly across the entire windshield of the truck. In the broiling Lahaina sun, I was bathed in an eerie light.

I couldn't wait to get to the Pequad bar and tell my friends about my important decision. They waited until after I'd paid for the first round, then they laughed uproariously at me. They told me that to buy a boat was lunacy. They said that a boat was a hole in the water that one pours money into. I know my friends. These people drink too much and their opinions cannot be relied upon for squat. I bought myself a double JB soda in a bucket with a twist, and sat in the corner, smirking at the bartender. I was, as we said in grade school, all *habut*.

But I was not to be deterred. At home was a Marine Catalog. In it was a boat that I had fallen in love with. If a boat is a *puka* in the water that dumb guys like me pour money into, then this was the most beautiful-est *puka* I had ever seen. In fact, just for fun, I decided to name her "Puka" in honor of my *lōlō* friends. This, my stupid friends assured me, was officially the dumbest name a boat could ever have.

"Eh Bra – you goin' name 'um Puka, she goin' get one *puk*a – one beeeeg one."

"Nah," I argued lamely, "she not goin' *puka*... she goin'..."

I was losing this argument, because my heart was just not in it. My voice was betraying me and I sounded like an altar boy operating a jackhammer. In retrospect, I should not have counted on my inner *menehune* to help me with this important decision. I was beginning to notice that he was in some sort of a funk. Perhaps he was suffering from low self-esteem. He sat hunched over in a corner, sleeping on the job and slobbering on his tiny *malo*.

Da Bank that says "Huh"

"Congratulations Mr. Beaner," the hesitant voice on the telephone droned, a week later, "your loan has been approved." Apparently, the bank was not informed of my tax difficulties. Maybe they gave me the loan because in the application I listed my occupation as "Sports Entusiast" and I said I made two million dollars last year.

I got down there as fast as I could and pried the check loose from the soon to be ex-bank manager's trembling hand. I ran immediately across the street to the other bank, where I cashed the check. "Small bills," I said, snickering. Then I took the cash I had just received and ran back across the street to the first bank.

I was convinced that by doing this, I was infuriating the people who approved my loan. Why did they give me the money when I had it all along? "HA HA HA!" I chortled with the magnificent sense of accomplishment that a Portuguese money launderer must feel after he's gone through a large box of Tide detergent. The teller was reaching for her silent alarm just as I dug into my plastic Foodland bag and dumped the cash happily on her counter. Hawaiians with large amounts of money really seem to frighten people. In a flash, the security guard was there. But I knew him. Japanee Dexter was a notorious *'ukulele* player who could never find work.

"Whoa – you score ha?" he said looking over my shoulder at the moolah and acting all nosy and funny kine. Jus' cause he get one uniform and one locker at *Hale o Wackenhut*, he thought he was cool.

"I won first prize at one contest."

"What kind contest?"

"*Ukulele.*"

He slunk away to the water fountain and sucked pipe.

My Puka

Puka was my first boat, my first nautical love, 24 feet of fiberglass bliss, with two huge blue Naugahyde chairs and a giant Igloo cooler. I especially liked the chairs, because I am a musician and we demand comfort. We can trace this back to a Union benefit that a decrepit and deodorant-impaired tuba player demanded way back in 1200 B.C. Unfortunately, I knew a lot more about chairs than I did about marine engines. I figured that the engine had two requirements. It had to be shiny and have a propeller on the end of it.

"Huuuu hoooo! Go get 'um bruddah!" cheered my slobbering little side-man, no doubt drunk again.

My beautiful Puka would have only the best: the best rigging, the best electronics, the best reels, everything except the best engine, which even with the bank's help, I couldn't afford. I settled for a used one, which I thought was a really good deal when a guy with two teeth told me:

"Only get couple hun'red hours, brah, I no keed you. Dis' engine – she go!"

Wheee HAA! I thought, imagining the wind blowing through my hair and my beautiful Puka blasting through the Moloka'i channel. Heee HAA! I thought as I laid the big bucks into his grimy hand. Whoa… I thought as we sealed the deal with a handshake and he walked off, purposefully scratching his *'ōkole*.

Puka's immense Igloo cooler gave me a feeling of great wealth. I saw myself filling its expansive space with many, many fish. In fact, I had spent several months reading fishing books that had taught me to be a lean, mean, fish-killing machine. Frankly, I knew all there was to know about fishing. Right then though, the cooler was empty, and after outfitting the boat, I was wondering if there would be any money left over for a warm beer and an egg salad sandwich.

After admiring my beautiful Puka, the hotel manager where I worked looked at me with a smile. Then he got me to agree to take him and his wife out water skiing on Sunday. In the meantime, he told me to call in on the CB. If I caught anything, maybe the Hotel would buy it. "Wow," I thought lamely, "gas money too!"

Captain Butch

I called my friend Butch, an experienced captain, and said, "Help me shake 'um out, Butch."

"I'll be dea. We go meet tomorrow at 4:30 in da mo'ning for one cup coffee."

I gasped, awestricken. 4:30 AM? Is Butch insane? Had Butch been smoking some really wicked Puna butter? Who in God's name holds a meeting at 4:30 in the morning?

"Uhh… Butch," I asked gently, "Why so early?"

"Gotta get dea befo' dey wake up," he said simply.

"Dey?" I asked timidly.

"DA FISH!" he boomed back.

I listened to the dial tone and struggled for sanity. "Fricka" muttered my little bummed-out *menehune* as he considered the ramifications of that ungodly hour.

The next day, at the appointed ridiculous time, we drank coffee at my house and Butch mapped out an elaborate float plan. "We goin' go DAT way." He was pointing towards the screen door with a lit cigarette. I was stunned by the detail of this navigational data.

"We goin' over da neighbors mock-orange hedge," my sleep-impaired *menehune* intoned, yawning.

To my complete surprise, it was dark at Mala that early in the morning. The ocean was so damn cold it was making my teeth chatter.

"Da mos' impo'tant ting, is dis bolt," Butch said ominously. Up to my knees in the water, I peered into the blackness with my new Eveready flashlight. I was aiming the beam at the big bolt in Butch's greasy hand.

"No foget dis," he said seriously. Then he took the wrench and locked the bolt down at the rear of the boat. The bolt that Butch referred to is a large bolt that we are supposed to remove when we trailer the boat. It serves to drain the water out. All boat owners in the entire world have one simple reminder burned into their collective memories. It is a mental post-it note that says "No forget the bolt!"

Forgetting to remove the bolt is not too bad. After a few weeks your new boat smells like a swamp and a fierce mildew eats the crotch right out of your best shorts. However, forgetting to put the bolt back in when you launch is much more serious! In fact, the U.S. Navy lost an aircraft carrier in the waters of Lake Kalamungai for that very reason. The Admiral forgot to put the bolt in. That dumb sonofabitch is still paying for it via a hefty deduction from his Navy pension.

Since that disaster, we have tried to be more observant of the whole bolt thing. Today, all over the world, signs hang on trailers that remind us of the importance of the mighty bolt. In Italy, a quaint, little placard notes: <u>No Fogeta Da Bolta</u>. In France, a delicately filigreed, lightly engraved epistle in the shape of a croissant suggests: ***Les Miserable Fishermen Sinko Sans de Stupide Bolto***. In Germany a black piece of magnetic steel reminds us to: **ATTACHÉ DE BOLTO DUMBASS!**

Salt Water Existentialism

After an hour of trying to get Puka's cranky engine started, we pulled out of the harbor. "Bugga needs work," Butch said disgustedly, banging his meaty hand on the cowling. The sun was coming up then and the water was like glass. Butch spotted a flock of birds and we were off. The smooth hull lifted up on the water and we were flying. I had a big grin on my face as the wind went streaming through my hair. I was so happy, I could have busted a testicle. My heart filled with song as we raced the sun.

"Dis is what life stay all about," exclaimed my inner *menehune* in a rare philosophical mood. I would have shared this with Butch, except that he was tangled up with a cold six-pack of Olympia. No matter. My life is complete now, I thought.

Somewhere into Butch's third six-pack, we got our first strike. "Ziiing," the reel sang.

"*HANA PA!*" Butch blurted out, drooling brewski on his T-shirt. Butch and I were now ready to begin the delicate choreography we had trained so hard for. This was the defining moment that all great fishermen face: the beer and adrenaline-fueled cosmic battle of human being vs. monster fish.

Humuhumunukunukunotquitegodzilla

I killed the throttle and Butch fell slowly backwards over the cooler. I lurched towards the stern to grab the fishing pole, while Butch on his back began excitedly paddling his big feet in the air. I jumped into the fighting chair and quickly strapped myself into the leather harness. By then, Butch had discovered that he was on his back and not in the best position to assist me. He muttered something indistinguishable and rolled over on his ample *'ōpū*. I was ready to fight the biggest, baddest fish in the ocean, but I needed to wait, as the captain of my vessel crawled forward across the deck on all fours. Strapped in the chair, my knees bent and feet squarely braced for fighting the giant fish, I felt the line slack. This fish was one devious and cunning bastard! He was playing me like a chump! It occurred to me then that time was of the essence. We couldn't let this monster get away!

"Butch!" I hollered hoarsely. I looked over my shoulder and saw Butch's large *'ōkole*, swaying port and starboard, port and starboard, about two feet off the deck. Frankly, this was a hideous sight, as Butch's fifteen-year-old shorts were sagging to reveal, in the bright Maui sunshine, his truly tremendous butt crack. An involuntary shudder racked my body. It was kind of like seeing a traffic accident. I didn't want to look, but I couldn't seem to tear my eyes away. When Butch finally reached the captain's chair, he gave me a shaky shaka sign, then he drunkenly gripped the steering wheel and, blinking and bleary-eyed, smiled the hugest smile I had ever seen. He was so proud of us! I looked at his big potbelly, his sunburned face and thick Portagee stubble and suddenly a feeling of friendship and *aloha* washed over me like the noxious exhaust fumes of Puka's big engine.

He's still standing! I thought to myself, dumbly, wondering if I would suffer post-traumatic shock from the horror I had just witnessed.

Steely-eyed, and with ferocious determination, I returned to concentrate on my finned prey. I whipped the pole upwards and I set the hook. I began the back-breaking effort required to reel in the HUGE fish. I bent at my knees, straightened my legs out, and working with my back, pulled the pole upwards. Then I dropped the pole down and cranked, cranked, cranked. I engaged in this strenuous activity for about 15 seconds, then suddenly, in the middle of a knee straightening, pole-pulling festival of ass and elbows, the fish came flying out of the water and landed at my feet on the deck. The silence was deafening. We gaped at the little guy incredulously. He flitted around in a small puddle on the deck, the enormous lure hanging from his diminutive lip. Butch, standing at the ready with the large flying gaff, aluminum Louisiana Slugger, and 12 gauge bang stick, realized that he was a bit overdressed for the welcoming party. We stared at our prey long and hard. We stared at him long and hard, again, a second time. It just wasn't getting any better.

"He not too big," Butch solemnly intoned.

O.K., I thought to myself, maybe he wasn't very big, but he was kinda' … what was the word for it? Cute?

"How much you figgah he weigh?" I queried, looking at the little flopper.

"Gee…uhh maybe uhh…could be…uhh…15 pounds," said Butch swallowing hard and looking at my face for any sign of — I don't know… tears? I guess I must have winced or something, because Butch, sensing my disappointment, reached deep into that big Portagee heart of his and kindly evoked the fishermen's "traditional embroidery of the truth."

This is an unwritten code amongst us brother fishermen who toil on the salt encrusted decks of tubs around the world. It was the balm for our broken hearts. It was our ointment for the bright red rash of ridiculous wages. It was the sweet brew that we guzzled from the enduring jug of human kindness. We bestowed this, without hesitation, on poor, sunburned anglers aboard money-pouring-down-the-*puka*-boats, who had spent all day fishing and stared in astonishing disbelief at a single tiny fish on a huge expanse of deck.

Flit, flit, flit went the little buggah. Butch took a deep breath, placed his fists on his hips and pronounced loudly, "Nahh…. Now dat I can see 'um mo' closely, dat fish… he gotta be… well… uh… 19 easy."

Nineteen pounds! Respectable! Even mentionable in casual conversation around the pool with the cute *haole* cocktail waitresses! For our first time out on the Puka, this was not too damn bad. "Yeaaaah!" I yelled out, jumping up and down on the deck, jiggling the pole and my 130 lb test line. Butch looked at me, belched loudly and shook his head in disgust.

"My beautiful Puka, you are my dream come true," I murmured, as Butch, butt crack secured in the deep Naugahyde nest of the first mate's chair, commenced to take a very long nap.

I dialed up the CB and called the purchasing office of the hotel. "Puka to Purchasing Office, Puka to Purchasing Office," I spoke clearly into the microphone. For a few moments, there was silence on the radio and I listened contentedly to Butch's snoring and the lap of waves against the hull. Then I heard what sounded like muffled laughter and a man's voice with a Filipino accent said—

"Ai! You name your boat, de *Puka*?"

After we got the formalities out of the way regarding the name of the boat, and the fact that this was not a CB crank-call, the hotel agreed to pay $0.50 a pound for our excellent *ono*.

"Deal," I said gleefully, forgetting to calculate that this was really only $9.50. What the hell, when news of Puka's prowess spread along the shore, we would command better prices and definitely make some real money. I cranked up the throttle and Puka lifted out of the water. We were on our way home.

When Butch woke up, he rummaged through the locker and found an *ono* flag. Considering how drunk he was, it was a brilliant acrobatic achievement to actually hang the thing on the outrigger. It would have looked even better right side up.

All the way into Mala wharf, my heart pumped with joy and I counted my blessings. We'd caught a fish and Butch <u>was still on board</u>. Wow! I thought, watching the sun sink into the sea. Having a Puka really does bring happiness.

We trailered the boat, washed it down, and stopped off at the hotel. It seemed to take us a while to actually find our little fish. There was a shit load of ice in the big cooler and da buggah was temporarily missing in action. Finally, aha! We grabbed his slippery ass and delivered him in a plastic trash bag to the purchasing office. I held out my hand and collected a measly $7.50. Apparently, the fishermen's code only works at sea. On land, those cheap bastards actually weigh them.

We went to my house. I made Butch some coffee, took a shower and dressed for dinner. "It's on me," I told Butch. We went to the hotel where I ate free, as part of my arrangement for playing music. We walked into the dining room and were seated WAY off to the side, by the banging steel doors of the kitchen.

"What kind of fresh fish do you have tonight?" I asked innocently.

"Well gentlemen, we have a nice fresh *ono* that just came in," said the waiter, turning down his nose at Butch.

"We'll have that." I spouted gleefully. "And make sure to put both meals under my Administrative Meal Account!"

Butch dive-bombed his stubby index finger at a wine selection and we dined heartily. The fish, OUR FISH, was delicious. Despite the occasional rude glance from the tourists at Butch's stained and smelly T-shirt, it was the perfect evening. Puka, I love you, I thought dimly, as we drank our third bottle of wine. With a flourish I signed the chit, appending a misspelled "Captian" after my drunken signature. Then Butch and I stiffed the waiter and stumbled out into the warm Maui evening.

Oprah Interrupted

A couple of months later, Butch was down on his luck and moved in with me, "jus' till I get on my feet" he said sheepishly. Butch informed me that his grandfather was coming to Maui for a visit. "Can he stay wid' us too?"

Sure enough, a week later, Butch's grandfather came in from O'ahu. He was a short, balding, old Portagee, built like a fireplug. I liked him immediately. According to Butch, he knew a lot about fishing and I could pick his brains for secrets that weren't in the book.

I asked him to come into the back yard with me under the mango tree. Grampa seemed a little nervous at first. It's not every day that a complete stranger says he's going to take you into the back yard to show you his beautiful *puka*.

"Whew," the old man said in relief, when he finally figured out that I was trying to show him a boat. He scratched his crotch and looked at the Naugahyde seats through his thick glasses. "Das not fo' catching fish, das for catching girls!" he said with a wink and a smile, affording me a generous peek at his brand new dentures. Day after day, I peppered the old man with fishing questions — about lures, about tackle, about technique; to which he mostly responded by scratching his chin and saying "Mmmm … das one tough one…."

Grandfather's main activity seemed to be watching Oprah on TV, eating boiled soybeans and breaking wind from his corner of the sofa. The stunning audio effects Grampa created rivaled any movie theater on Maui. Grampa's flatulent interruptions to the Oprah program didn't seem to bother him a bit. He certainly wasn't shy about it, either. "Wha dat she wen say?" he'd ask sincerely, straightening his big, black glasses after a really good one. If Oprah could have magically appeared as a fly on the wall during our afternoon reveries, she would have quit the business immediately. Nobody can take that kind of abuse.

"He get def e'ah," Butch hollered one day as Grampa stepped on yet another large duck. Well, no shit, Sherlock, I thought, opening the jalousie windows. The next day, after a particularly stunning display of windage, I looked across the way and saw my neighbors lighting a match.

Karaoke Grief Consuling

One night, I got home and Butch told me that Grampa was feeling a little down. Why, I wondered, were we out of soy beans? Butch said that ever since his grandmother passed away, Gramps was feeling like nobody needed him. Butch and I hatched a plan to cheer him up. We had to do it on Monday night when I wasn't working.

The Karaoke Bar was completely deserted. It seems that few people enjoy singing off key while being seriously inebriated on the first day of the week. There were just the three of us there: Butch, me, and Grampa. Oh yeah, and an old Korean waitress who had been recently embalmed. We drank quite a few double scotches, grinded some *pūpū* and told Grampa how much we loved him and how much we needed his advice on fishing, since we were presently catching doo-diddly. Then we launched into song. Butch and I warmed up for Gramps, me with a rousing rendition of the Kikaida theme, which I think is called "Jiro changie Kikaida" or some shit like that. Butch sang "Lui Lui" in Pidgin, which actually is more intelligible than the English version. Grampa stood up slowly, wobbled up to the stage and did a 20 minute intro, pouring his heart into the microphone about how much he missed his best girl. Then he sang "You Are My Shunshine" and bought the house down, or at least the old waitress who begged us to "please... for god sake...turn down..." as Grampa continued to belt it out. Butch began crying and rubbing his runny eyes with his cocktail napkin. By the time Gramps got to the last chorus, I was crying too. "Morons," griped my *menehune*. He simply did not appreciate Karaoke technique or the exquisite irony of Grampa sharing his bus'up heart with a pissed off old Korean waitress.

Tea Time in the Executive Office

The next day, as I was attempting to recover from a slight hangover, the assistant manager of the hotel called me at home.

"Haddo," I said slowly in the high, trembling voice of a ninety year old mama-san.

When I realized it was the hotel, I took the phone away from my mouth and said authoritatively, "It's O.K. Hiromi. Go back home, now. Thanks for doing the laundry."

The voice on the phone asked me to meet with him in his office, to "review a matter that had come up."

I placed the receiver back in the cradle. I did not like the sound of that very much. Hmm… review a matter that had come up. This could be serious. I was not a complete dunce. I could feel the reach of the long arm of the law.

For a musician, a meeting in the "Executive Office" usually means one of several things:

The Bar Tab has not been paid.

There is too much drinking and not enough playing of music.

One of the young *haole* waitresses has ratted you out to the general manager.

Once again, you were caught napping behind the microphone during the chorus of the song, "Tiny Bubbles."

All of the above.

At 4 p.m. sharp, I went to the executive office and waited in the reception area while an unpleasantly robotic, perfectly coiffured woman offered me a cup of coffee, or "some herbal tea, perhaps?"

"OK," I whispered morosely and stared at her slack-jawed.

"How about one Valium, Mrs. Barnacle-Up-Butt, an while you at 'um - why no you bake one cake wid' one saw insai 'um, so us guys can bus' out of hea?" chirped my inner *menehune*. Ho, dat little buggah had one mean hangova'.

I was trying to prepare— as best as a condemned man could— for what was surely the awful news of my termination. What about Butch and Grampa? Were we all going to be living in a cardboard box by the *haole koa* bushes behind the cannery? RoboWoman nuked something in the microwave for what seemed about 30 minutes. She then placed a red-hot little tea cup and serving platter on the marble table in front of me. I reached towards the cup with my index finger, but I couldn't seem to fit my finger in the finger thing. It was clearly designed for a *kanaka peke* – a dwarf. "Ahh shit," I muttered, because the tea was boiling hot and I didn't have an asbestos oven mitt. RoboWoman's inhumanly precise hearing picked this up and she cleared her throat and monotoned,

"Well I shouldn't think it's going to be that bad."

She moved back to her desk and came to a halt, smiling into the lacquered finish of the far wall. Ho, da eerie.

The intercom buzzed. "Let him in," the deep voice said.

Hatchet Hitler

At our hotel, as in most hotels in Hawai'i, there were two managers, the general manager and the assistant manager. The general manager was an idiot with really nice, white pants. I may speak Pidgin well and English poorly, but the big cheese of the hotel spoke English even worse than I did. He was from an unknown province in Slobovia that manufactured white pants.

The real work of the hotel was done by the assistant manager. Years ago, the guys at the bell desk gave him the nickname "Hatch," which is an abbreviation for Hatchet Hitler, pronounced in a thick Filipino accent. When the door opened, he was standing behind his desk with a slightly annoyed look on his face. Hatch was an old friend, or so I thought.

"Come on in, buddy! Good to see you! Would you like something to drink? Something non-alcoholic for a change?"

"No thanks," I said, patting the wrinkled aloha shirt covering my flabby stomach, "I've got to watch my girlish figure." I had some decent social skills when threatened with poverty.

Pleasantries exchanged, Hatch got down to business. "We're concerned that your bill at the Pequad Bar is getting up there." Mystery solved. It was the dreaded numero uno on the list. "You know of course, that your administrative meals are complimentary, but we can't comp the booze."

"You can't?" I remarked, the tears welling up uncontrollably.

Satan's Printer

Hatch punched the intercom button. "Mrs. Hinglemier, transmit to my computer the accounts payable that we discussed earlier. I'll print it out here." He pecked away at the keys. We waited in silence. The printer stirred to life and began clackity-clacking, the print head flying from side to side. I couldn't see the numbers, but I knew what the damn thing was printing. Butch and I drank the same thing every night after work; it was a weakness that we shared, except Butch never had any money. So I signed and I signed and I signed. Double JB soda, bucket, twist, $4.97. Double JB soda, bucket, twist, $4.97. Double JB soda, bucket, twist, $4.97. Double JB soda, bucket, twist, $4.97.... The damn printer rolled on, and on, and on.

My former friend, Hatch, laced his hands behind his head and leaned back in his chair as the horrible machine continued its treacherous path through yet another tree. Double JB soda, bucket, twist, $4.97. Double JB soda, bucket, twist, $4.97. Bastards, they had kept track of every single drink! Who knew they could do that? A tear dripped from the corner of my left eye.

My former friend, the assistant manager, now began whistling, "Swing Low Sweet Chariot," smiling and rocking in his chair. The clackity-clacking continued unmercifully. After about 10 minutes, Hatch removed his hands from behind his head and placed them on his belly, now whistling "Camptown Races" and tapping his index fingers together, in rhythm with the carriage return of the infernal printer from hell. Clackity-clack, clackity-clack. Tappity-tap, tappity-tap. Crappity-crappity crap. The cruel bastard was nodding and still smiling at me as the printer from hell detailed the explicit and hideous perversions of my alcoholic lunacy. I bit my lip, because I was ready to roll around on the carpet and bus' out crying.

My Pequad bill had long since scrolled down to the floor and clearly there was no room for me there. The perforated computer sheets kept folding over on themselves, in a grotesque *pu'u* at the front of his desk. When the horrible din finally ceased, my bar tab was in a whopping pile on the floor. It loomed up from the carpet like frickin' Mauna Kea. "Holy shit!" hollered the little *menehune* in my head.

"Whew!" Hatch said, sitting up. "Might need a new one of these!" He patted the smoking machine from hell and tore off the final sheet of paper. "How are we going to handle this?"

My oh-so ex-friend, the assistant hotel manager looked at me, putting his hand under his chin and his skinny elbow on the big polished desk. You could have driven my beautiful Puka through the humongous silence between us.

"Well…. Suicide comes to mind," I said darkly, choking back the tears.

Ōkole In A Sling

"That may not be quite necessary," Hatch said wincing slightly and straightening up some papers on his desk.

"What do you mean?" I squeaked out.

"We need a favor."

Hatch began in earnest now. There was a very wealthy guest that visited Maui and spent big bucks at the hotel. He came every year and stayed in the Presidential Suite for a month. Hatch said the fellow had amassed a huge fortune. Hatch paused dramatically to make a very succinct point.

"He is the most VIP guest in the entire history of this Hotel's operations."

"And...?" I peeped.

"He wants to go fishing, but he doesn't want a commercial type of experience. He wants a more authentic experience, a real connection with the culture of our islands and its people. He wants to fish for a day off the K-buoy with some local guys. He wants to have some fun and learn a little bit about our ways and our techniques."

"And so..?" I squeaked.

"So if you take him out on your new boat, hook a decent size fish and show him a great time, we might be able to make this unfortunate mess disappear." He gestured to my pile of sorrow on the carpeted floor and raised his eyebrows.

After I heard the phrase, "hook a decent size fish," my face went completely white. I was just beginning to understand that this was much easier said than done. Perhaps in all those nights of debauchery and drinking at the Pequad Bar, Butch and I had severely abused the fishermen's traditional embroidery of the truth. Now it was coming back to bite us in the keester.

"You don't have to make a decision right now," Hatch said, looking at my red, watery eyes. "Just meet the guy in a few days and let me know your decision." We shook hands politely. "Do you want to see this?" Hatch said, looking down at the pile.

"No...uhh...thanks," I whispered hoarsely and slunk away towards the door.

"One more thing," Hatch said flatly, when my trembling hand reached the brass door knob. "He's a bit eccentric."

"La dee fuckin' daa" muttered my peeved little *menehune* as we skulked through the door.

Grampa Gepetto and the Pinocchio Boys

After work that night, I slumped down on the couch and poured out my guts to Butch and Gramps. We were drinking beer and eating cold hot dogs. It was our typical family-style dinner. Each guy grabbed a wiener, dipped it into the communal *poi* bowl and chomped away. With this clever dining technique, we didn't even need a fork. When a wiener was consumed, we busted another one out of the plastic wrapper and began dipping it into the *poi* all over again. I laid the whole thing out about the ridiculous bar tab and the rich guy in the Presidential Suite. "Plus," I whined, "I get da feelin' from Hatch, if we no catch, then could be da whole deal is off!"

"Das not one problem," Butch said confidently, biting his *poi* topped wiener and lying to my face.

"Butch," I yelled hoarsely, "GET REAL! WE ONLY CATCH ONE TIME OUT OF TEN!"

We were stumped. Our brains were in overload. What to do. What to do. My life was over. They were going to fire me and I was going to have to sell my beautiful Puka to pay off the Pequad bill, then I would be penniless and the IRS would take my clothing and I would die naked in a cardboard box. "Ho… and goin' smell funny kine you know!" my *menehune* reminded me.

To our complete surprise, Grampa pushed his big glasses up on his nose and said clearly, "Us guys can fake 'um…. I know how."

Butch and I sat up on the couch, stunned. Whoa! Did we hear what we thought we heard? The old man smiled mischievously, leaned towards us and spread open his calloused hands. Butch and I were stuck to his every word, like mayonnaise on a Spam sandwich. Grampa's eyes sparkled in the light of our total and undivided attention. His dentures were sticky from the *poi*, so he pulled them from his mouth and plopped them into a water glass on the messy coffee table.

We leaned closer as he mumbled, "Coupla years back, me an small Jimmy was on one boat and one *haole* guy wen fall asleep. He was complaining dat he pay good money and no mo' fish, so da firs mate wen get piss off. He wen hook one lure to da bucket handle and he wen trow da bucket 'ova. We wen keep goin' fo' awhile, da bucket sinkin' down and driftin' mo' fah away. Den da firs' mate, he wen lock down the reel and da captain wen gun da boat. Da drag from da bucket wen bend da pole and crank da bearin's in da reel. Ho, da reel wen go 'ZZZZZZZ'. Seem like one big Marlin wen hit 'um really hard. Da guy, he wen wake up, get all futless, jump insai da chair and den he wen give da bucket da fight of his life. He stay pullin' 'um in from maybe 250 yards, struggling and sweatin'. He wen broke his ass! Ho, he was so piss off wen he finally see da bucket come up behind da boat!"

Butch, me, and Gramps busted out laughing. We laughed so hard we almost fell off the sofa. It was so funny, just imagining that poor guy, busting his hump for a bucket filled with salt water. Ha ha ha, what a dork! After a while, our laughter died down. We started thinking. We took a few more swigs of beer. Butch retired a half eaten wiener, standing it upright in the thick bowl of *poi*. He lit a Camel.

"Wait a second, Grampa! I get it! I get it!" My heart was pounding. "We switch da bucket with one dead *'ahi* dat we buy from Nagasako's. Gramps, das brilliant!" I exclaimed. Then I had another thought: "But what if da rich guy no like take one nap?"

Grampa stretched out his right leg and reached into the pocket of his old shorts. He removed something from his pocket and extended his closed fist. As Butch and I looked down in puzzlement, he turned his hand over and opened his fingers. It was a little plastic vial. On the label it said: **Kaiser Lahaina Pharmacy, RX- 8-774-918**

Cabrall, Wilfred. Percodan, 300 mgs. Do not drive or operate heavy equipment, after taking this medication.

Da light went on. I put my arms around his thick shoulders and gave him a big hug. "I love you, Grampa," I said, and my inner *menehune* started giggling like a little girl.

Grampa's plan was a wiener ... I mean winner. How could he have hid his genius from us for all these weeks? Was all that Oprah stuff merely a subterfuge for his blazingly brilliant intellect? Was grampa solving quantum equations in between machine gun bursts of methane disbursement? Butch and I were putty in his hands, the gentle and wise hands of a great master. Yes, grasshopper, he seemed to emote, it can work. It will work! Butch and I looked at each other and enthusiastically voiced our approval. "We goin' go fo' it! Grwampa!" we cheered.

Grampa's eyes lit up, he smiled and licked his lips with his big cow tongue. To my surprise, he grabbed my ears and pulled me into his chest. Then he planted a really wet one on the upside of my head. "I love you too, boy," he said happily. Grampa slobbered wetly, minus his teeth, on the side of my forehead. Grampa Wilfred Cabrall - my personal savior, smelling like wieners and beer.

"Gramps," I said, headlocked and wheezing, "No foget Butch. He like some shuga' too."

Anesthesiology and Tourism

"Did I tell you that he's Canadian?" Hatch said as we walked past the lobby. "They talk funny, but don't let it get to you. AND REMEMBER – we want him to have a great time. Catch a fish for him, give him a good time and you're home free."

When we first met, Mr. Heavy Pockets had just put away a bottle of expensive French wine. Emerging from the men's room of the fine dining restaurant, Mr. Beaucoup Canadian Coinage was a big, jovial fellow, kind of like that Russian opera singer, Pavlov. He was jaunting merrily along as the waiter trailed him through the etched glass doorway with the unsigned bill. My wonderful new friend, the assistant manager of the hotel, shooshed the waiter away and mentioned to me, under his breath, "He always forgets, so we just add the charges and he pays them later."

Hatch briefly introduced us and, peering through his expensive sunglasses and with a voice that achieved the musical subtlety of a giant accordion, Mr. I Just Took A Two Hundred Dollar Leak pumped my hand enthusiastically and in a very loud, very strange accent, told me how much he looked forward to going "ooot" fishing.

"What the hell is an 'ooot'?" my inner *menehune* wondered as my hand was jiggled all over hell and beyond. "Is it like a *mahimahi* or something?"

Being a musician, I am generally in favor of eccentricity, but more to the point, I was desperate to keep my boat and my gig at the hotel. On the way back across the lobby, I said, "O.K. You got a deal." I told Hatch to have the limo at the dock on Saturday at 9:00 a.m.

"Good." he said confidently. "Call in the catch to Purchasing on the CB. We'll give it to the head chef and they can prepare it any way he wants." Hurray! My *kookah pilah* misery would soon be delivered to the shredder! I went home and told Butch that we could get a late start in the morning. "After all," I said, glugging a beer and whispering conspiratorially to Butch and Grampa, "dead fish, dey no wake up early, eh?" We busted out laughing. We patted Grampa on the back, congratulating him for the brilliance of his plan. Then he asked if we could go to the Karaoke bar again. Apparently he had an eye for the old Korean waitress. Grampa smiled and jiggled his thick, bushy eyebrows. I called in sick to work. We piled in the *kūkae* mobile for yet another night of debauchery.

The Seaweed Safari

It was a beautiful Saturday morning at Mala Wharf but we weren't appreciating it too much. Mostly, it just seemed really bright. It was crowded. There was a line of small boats waiting to launch. Butch boarded the trailer and started rigging my beautiful Puka. He looked in the cooler and slammed down the lid disgustedly. He seemed pissed of at me for some reason that I couldn't quite understand.

I was hung over. I felt nervous. I felt rushed. I felt extremely anxious to succeed by any means possible. The concept of drugging the angler seemed to cover some completely new territory. Would this work for other tourist activities? For instance, helicopter tours could save a bundle in aviation fuel. They'd just stay parked on the runway for two hours, then the pilot would say, "Aww, shucks, too bad you folks fell asleep." Then I had a darker thought, like, what's it really like in prison?

Hopefully, we would slip the Percodan into the big Canadian's brewski, rig the dead fish up on the lure, wake his *ʻōkole* up and cheer heartily as he reeled it in: "Yeaaa Mr. Tubby Pockets!" Then we would get the eccentric SOB off of our boat, run home to Grampa Gepetto and be home free! My *menehune* started to say a small prayer:

"Akua, if you get us thru dis one, we neva going to lie again to da cocktail waitresses about the size of any fish we catch. Including da 30 pounda last month… sorry… I mean… da… uhh…9 pounda."

I went through the checklist that I had scribbled during yesterday's Oprah show.

Grampa went out and bought a nice size *ʻahi* and put 'um on ice. It is in a hidden cooler in the bow. CHECK.

Butch assures me that he has got the Percodan in his pocket. CHECK.

Full tank of gas. CHECK.

Poles and lures. CHECK.

Rigging and (I couldn't quite remember the last part of this one).

I took a deep breath. Nothing can possibly go wrong. K' den ... we ready!

The Duke of Dork arrived at the dock at 9:00 sharp. Butch and I stared in wonderment. Out of the hotel limo stepped a huge Canadian man dressed like he was going on a big game safari to frickin' Africa. He had a helmet on his head, the kind that Butch and I had last seen in a Tarzan matinee. He slowly exited the limo, then leisurely strolled over to the boat and confessed loudly that he was actually quite excited, but worried that he'll get seasick and "have ze epi-sode." Butch, smoking a Camel and flicking his ashes perilously close to the spare gas tank, assured him that he need not worry, and that he, Butch, an experienced fisherman, "blows chunks" all the time. The Earl of Hurl looked at me sharply now, and his eyes darted furtively in the direction of the departing limousine. Together we walked over to the dock. He looked at me again with wide eyes, as Butch haphazardly splashed my beautiful Puka into the water and roared away with the trailer. I helped His Royal Giant Numbnuts into a just-cleaned and shining interior and we exchanged brief pleasantries. The boat creaked as it settled beneath his weight.

"Uhh... welcome aboard," I said, acting all professional.

"Fine. Thank you," he said, his gold chains glistening in the sunlight. "I am prepared for ze mighty battle, to catch ze big fish."

"And we are prepared with the ze big dose of Percodan to knock you on your *'ōkole*," my *menehune* chimed in a very bad French accent.

I turned on the ignition and an emergency light on the dash glowed bright red. Immediately, Puka's bilge pump roared to life, shooting a hefty jet of water from the side of the hull. "Strange," I thought, as I offered Lord Queasy a cold one. I was holding on to my beer and thinking about opening it when something began niggling at the back of my mind.

After a few moments of studying the gauges and still puzzled about the bilge pump, I turned and noticed that the teak floorboards on my beautiful Puka were floating and behind me. The Incredibly Wealthy Baron of Barf was ankle deep in salt water.

"Is there ze problem?" he asked, an expression of confusion on the pink face beneath his helmet.

Suddenly, Butch's words came rushing back to me, "Da mos' impo'tant ting, is dis bolt." The bolt! THE GODDAMN BOLT! I leapt up to the dock and yelled at the top of my lungs—

"Butch! GET THE TRUCK! GET THE F**** TRUCK! GET THE F****** TRUCK! GET THE F****....AWW SHIT...BUTCH!!!!"**

Of course, Butch was nowhere to be found. He was pissed off at me because he didn't think we had enough beer in the cooler, so he had taken the *kūkae* mobile and trailer into town for a delightful little booze run. The bastard was three miles away.

"You fricka!" yelled the *menehune*, so pissed off he almost passed out.

Tiny Bubbles

It did not take long for my beautiful Puka to sink. The tether lines snapped like cheap guitar strings and down went the Duke of Puke, the custom electronics, the Penn Senator reels, the cranky 300 HP engine, the blue Naugahyde seats and gigundo Igloo cooler. In fact, His Royal Turdness made a big effort to save the damn cooler, like we were going to be stranded on f****** Gilligan's Island or something.

"Call ze Coast Guard!" he gurgled up at me in that stupid accent, dog-paddling in his safari jacket while attempting to rescue the large plastic cooler.

"Ah... go **** yourself," I muttered disgustedly and popped open the can of beer I still held in my hand. I chugged half of it down and tried not to bust out crying.

My fellow fishermen, who I'd regretfully come to know, finally attempted to help me, but their faces were red from trying not to laugh. They weren't of much help either. Basically, they climbed up on the dock, looked down into the water and shook their heads sagely, as together we enjoyed a drifting Bwana helmet and about 10 feet down, my beautiful, blurry Puka, beneath a lather of tiny oil bubbles.

With the pockets of his safari jacket ballooned out and draining copious amounts of water, the wet Prince Dingleberry trudged up the boat ramp and squished over to the payphone to call for the hotel limo. There was a little strand of seaweed draped over his shoulder. I did not actually see him leave, because I was too mentally occupied with the formulation of a new strategic plan. It was called "pre-meditated murder." As soon as Butch parked the truck with the attached and formerly unavailable trailer, I was going to leap out of the *kiawe* bushes and kill him with a nut wrench.

As I stood there on the dock, trying very hard not to have a nervous breakdown. I heard a little bloop and the secret cooler surfaced. It rolled over and spilled out a beautiful *'ahi*. I began to laugh uncontrollably. Grampa Gepetto, Master Puppeteer and Weiner Inspired Genius, had overlooked one small-kine detail. The long straight cut along its belly flapped open as the *'ahi* sank. The son of a bitch was cleaned.

Monsieur Lunatique

Mr. Bodacious-Bucks-Ratfink-Bastard arrived at the Hotel bar, had several Mai Tais and joyously spilled his guts about my skills as a captain and the fate of my beautiful Puka. In fact, everywhere he went for the next two weeks, His Lordship, The Don of the Dripping Dingus, told his sordid tale. Soon he was elaborating, finessing the details, and even making up some new crap as he went along. Every day he spun his gleeful story with a belly full of rum, twinkling eyes and an enormous glass-shattering laugh. The honking fable got bigger and better with each telling. He certainly had enough practice, because His Royal Weaselness of the Mommy My Wet Buns Are Burning From My Salt Water Limousine Ride, blabbed it with unabashed glee across the entire West Side of frickin' Maui.

Bastard!

The story of my beautiful Puka spread to every employee and hotel along the strip with astonishing speed. For months afterwards, every bellman, front desk clerk, secretary, housekeeper, bartender, security guard, receptionist or whateva, would sneak up behind me during an admittedly less than spirited musical performance and yell out in a Filipino, Portuguese, Korean, Hispanic, Japanese or Hawaiian accent—

"Get Da Truck! Get Da F****** Truck!"

This was usually followed by hilarious giggling and the swift running of feet down the carpeted hallway. Since it was difficult to get untangled from the guitar cord, I was continually unsuccessful in my further attempts to kill someone. I developed a begrudging respect for some of my elder co-workers. Some of those old Filipino maids can run surprisingly fast.

The hotel forgave my Pequad bill, because The Sovereign Monarch of the Drifting Peckerwood said it was his best trip to Maui ever. When he checked out, he gave Hatch a rather large check for our services. It was a sum almost equal to my delinquent tax bill. Hatch said it was in exchange for one little piece of information.

"What was that?" I asked curtly, still pissed.

"Your home phone number," my ex-friend the assistant hotel manager said flatly.

The good news is that Butch got another ride on a really stylin' 38 foot Bertram, a first class boat all the way. He and Grampa bought their own place, up on Lahainaluna Road. Every so often, I go down to the harbor in the afternoon and watch Butch come in. Lately, he's sobered up and he almost always gets the flag thing right. When I stop by their house, Grampa gets all excited. Kyung Sun comes out of the bedroom, all embarrassed, buttoning her pink bathrobe as Grampa circles his huge tongue around his lips and nails me a good one. Then the three of us watch Oprah.

The best news of all is that one morning after my settlement meeting with the IRS, I met an extremely beautiful woman. I fell in love. We got married and have a happy life together.

She finds it very curious that once or twice a year I get a call at 3:00 in the morning from a jovial man with a Canadian accent calling on an air-phone somewhere over Tinyturd, Yugoslavia.

"Haaado?" I answer real Japanese-like, never, ever managing to fool the bastard.

"Get zeee Trock! Get zeee F******* Trock" he chortles merrily. Then he hangs up before I can reply.

His Royal Dumbass is getting quite advanced in years. Maybe he will remember me in his will, which I hope will be executed soon.

These days, I get up in the morning and look at my beautiful wife, brown, golden and gorgeous against the white sheets. Her long, brown hair is scented with coconut oil and shining in the morning light. Life is good. I pour a fresh cup of Kona coffee and open the window. In front of me, the massive expanse of the blue Pacific sings softly of adventure.

"We should get one mo' boat," my inner *menehune* says. Then he strips the *malo* off his tiny backside, wiggles his *'ōkole* and busts out laughing. "Nah nah nah nah," he says and jumps back into his bed. I noticed the other day that he was wearing a pair of extra, extra, small biker pants. My little *menehune* is leaving soon; I think he's found himself.

"Thanks for the *kōkua*," I whisper, trying to keep a straight face.

I'm going to miss dat little buggah.

Author's Note:

I will never ever buy another boat. I will never ever buy another boat. I will never ever buy another boat. I will never ever buy another boat. I will never ever buy another boat. I will never ever buy another boat. I will never ever buy another boat. I will never ever buy another boat. I will never ever buy another boat. I will never ever buy another boat. I will never ever buy another boat. I will never ever buy another boat. I will never ever buy another boat. I will never ever buy another boat. I will never ever buy another boat. I will never ever buy another boat. I will never ever buy another boat. I will never ever buy another boat. I will never ever buy another boat. I will never ever buy another boat.

Hānau Hope

The moss remembered the shape of their boots, the wet earth clinging as they lifted their feet. On the Island of Kauaʻi, along the trail leading up through the Alakaʻi swamp, trees heavy with fresh rain dripped their sweet nectar to the ground. When the wind approached, the men could hear it coming from several miles away. First whispering, then growing louder and louder, sweeping from the ridge then flowing down through the spaces between the trees.

As they approached the 4,000-foot level, it became noticeably colder. Dew dripped from the buds of *liko lehua*. Wisps of clouds moved ghost-like through the thick, green canopy.

The three men were experts in different fields, carrying sophisticated, well-designed technology. Traveling on foot, their progress was deliberate. They climbed across the high ridge, their heavy exhalations misting in the cold mountain air.

The trail was arduous, testing their physical conditioning. Their packs weighed upon their lower backs, while the terrain stressed their thigh and calf muscles. Despite the slow, methodical pace of the team, ankles and knees absorbed the constant punishment. They moved meticulously across the ridge. The path was steep, slippery, and unforgiving.

In the rear was Solomon Kamahana. He was new to the team. He had recently graduated from the University of Michigan, a young Hawaiian scholar with a newly minted doctorate in ornithology. Although Sol was inexperienced, Marchais and Wilson welcomed him immediately. Somehow, Sol had a way of drawing people in to him. During their initial meetings, Sol's smile would light up the entire conference room. When he interviewed for the position, the staff were delighted. There was a warmth to him that people appreciated. Marchais and Wilson had reviewed his dissertation, and suitably impressed, agreed that it was time to add some new blood to their group. It also occurred to them that having a native Hawaiian in the field might present their future funding requests in a more favorable light.

For years, Marchais had been the senior scientist on the team. He was a thorough professional, and so was pleased that the equipment they had chosen was functioning reasonably well. There were the laptops, electronic counters, range-finding binoculars and digital audio equipment. Each team member carried a radio linking him to their base and in the event of a serious injury, to a helicopter available from Līhu'e. Wilson carried a Global Positioning System that tracked them reliably, except when the forest canopy grew too thick and the unit dropped a satellite, skewing the data. Marchais struggled with his opinion of this technology. He felt that some of its usefulness was overrated. What use was satellite tracking in the rain forest, he reasoned, if the idiot thing couldn't find the satellite, because it was under an overhanging tree?

Marchais had never relied much on technology; he'd begun his education long before there were small computers. In his day, the computer at the *Université de Paris-Sorbonne* was the size of a gymnasium. Since safety considerations weighed so heavily in the planning concerns of the center, Marchais agreed to take some of the newer equipment with him, but he wondered if they had been talked into taking more gear than they actually needed. The equipment grew heavier with each step.

Marchais had been at this for many years. He could recall in early '83, when the survey yielded a deep sense of dread. It was their first excursion to the area after Hurricane 'Iwa. 'Iwa was named for the frigate bird, an aggressive man-of-war, who often fed by forcing other birds to disgorge. On November 23, 1982 'Iwa struck the

Islands of Niʻihau, Kauaʻi and Oʻahu. 7,426 homes and apartments were damaged or destroyed.

Survivors said that the sound of ʻIwa was probably the most unnerving element of the experience. In the graying darkness, it moved inexorably forward, shrieking and beating the earth below with its tremendous wings. It was merciless and unrelenting. During the eye of the huge storm, many residents thought that the worst was over. Then, the great feathered beast circled around and came in once again.

Months before the '83 survey, several volunteer crews had cleared the lower elevations of the trail, but in the upper portions, it was still pretty much as ʻIwa had left it. The going had been so slow that year: the men had to ease over and around the fallen trees. Marchais had seen the tremendous destruction of ʻIwa. In the old growth areas, many of the trees were broken and splintered, boughs and limbs hanging downward towards the scarred earth. The floor of the cloud forest was littered with debris. There were so many broken trees that as darkness approached, Marchais felt they had entered some kind of an alternate world. It seemed that war had been waged against the trees of the forest. Marchais took out his notebook and tried to comprehend the damage. Trees hung from the canopy at all kinds of odd angles, creaking in the wind. Mangled limbs, swaying, dangled from vines and twisted ropes of bark. Amidst the wounded and dying battalion of trees, Marchais shivered in the misty cold and pulled his jacket in tightly around him.

He was hoping that this survey would be a lot less depressing. After about six miles though, Wilson slipped and gouged his hand on a sharp wooden splinter. The injury was neither deep nor disabling, but it was not a good omen for the team. Luckily the medical kit was well stocked. After they had cleansed the wound, applied astringent, gauze, and tape, the men again pressed forward.

They started out as they did every morning on the trail, by noting their GPS coordinates. Marchais, who always led, remembered a time before they had GPS. It was the time when he and Wilson got so turned around, they spent an excruciatingly long three extra days trying to get out of the swamp.

"*Merde*, Wilson," Marchais complained in exasperation on the second day, "we are lost like ze stupid sheep." Marchais had spent most of his professional life in the United States and over the years, his French accent had diminished, except when he was upset.

His pronunciation of the word "sheep" was quite amusing to Wilson, who recalled it three months later, coming home from a faculty party with his wife and son. He'd had a few glasses of wine and thus a few navigational problems. "*Merde*, Margareet! We are lost like zee stupid sheeeeep."

"What's a *merde*, daddy?" their nine-year-old boy asked from the back seat as they drove through yet another unfamiliar neighborhood in Mānoa Valley.

"A *merde* is a scientist who is lost," said Wilson, looking in the rear view mirror at his son's earnest face. "When you grow up Tony, try not to be a *merde*. O.K.?"

Wilson and Marchais had learned that year the reason that the Alakaʻi swamp was so dangerous: *it was so confusing*. With a numbing regularity, the low clouds came and went, and one little path through the trees looked exactly like the next. Physical fatigue kept the men in a kind of mental fog. Over the years, there was no telling how many people had gone in and simply never returned. It was easy to get disoriented and then desperately lost.

Wilson loved his work and considered himself fortunate in life. He had a good job, a beautiful wife, a great kid, and a small wine cellar excellently stocked with German wines. Margaret especially enjoyed the Lembergers and Rieslings. His wife of 10 years was fashionable, gorgeous and *"très belle,"* as Marchais once noted, looking at her picture in Wilson's wallet and stroking his gray beard. Almost everyone on the faculty appreciated the fact that Margaret had spectacularly beautiful breasts. Wilson agreed totally; he had in fact paid for them. At University functions, Margaret usually clung to his arm in a stunningly low-cut outfit. All manner of colleagues sidled up to Wilson feigning an interest in his work, when they were really just there to ogle Margaret.

It didn't bother him a bit that other men stared at Margaret. In fact, most of the time, he barely noticed. He just kept smiling and talking about his third greatest love in life, which, after Margaret and the wines, were the bugs. Big, beautiful, hairy, segmented, multi-legged, antennae-waving, chemical-excreting bugs. Wilson was in the top echelon of his field. He was one of the finest entomologists in the world. He was also a gifted and skilled natural photographer, an ability that he had inherited from his late father. Consequently, in the field, Wilson was invaluable, for he did the work of two people, both collecting his unique specimens and skillfully photographing the subjects.

During the year of the 'Iwa survey, Wilson had struck a gold mine. Insects that no one had ever seen before were falling from the trees. He was collecting so much data, he could hardly keep pace with Marchais. Some of the specimens he found were still being identified in museums across the world.

That evening at camp, Wilson checked the dressing on his hand, then found his brandy flask and took a big swallow. He lit his pipe, the sweet fragrance drifting down the mountain. Dr. Wilson enjoyed his comforts, even in the field. Though Marchais was never happy with any of the team smoking or drinking, he had learned over the years to leave Wilson be. Despite the occasional urge to pickle his cerebellum in a bottle of '86 Trollinger, Wilson was truly one of the best minds he had ever worked with.

Marchais removed the strap of the binoculars from his neck. Feeling severe muscle-ache and fatigue, he swallowed two Tylenol. He cursed softly in French as his laptop crashed. After it re-started he began fiddling with it again, clacking away on the dirty keyboard and muttering in his native French.

Darkness descended and the deep forest grew colder and colder. When the moon rose up majestically from behind the mountains, Sol rested his head against his backpack and stared in wonder at the night sky. Despite the brightness of the moon, he could still see an ocean of stars. Through the bent frames of his glasses, the celestial display overhead seemed to call him back to an earlier time. He knew that by understanding the paths of those twinkling stars, his ancestors had navigated across huge distances.

Sol closed his eyes. The earthy smell from the forest was lingering in his nostrils, so close, so pungent. He inhaled deeply and remembered an old song his grandmother would sing to him when he was a boy. It was called *Manu ʻŌʻō*:

ʻO ka manu ʻōʻō i mālama	Precious honey-eater who cared so
A he nani kou hulu ke lei ʻia	Your feathers are beautiful, woven into a lei
Mūkīkī ana ʻoe i ka pua lehua	You were sipping from the *lehua* flower
Kāhea ana ʻoe i ka nui manu	And calling the many other birds
Hō mai, ʻoni mai	Come fly hither, come close
Kō aloha ma nēia	To your beloved
Kīhene lehua	*Lehua* cluster

Marchais powered down the laptop and Wilson inhaled the last red embers in his favorite pipe. Sol's languid thoughts seemed to quiet, as a fine mist rolled in above the trees. The men prepared for sleep, as a silk-enfolded moon made gentle passage towards the sea. Sol opened his eyes. High above the green mountains, Hina, the moon goddess sailed onward, flecks of light eddying behind her and falling softly down through the leaves.

Sol tossed and turned in the confined space of his sleeping bag. He began to dream that he was soaring high above the emerald green forest. The cool, moist air flowed in around him, tumbling and eddying beneath his own feathered wings. Sol was covered in contour feathers of yellow and green. They cascaded down the back of his head and the front of his chest. He could see the minute details of the *'ōhi'a* forest so clearly. Ahead of him, the *lehua* blossoms swirled in the mist, beckoning. He rode the currents effortlessly, gliding and banking in long, graceful arcs.

In time, his muscles began to weaken. He was getting tired. A steep descent brought him dangerously close to a stand of *koa* trees. The ground was coming up quickly now, looming larger and larger. He was heading at great speed for the thick branches, his own wings heavy as he struggled in the stagnant currents of air. He awakened with a sharp gasp. He breathed rapidly, the perspiration beading on his forehead.

Sol had loved birds since he was a little child. He knew in his heart that the *aloha* he felt for the small creatures was passed down to him from his grandmother, Manulaniheihei. When Sol was growing up, Tūtū Manu had shown him several feather lei that belonged to their family. She told him of how the Hawaiians had trapped the birds, then plucked only the one or two feathers they needed. Then they'd release them, she said, to again fly in the green forest.

Years later, in a cubicle at the University of Michigan library, Sol reviewed an estimate suggesting that a single feather cloak, worn by the great chief Kamehameha, contained the feathers from some 5,000 individual birds.

Manulaniheihei passed away during his senior year. Before her journey, she waited for him. He flew home to her side and stroked her hair, so white, soft and silken. He told her of his studies in ornithology and she was very proud of him. She took Sol's hands and told him not to worry, that the birds she loved so dearly would carry her spirit up to heaven. She would be in God's Nest then, she told him and gently squeezed his hand.

The men were in the forest for a simple reason: to survey the birds. They were there to discover the offspring of the mating pairs that Marchais and Wilson had last seen years ago. Sol had only seen pictures in his textbooks of the species *Moho braccatus* - the Kaua'i *'ō'ō*. He eagerly anticipated observing them with his own eyes. A sudden gust of wind caused the leaves in the *'ōhi'a* above him to tremble. He watched several of the dark leaves fluttering to the ground. The dream of crashing through the trees in the forest still troubled him. "Help us," he prayed silently to Manulaniheihei. "Help us find the birds."

In the early morning, the men paid careful attention to the "dawn chorus" of the birds. This was the sweet resonance building in the surrounding forest, starting from the first call in the pre-dawn silence to the loud singing of multitudes of birds. The men listened very intently but were unable to detect the *Moho braccatus*.

Marchais, feeling rested, prepared a small breakfast for the team while Sol helped Wilson change the dressing on his hand. The men ate quickly and packed up their gear. Wilson lit up the GPS and compared the readings to Marchais' scribbled map coordinates. "About four miles," he announced.

The men had been traveling for over an hour when Wilson noted their arrival. They paused to observe and listen. The listening was particularly important, as they had trained to identify the high, flute-like trill of the Kauaʻi ʻōʻō. Sol could visualize the little bird in his mind, as captured by an artist's brush in *Studies in Avian Biology*. In those musty pages, the ʻōʻō was beautifully bedecked in black, with what looked like some deep, mysterious blues. In his mind, he saw the artist's depiction of the bright yellow bottom feathers so cherished by his people. Sol blinked his eyes, then took a handkerchief and quickly cleaned his glasses. Looking up high and towards the north, he gathered his thoughts and took a few deep breaths. *"Hoʻolaukanaka i ka leo o nā manu"* his Tūtū Manu would say. It was an expression used by those who traveled or worked in lonely places — *life is made happy by the voices of many birds.* Sol smiled. They were getting closer.

The team understood the plight of native Hawaiian species extremely well. They had studied a theoretical limit called *"the minimum viable population size."* This was the integer below which a population of living creatures cannot escape going out of existence. They were hoping that the Kauaʻi ʻōʻō as a species had not dipped below this number.

In truth, the extinction of most of Hawaiʻi's native birds could be laid at the feet of one renegade seaman. It was his immoral act of vengeance that brought down the birds. Angry at the missionaries for preventing his men from fraternizing with Hawaiian women, he purposely dumped mosquito larvae into the mouth of a fresh water stream. The larvae contained in the rain barrels and bilge water of the sailing ship were purposely transferred to the little fishing village of Lahaina. It wasn't long before millions of the horrible things twisted and convulsed in streams and *loʻi* across the island of Maui.

The *Culex quinquefasciatus* adapted quickly to Hawaiʻi's climate, riding in the winds to the neighboring islands. At this same time in Hawaiʻi's history, exotic foreign birds were being introduced. They were quite the rage in their day. People were very cavalier about it, importing foreign species without much thought: parrots, songbirds, and doves. Even the young Princess Ka'iulani had imported peacocks to grace the lawns of her scenic estate.

Unfortunately, those foreign species brought with them a form of avian malaria. The mosquitoes served as a carrier for the disease, transmitting it from the sea to the mountains with deadly efficiency. Avian malaria moved from the introduced species to the native birds. There would be no more golden feathered capes for the *ali'i*. The holocaust had begun. Hawai'i's native birds died in untold numbers.

The carrier mosquitoes could go only as high as 4,000 feet, so the catastrophic decimation took a while. In 1891 the 'ō'ō were plentiful; they could be seen from sea level to the highest mountains. At the turn of the century, observers noticed a clear decline, and specimens shot for museum collections had sores on their bills and feet. In 1928 they were rare. Finally, in 1960, the population stood at approximately 36 birds. After 'Iwa, Marchais and Wilson made a few sightings of pairs. It was the descendents from this group that the men had hiked so far to find.

They headed for a small clearing, studied the area and agreed that it was a good a place to set up the equipment.

"Excuse me, Dr. Marchais, Dr. Wilson," Sol said, easing his pack to the ground. "We have traveled so far for this opportunity. Please allow me a moment." Wilson and Marchais nodded respectfully. Sol smiled and raised his hands to the sky and thus began a simple chant in the forest clearing. In the mist, the graceful movements of his hands with the sound of his *oli* rose and swelled with the gentle wind from the forward slopes. Tiny drops of rain speckled his glasses as Sol reached gently upwards, towards the morning sky.

Eia mai au i ka malu	Here I find myself in the calm,
I ka noe e pōʻai nei	The mists surrounding me;
Me nā kūpuna lā	I have my ancestors to watch over me,
Nā ʻaumākua oʻu	As well as my family guardian spirits;
Hea aku nō au	I call out to you,
Ualo i ke kualono	The mountain ridges resound;
E hoʻolono mai ē	Hear my voice,
Nā manu o uka nei	Birds of the upland forest;
Hē mai, hē mai hoʻi	Come to me,
I ka pōʻai noe hoʻokahi	In the clearing of the misty circle.

The men felt a true kinship. They were from different fields of study and from different backgrounds. They were born and raised in different parts of the world; yet in some magical way, Sol's chant had united them in purpose and bought them closer to the forest and each other. They were filled with hope for the success of their mission.

"*Merci, mon ami,*" spoke Marchais from his heart.

"Thanks, Sol," Wilson said warmly.

Marchais retrieved a DAT from his pack, loaded the tape in the machine and set it on the forest floor. The machine whirred quietly, scrolled up to the first program and paused. Wilson had gathered materials to camouflage the equipment and now covered the top of the mechanism with earth, dry moss and twigs. Sol hooked the miniature DAT recorder to his belt and aimed the parabolic microphone up into the sky. If a flock of ʻōʻō entered the perimeter, he would record the new birds' calls from the machine attached to his side.

Marchais looked into the eyes of his men. They nodded. They

were ready. He reached down through the twigs and moss, and engaged the PLAY button. The speakers hissed slightly. Marchais cranked up the attenuation.

They moved back under the cover of the ʻōhiʻa trees as the VU meters on the machine pegged. The forest filled with a high, beautiful trill. The sweet flute-like call of an ʻōʻō, long dead and gone, was being broadcast through the woods. The pure sound filled the air, trilling in the early morning light. Sol was so excited, he could hardly hold the microphone. Wilson pulled out the Nikon with its specially silenced mechanism and smiled hopefully at Marchais.

After a long wait, a very slight rustling could be heard in the far canopy of trees. A single black bird flew overhead. Its feathers were midnight black. There were yellow tufts down near the legs. The small bird was incredibly beautiful. In the sparkling sunlight, it alighted on a branch and called out in the direction of the clearing.

"Uueeee, keet-keet," it sang. "Uueeee, keet-keet."

The ʻōʻō cocked his head, listening for a response. Hearing again the voice on the recording, it flew straight down to the location of the machine. The men could study it in more detail now, for it was much closer. Marchais raised his binoculars and focused. Wilson's Nikon whirred, taking pictures as fast as the mechanism could manage. Marchais could see clearly that the ʻōʻō was an older male of the *Moho braccatus* species. He noticed the ends of some of the feathers were frayed. There were areas of faded coloration around the eyes. This one would not be around for much longer, thought Marchais.

Moving quickly with his small beak, the ʻōʻō cast aside the camouflage of twigs and moss. He scraped at the earth with his beak and with his feet. It took him a while to finally reveal the machine.

The beautiful ʻōʻō paused, confused.

"Uueeee, keet-keet," it sang. "Uueeee, keet-keet," scratching with its small feet again and again at the surface of the mechanism.

"Uueeee, keet-keet?" queried the ʻōʻō, pecking and probing. "Uueeee, keet-keet?"

Marchais felt a deep sinking feeling in the center of his chest. He stumbled back and leaned on the stump of an old ʻōhiʻa log. Marchais was witnessing something that his entire professional life had failed to prepare him for. He stroked his gray beard, slowly shaking his head.

The morning light pierced the leaves and shattered on the forest floor. Wilson, watching the clearing, began to comprehend. "No, no, no," he whispered to himself.

Sol finally lowered the parabolic microphone and placed it on the ground. His hands were trembling, his arms as heavy as lead. Marchais turned to look at Wilson who had already stopped taking pictures.

There were no other birds, none at all.

Sol studied the face of the small black creature in the center of the clearing. So beautiful, so delicate. Sol's mind drifted back to a time when thousands of ʻōʻō flew through the surrounding forest, when they sang from the highest peaks, their voices flowing from the windy gorges, the green hillsides, echoing through the mountains and ringing from the branches of the tallest trees. "Uueeee, keet-keet," they sang for centuries. Then one fateful day, their world changed. The evening sun still flew towards the sea, but now, each time it made its nest, the sweet voices of the birds grew fainter and fainter. Finally as the years passed, they made no sound at all. The ʻōʻō had fallen, one by one, spiraling down from the sky.

Seeing this single, small creature in the clearing, a feeling of indescribable loss gripped Sol's heart. He felt the weight of it in his chest, pulling him down from the sky, down towards the brittle earth.

His ancestors reached for him now, their words, soft and low, entered his being on the wings of *'ōlelo makua*. Tūtū Manu's spirit flew down from heaven and formed a continuum with the little creature, as if a feather lei had been entwined with the mist of the upland forest. In that single moment, a bridge between two worlds extended and Sol felt an eternity. When the little 'ō'ō lifted his head and stared straight into Sol's eyes, his heart broke. The tears poured forth, streaming down his face, falling down the front of his moss-stained shirt.

Manulaniheihei had told him that she did not want the little creature to die without a name, so Sol named the little bird *Hānau Hope* — the last born.

He reached into his pocket for the remote and shut down the machine.

The forest was silent now. The lone and beautiful 'ō'ō stood there for a long time. The men watched silently, their breathing ragged and slow. Marchais lowered his head.

The men had struggled so hard, and come so far through the mountains only to unearth a deepening hush in the swirling mists of Alaka'i. From this time forward, the world for Marchais, Wilson, and Kamahana would be a lesser place. Their's would be a journey much less interesting and far less beautiful, because their years of study had led to a different kind of discovery.

They had found the ache that extinction leaves in the human heart.

There was a quiet rustling of leaves in the air. A cold wind ruffled the soft feathers, pushing him slightly off balance. He righted himself and looked to where he once had heard so sweet a voice.

With an unfolding of small wings, the last 'ō'ō soared upwards into the heavens.

Hānau Hope

Author's Notes;

I was doing an interview at KCCN Radio for the release of my recording, "Island Born." The person I was speaking with was noted island radio personality Keaumiki Akui. I have always liked Keaumiki: he is an intelligent and interesting person. He has a feeling for things Hawaiian and a love for the culture. One of the songs in my CD had a recording of birds in the forest. The conversation shifted to the plight of Hawai'i's native birds and Keaumiki told me this story. "Hānau Hope" *is based on an actual event.*

I went to see my old friend and former neighbor Dr. Samuel Gon III, who is Director of Science at the Nature Conservancy. He was gracious enough to spend some time with me, to open up the textbooks and help me understand the science behind the extinction of Hawai'i's native bird populations. I am so glad there are people like Sam in this world. He is a person that I admire very much.

I am very grateful for the aloha and kindness of both these gentlemen.

Sol's oli *in this story was co-written by my mother, Nona Beamer, and my* hānai *brother, Kaliko Beamer–Trapp. The song* Manu 'Ō'ō *is a traditional Hawaiian mele from the Beamer Family Collection. Tūtū Manu's expression, "Ho'olaukanaka i ka leo o nā manu" is from 'Ōlelo No'eau – Hawaiian Proverbs & Poetical Sayings by Mary Kawena Pukui, in Bernice P. Bishop Museum Special Publication No. 71, Bishop Museum Press, Honolulu, Hawai'i 1983.*

Stalking Haunani

Haunani Freitas is one angel dat wen come out of heaven foa hang out on da eart with da res of us doodoo heads. She live at 457 Wai Nani Way in apartment numba twelv. I know dis because I was stalking her so hard, I almost drove myself nuts.

Me, I was tryin foa learn from my past mistakes. I was married twice befoa, but I neva kno how foa act. Moa worse, my second ex was part Korean eh? Ho dey get mean tempa, I tell you. Living wid dat *wahine* was like trying foa sleep next to one firecracka, five seconds befoa midnight on New Yea's Eve. In fact, dat whole second marriage ting wen blow up in my face like one big can Spam, filled with dynamite. I still trying foa heal from da blast. At da final court ting, da judge wen say, "Honey Boy Rodrigues, you gotta do dis, you gotta do dat, you gotta pay dis, you gotta pay dat. I wen home, try look myself in da mirror, ho, my face stay all covered wid black soot and my hair was pokin out da sides, all funnie kine, like Neil Abrahcromby afta he run tru one wicked brush fire.

My hair was alredy spooky lookin anyway, from wen I was baby. My modda, she look at me, an say,

"Look Daddy, he get *ehu* hair!"

But Daddy no moa *ehu* hair.

"We go call him Honey Boy," my moddah said, "cause his hair jus like honey!"

Den Daddy said, "Nah, we goin call um Bozo, cause his hair just like dat clown, Henry Santos who live next doah!" Ho, my moddah was ready foa beef my foddah afta dat. Eva since I can remembah, dea relationship had its ups and downs.

I figga, from now on, I no go make da same kine stoopid mistake in marriage again. I goin take my time and no make no moves, until I get um all scoped out, li' dat. I was tired loose erying. In fact, I was tinking, maybe next time, I save erybody planny humbug. I jus goin pick out some pretty *wahine* dat I no even like and give her one house.

Dis my story, my *kapakahi* love story, of how I wen stalk Haunani Freitas.

I was workin at da A1 Transmission Service on Sout King Street. Was one good job, cept even in Decemba, was hot and da shop smell like transmission fluid. Not da new kind, but da stink old worn out kine. Da exhaust fan wen broke insai da shop, and da boss so dam cheap, he no goin fix um. Da smell, he no leave. He jus stay and linga around yo head all day, like one frickin hat. But I wen work planny worse places befoa. Plus, us brokanics made some pretty good dough. I still remembah da time, one Filipino kid from Mayor Wright Housing wen pay us $300 for change da fluid in da tranny of his Sentra. Tree-hunred bucks! So us guys wen trow in one lube foa free! Ha Ha. We wen bus out laughing afta da kid pay da bill. Ho, shet foa brains, you got lubed alright. And because you so stupid we all wen grind at Benihana and drank sake till dey wen trow us out. We got all bus' up and no can drive home. Me and Harlan Miyasaki had to ride bus. We was so *pilute* dat we no can even score wid da ugly cocktail waitresses.

Afta Su Yen wen divorce me, I was feeling jam-up kine. My big seesta Bernice da butinsky, told me "Eh, go buy one cat. Dey keep you company, you know." So I wen down da humane society and get one small black one. Foa real kine cat. Had tail and fleas and whiskas an erying. And cheap! I wen name him "Rocky" foa Rocky Galunta, who wen grad wid me, Farrington class of 79'. Rocky was da bull of automotive shop class, except he was kinda on da short, cranky, piss-ant side. He carried one big frickin chip on his shoulda and a 15 lb tractor wrench in da back of his truck cab. One time he got stopped and da cops dey acks him if da big wrench was one weapon. Not even, he said, he needed um for fix his radio.

Rocky was always beefing and afta high school, his fadda told him, "Eh, shet for brains. Go get one job, prefably in one nodda country." Rocky wen move to Oregon foa cut down trees and beef. I tink he still up dea, kickin da shet out of da trees and waitin for kill *haole* day, which I pretty sure, dey no get in Oregon.

I wen name da cat afta him, cause he all aggressive and mean too. Sometimes I walk down da hallway and dat cat, he look at me like, "What? I owe you money?" Den he like try foa duke um out wid da cuff on my work jeans.

Was coming up to Cristmas time. As da worse time foa be single, I tell you. What? I going wrap one present foa myself and pretend I no know what get insai? Shet. Worse, yet, I still neva had one tree so Rocky could spray um wid his Merry Xmas cheer. My oddah seesta Nadine da Queen, kept calling every oddah night, acting all nosey, and whining in her high pitch voice, like one burnt bearin in one 82' Pinto, "What... you neva get yo tree yet? You no get um yet?"

"Uhh... I neva get um. Becuz, no moa. Star was... all... sol out."

"NOT! – I was jus dea! No Lie, Honey Boy! You jus too dam lazy for put um up! I not goin bring da kids by, den. What kine Chrstmas dat? Dea own Uncle, too lazy foa get one tree. Foget it. And Merry *#@#*^* Christmas to you." Nadine was da drama Queen and since small kid time, I had it wid her alredy.

Trutfully, she wen bug me so bad last yea', I wen make da tree but Rocky was only baby kine yet, eh? And he wen climb on top'yom and hang on da branch, like one small black monkey. Da tree wen *huli* ova. TimBAAAAH! Jus so happen Nadine was visitin and ackin all high makamuk and feeding her rugrat some candy cane pieces, when da tree had *huli* and da ackspensive glass ornament she wen jus give me wen bus' on da cement. Da rugrat was kickin his stubby legs and crying like da sky stay fallin in. Ho, Nadine was so piss off. Like Rocky wen do'yom on purpose, but he neva. He was jus small and made planny kine Christmas *pilikia*. His mind was all futless and any kine movement or shiney kine stufts, he go jump on um. Da Christmas angel ornament Nadine wen give me neva make any humbug, but dat liddle buggah Rocky wen dive on um all fierce and mean-like, anyway. Like da ting was some kine terrabal insult. Remine me of da way Andy Mirikatahani used to dive on dose small Korean nudie clubs, befoa he went up da riva. In fact, Andy and Rocky get lots in common, dey like grab stufts dat no belong to dem.

Anyway, was goin OK, but da nights was still long and only had "Its A Wondaful Life" on TV, ho I seen um so many frickin times, I like bus' da TV alredy. Eh KITV, why no show um 50 times a night? We want moa!

Den one Decemba night, around dat same Christmas time, one Kona wind stay come slinking up da Ala Wai from behind da Zoo. Ho, dat wind was all warm and *hapai* wid dakine elephant shet scent. I had one funnie feelin in my guts dat night. Like wen I wen swallow one fishing lead, small kid time. I wen open da drapes and crack open da window. Ho, Rocky's eyes wen come beeeg. He krinkle his black nose, an smell da zoo smell, an tought, "Africka!" He wanted to beef right dea! He wen run all around da place, but no can find no wild Afrikan tigas foa beef wid. He look at me like, "What, I owe you money, again?"

"Rock," I tol him. "Get one grip." He went sulk unda da bed, wea I wish he would spend moa of his time, da bastad. Dat night also had dakine high, tick, humi ditty. You know what I mean, eh? You go put on one t-shirt and walk tree feet foa turn on da TV. Wen you get back to da sofa, you stay soaking wet, and you get one terminal case BO.

I was kine of antsy too, eh? So I wen pop open up da binoculars dat I wen buy for one Moloka'i hunting trip tree yeas ago. I was trying foa spock some Chrismas decorations across da Ala Wai. I was lookin at one string of lights on one balcony in da distance, when dat dam liddle Rocky wen punctcha my big toe wid his claw. As I wen lurch foward, cuz of da xcrutiatin pain, I wen drop da binoculas down and saw right insai da apartment across da street! Holy Frickin Moley and Deah Moddah of God. Deah she stay. My dream come true. My Christmas Angel. God help me. I wen stalk my first Haunani stalk.

She was mosly naked except foa one short, pink neglahjay dat showed off her nice chimichangas and one pink lace pantie. She was watching da ESPN hockey game, brushing her hair and drinking from one small kine tea cup. Even tho Rocky was engage in some kine surgery of my big toe, I wen make da focus even moa sharp. Haunani stay undaneat one really nice, tick, Douglas fir Xmas tree. She when put one red ribbon on her hair. She was so bootiful, like one goddess, floating in one sof, pink cloud. Ho, I tell you, da whole pikcha look like one Longs Drugs Christmas card, dakine so nice, you gotta keep um all year, even if fall down so many times from da shelf, you like scream.

Da Xmas lights was all shining and making nice kine disco on her skin an I wen look around her place wid da binoculas. I could almos hea da music from her stereo speakas playing, "Come Dey Told Me, Gadum Pa Pa Pum." Wen I stay look her face, she seemed so innocent, I felt bad for ereyting bad I eva did in my dumb life and worse yet, I felt bad foa stuff I neva even do yet! Dat is da powa of one angel, I tell you. I almost busted out crying, because of da murda of my boss. Den I wen remembah, I neva kill him yet.

Afta couple minutes, she wen notice dat da drapes stay open in her place and she wen pull da cord ting. Aw shet. I was alone again in my sad, cruel world. I trew down da stoopid pair of binoculars on da empty bed. I wen into da living room and turn on da TV foa watch da same hockey game as her. Was kine of interesting, but I neva unas-tan um. I wen make one mental note, foa go down to da library and try foa figa da ting out. Afta a while, I wen get up cuz dey wen show da commercial and Rocky, sensing movement and possible beef conditions, wen come flyin out from unda da sofa foa try kick my ass. I was so depress, I neva even notice. I jus kept goin. He wen hitch one ride on da top of my right foot to da fridgerator and back, his tail all puffy and his front paws wrapped around da back of my leg, holding on foa deah life. When I finally looked down, his eyes was all wide and his liddle black ears were pressed flat against his head like da small horns of one mentally challenge billy goat.

Of course, I neva even know her name was Haunani. I had to find dat da hard way, by bus'ing into her car and stealing her registration. I felt kinda bad about dat too. But, I neva mess up anything on da car, I jus when use da slim-jim from da tow truck dat Binky Ka'ahane from "Unreal Toeing" wen loan me.

Binky's shop was right next to us guys. I wen acks him one day, why he name his company "Unreal Toeing" anyway. Binky was huge. He looked at me, like one bullfrog sizing up one pipsqueak fruit-fly. Binky was wondering if da effort foa open his mout' was really worth it. Da whole worl got really frickin quiet in dat instant. I could hea one mosquito fut in shop #108. Den he wipe da swet from his head and acks, "What you tink dey say, wen dey find dat da car no stay?" He squinted at me.

I gave up, shrugging my shouldas.

"F*@#*#* Unreal!" he wen roar, his deep voice shaking da dust down from da roof of da ol' warehouse. Wen fall down easy-kine, like da midget snow insai one small kine Xmas papahweight. Off in da distance, somebody's shop radio was playin, "Da First Noel" as da tiny warehouse snow wen fall tru one sunbeam high above bruddah Binky's big ballahead.

Afta I busted into Haunani's car, I wen copy her registration at

Kinkos and wen slide um back insai da glove compartment of her Mazda. Den I saw da security camera in da garage looking at me. Ho, I wen dig out of da building moa fast den Jeremy Harrits wen bail from his 2002 campain.

I pretty shua Haunani wen Kam school. Cuz on her Mazda had one "The Kamehameha Schools Est. 1887" bumpa sticka. Erybody in da whole worl know dat if da cops see dat, you can make anykine and still no go jail. Dat bumpa sticka not jus one piece papa, das one Hawaiian cloaking device. You can be driving one M1 Tank goin freakin nuts on H1, an dose *kanaka*s dey no stop you. Why? Cuz dey all wen grad Kam school, as why. Dey get dakine secret handshake and decoda ring. Da machinist down at work, Milton Kamanu wen grad from Kam School in '82. Milton can go 500 mph in one 15 mph School Zone, wid his frickin stereo blassin M&M's "Shoot da mother*#@#*@* Cops", and as long as his "The Kamehameha Schools Est. 1887" bumpa sticka stay in good working orda, dey jus goin smile and nod, dose dam *kanaka*s. "Ahh…. Kam School", dey whispah, flashing da warrior ring and shaka sign. Den dey sing da school song, make one small *ami* and salute, as Milton, dat rat bastad, goes and brok tru da sound barrier in his red Tundabird.

Das what wen happen to dakine… uhh… Pokelani Linndsay. She neva remembah to put da sticka on her Mercedez and pooah ting, she wen wreck her career. Even though she still try foa weasel her way into first-class on Hawaiian, too late. Pokelani could be da only person in da whole worl whose bumpa sticka wen acktually expire.

Kam School '98 grad, Mapuana Kanahele—flight attendant, jus look at her, smile really beeg, point one manicured finga-nail at da hine end of da plane. Her nice kine heirloom bracelets jingle je'like Xmas bells, wen she go tell Pokelani, in one loud, *tita* voice, "Open seating past row four damnit. What Pokelani? You no can read?"

I went down to Haunani's building foa hang out. I took one quick look at her laundry in da machine. Ho! Nice! Den I wen go by da dumpsta. I discova'd dat you can learn a lot about one angel from her trash. Even angels from heaven gotta trow away dat *manapua* cardboard ting. And ho, planny kine Jasmine tea bags, dis girl like her tea. And she no drink alcohol and no smoke. Lucky ting was one small building, so not dat much trash foa go thru. Da worse part was da lef ova hum-ha from da *Pake* family in 17. Strong I tell you, da smell hide insai da dumpster foa days. I almost no can dive some days, even wid da spray paint goggles from Duke's Auto Painting. Dat hum-ha smell started to give me one mean headache and blurred vision. Pretty soon I was going file workmen's comp against my boss, Freddy Pacheco, foa no reason, oddah den da fact dat he wen hire me for fix transmssion.

By nosing around li dat, I found out so many stufts about Haunani. She was working foa one Polynesian review in Waikiki and she was dating one rich punk named Bobby Renton. Ho, I wen lay net foa dat bastad.

Stoopid head Bobby drove up in his new 40 tousand dolla Lexus and wen park um on da side street. Da leatha seat was still warm from his skinny ass when Binky had da Lexus up on da crane, and on da way to da shop. Us guys made some quick "adjustaments" and Binky put um back in da same place. Next mornin' dat stoopid shet Bobby wen go outside and da Lexus no start, why? Cause no moa transmission das why. Also no moa engine. Binky needed um foa one trade deal or someting. I remembah Binky acksin' me, "What, you guys need da muffla?"

"Nah, you get um," I said. Jus like was my car.

"Gee, bruddah, you not too bad for one Portagee," Binky said laughing. His son was wid him. Another big ballahead bastad. Dea was two moa of dose guys at home in Waimanalo, all huge. Ho, I pity anybody who make pancake at dat house.

Dat jackass Renton stay poundin on da steering wheel, wen he notice da small note I lef on da passenga seat;

Eh Bobby,

Dis time, its just da car. Next time we goin take out your guts and feed um to da SHARKS. No eva come back dis way again. Stay away from My Christmas Angel. We know wea you live, and we see you again, we goin bring one gas can wen you sleepin and make Bobbyque.

Signed,

Bozo and da sout street boys

Bobby wen jump outsai da Lexus, acking all futless and came around to da front. His legs was shaking when he go pop da hood. He look at da big black *puka* of what use to be da engine. I was idaling in da black Camaro across da street and see Bobby's face insai da binoculars. Ontop da radio had Nat King Coal singin "Chessnuts Roasting On One Open Fi-ah." Ho, dat Jack Fross must be one mean chihuahua.

Anyway, I try look foa Bobby again and shua enough, dat buggah's chessnuts was roastin. Ho, he go slam down da hood down and yell out:

"F*&#*****^@ Unreal!"

Den he walk away, real fast like, looking behind him every coupla feet. I grab da chrome ball on dat short trow gear shif and bang um into second. Den I pop da clutch and floor um. I come up behind his ass and flick on da nitro switch. Da Camaro, she scream sideways down da sidewalk, da rubba burnin' an smoke pouring out from da jacked up reah end. Da ting mus have look like one Sherman tank bearin down on pooah Bobby. He take one look behind him, run like one *mumu* orangutan and go make one ugly ass swan dive right into da Ala Wai Canal. I lean ova da window, foa spock him and give him da bird. SPLAAAT, he go, swirl around in da oily wata and dissapeah from view, like one lef ova fruitcake goin down da garbage disposal. I pretty shua, in da next few days, da buggah goin get one mean earache. Not to mention, goin have to burn dose nice clothes. Cuz, ho, you know, dat wata so *pilau*!

Coupla nights lata, Haunani was watching da Wings – Hurrahcaines game and writin Xmas cards. Dat wahine was scrumptious. I spent some moa time admiring her in one blue neglahjay. I guess nice chimichangas is nice chimichangas no matter what kine color bra dey stay cuddlin' insai. Den she drank some tea. I let da binoculas drif around her place, you know, jus checking um out. On top her stereo she had tree Willie K. CDs. Ho, you gotta love dis girl. I wen to sleep reading my "Rolla Hockey, Skills and Stratagey Foa Winnin On Wheels" book dat I wen borrow from da Waikiki-Kapahulu Public Library.

I like foa watch her dance, too. But I no like come on too strong, eh? I had also was tinking dat that she might wea dakine fancy-kine shells foa brassiere. Ho, toughts of dose sweet malasadas snuggling in da moddah-of-pearl shells was enough foa make me all futless. While I was tinking des toughts, Rocky was prancing down da hallway, wid one dead geccko hanging from his mout. I said to him, "Rock, I goin out tonight."

He look at me, like, "You Shet. Even if I do owe you money, I still not goin pay!"

I thought about dose sweet *pan duce* all day at da transmssion shop and I no can even work. At lunch break, Harlan told me Nadine lef one message on da machine, dat her oldest boy Derek wanted one Pokemon for Christmas. Harlan was moa smart den me. He wen graduate MIT wid one doctarite, but now he gotta work transmsssion, cuz, je'like dat guy Seve Homes, he no can fine his diploma.

Eh, Harlan, I acksed, between moutfuls of saimin. "What's a Pokemon?"

"One Jamaican Proctologist."

He wen bus' out laughing and almost brok one gut. "Ha Ha Ha! I wen fine dat joke on da intanet… " he wen wheeze, and bus' out lauging again. His face got so dakine red, look like his Japanee nose was changing color. In fact, da sound system insai da coffee shop was playing "Rudolph Da Red Nose Raindeah" while Harlan's honka was turnin red and and lightin up da booth. He was still laughing, dakine Kaneohe-bound nuthouse laugh, wen I lef. Stoopid bastad. I no like stick around too, cuz wen Harlan laugh li' dat he catch azma, and me, I no like catch um too.

Back at da shop, still no can concentrate. I drop one bearin and da buggah roll down da street and was gone. Ah shet, what's a bearin or two, I tought, and I put back da tranny of one '98 Oldsmobile Cutlass, missin bearin an all. I put dakine special ingreedament insai for keep da noise down. At 4 PM sharp, I wen dig out, jus wen Freddy was goin acks me about da hubcap filled wid sawdust by my worktable.

I drove home. I took one long, cold shower. I wen shave. I put da maximum amount of Brut Cologne dat one man can put on, befoa crossing into da treshold of *mahu* status. I wen comb my hair and put planny Pomade. Ho, da sticky da hair came. I hope one fly no land insai um, cuz dat buggah goin be hanging out wid me all night. I wen bus' out my best shirt from da closet. I wen shine my shoes. I wen spray one tremendous blast hairspray in my left ear, foa good luck. "U da man!" I said to myself, den I look moa close and tought, "Shet. Too much pomade! Look like Behn Kaiatano." What da hell. If dey ever was goin make one "Transmission Repair Specialists that Stalk Haunani Freitas Calandar" I still in da runnin for Mr. Decemba.

I jumped insai da Camaro and dig outta da garage. Half way down Kalakaua, by da Waikiki Theater, I hit da nitro button and da racing tires on da back wen smok one good, long patch. Ho, da Japanee tourists by da curb wen get all futless and run back insai da Royal Hawaiian Shopping Centa; dea papah bags all *hemo*, da cameras all fallin down. "Godzilla approaching Tokyo! Godzilla approaching Tokyo!" I wen yell in my best Japanee movie accent. Felt good! Den I saw da motocycle cop in da rear view mirror. He look at da bumpa of da Camaro. No moa sticka. Da blue light go on. Shet. Busted.

"I like give you some advice dat I wen learn at Kam School," Offissa Joseph Kamuali'i said, all police like, afta he wen write da ticket.

"Uhh ... OK."

"No use so much Pomade, Meesta Rodrigues. Wid yoa *ehu* hair, look like Behn Kaiatano wen get one dye job. Da chicks dey no dig it. Seriously. You remembah how long dat bruddah Behn wen stay single?"

"Tanks Offissa" I said unda my breath. He wen hand me da citation. Den I drove away slow and easy. Lucky ting he neva see da nitro button by da cigarette lighta.

Because of da stoopid ticket, I arrived late to da *Luau* show. Was late too, because I had to figa out how to get in from da beach side. Shet, I no care if Reen Manshow was playing *ukulele* by da Lurline, wearing nothing but giant eyelashes, and singing "Hea Come Santa In One Lectric Car." I not goin pay $32.50.

I had snuk in and wen in da back by da tree. Da band began to play one lame-ass version of "Mele Kalikimaka", wid da girls whacking da small bamboo at each other. Ho, catfight! Could be some kine choreography or someting, I guess, but still look sexy to me.

I neva have dakine female companionship for long time and

unlike dat piss off and mean ass Rocky, me an my *laho*s was still traveling on da same bus. Hey, no wonda Rocky so piss off at me! Mines was lonely, shriveling and unused, but dey was still dea for Christsake! "*Hui* Haunani!" dey wen sing insai my nice grey slacks "Ova hea! See da buggah dat goin sweep you off yoa feet! And who you goin fall in love wid and den live happily eva afta!"

I drank a big Mai Tai and grab one nodda one. My foddah used to have one saying wen trying for fix da car, but actually getting drunk in da backyard, it was: *"Godfannit! Go get dat frickin ting and bring um ova hea,"* meaning, "Attention, my beloved first born son Bozo Rodrigues, please get me da socket wrench from insai my red toolkit." Dat was my deah Dad, always needing one translata.

In da flickaring torchlight, da drums was beatin sofly and da rum was goin right to my head. I was feeling kine of mental. Could be I was nergeous cuz da angel of my dreams stay only a few yards away. She came on stage, perspiring slightly in da warm tropical night. Da music came so nice. She wen dance on one small kine platform, da brown skin of her naked back glistening in da sof moonlight. *"Godfannit! Go get dat frickin ting and bring um ova hea."* I wen say liddle bit too loud, sounding a lot like my deah departed foddah. In fact, I was beginin to tink I was a lot like my pooah foddah, and so far wasn't workin out too good.

Da Pomade was starting to melt down my sideburns, I could taste um if I stuck my tongue out da side of my lip. I put da Mai Tai glass against my sizzling forehead. "Lawd take me now," I wen mumble stoopidly. Next to me, had one nice old white-haired lady from Nebraska. She wen drop her napkin and in da process of pickin um up, had noticed da impressive garage I had build on my own premises. I smiled at da old lady and wiggled my Behn Kaiatano hair. A transmission specialist, if drunk enough, mus sometimes service olda vehicles.

The stage manager of da Polynesian show was one Samoan kid. To tell you da trut, I tink dat buggah wen bus' trough da Brut Cologne barrier back in grade school. Still, dat bastad still held da key to my futcha. At first, he seemed upset by my approach to da backstage area. Could be he was tinking foa call da cops. But in my pocket had one $20 bill, and da chicken-scratch love note I made foa her on one napkin from my pineapple spear. "Exquiseme," I said all polite like, and *haole*-fied, handing him da note and da $20, "You tink you can help me out?" He looked at da $20 in his hand and da note. He try foa figure out exactly which shiney socket in da tool kit da brokanic was reaching foa.

"Hmmph," he snorted, "an foa whom do you wish foa me give dis?" he said all sassy, li' dat. Sounded like he was talking to me tru his stuck up nose.

I was confuse. "Uhh ... da 20 bucks is foa you."

"Duuuhhh..." da Samoan kid said even moa sassily, "I kno dat! I MEAN DA NAPKIN!"

Da ring and pinion gears was stripping in my differential. My pressha gauge was moving rapidly towards da red. Soon, da smoke was goin come out my ears. *Mahu* or not, I would disconnect dis bastads driveline right now, if he keep acking all sassy to me.

"Hau ...... Da girl on da pedestal!" I slobbered loudly.

There was silence.

"As what I wen figgah," da Samoan Kid said finally, shaking his head disgustedly, "she always get da weird ones." He fluttered made up eyeballs, threw his hair ova his shoulda and said, "MEN!" Then he run over to da girls' dressing room.

"Wait!" I said, kine of pleading like. I was desperate eh? "What kine flowa she like?"

He look at me with dakine pity on his face, "Carnation— pink, da long stem kind and no get da cheap one." Den he wiggle in da door.

I goin let him live.

My Christmas angel was mos likely removing her makeup in front of one of dose zillion watt mirrors. In my futless mind, I wen imagine her naked back glistening, as she opened my sticky, pineapple-scented napkin to read:

Howzit honey,

you dance so nice, an you so talented.

I hope I get to meet you sometime.

From,

Honey Boy Rodrigues — Hockey Playa

I wen go beneat her dressing room window, da gears of my heart twistin in da red transmission fluid of my boilin blood. I tink I was in love, becuz I stay spinning in one weird kine auxiliary overdrive. Das da kine, you no can touch um. Only da factory can repair.

I heard some sof kine laughter, then da Samoan kid's voice said, "Oh he not too bad foa look at, but I no tink he too smart."

Ho! I tell you! My differential wen slip into 4 wheel positraction. One moa Mai Tai and I may have to rebuild dat rat bastad's transfer case. I stumble back for fine one seat at da bar. "Coffee!" I wen blurt out drunkenly.

As my ancestor, da great Portagee-*Kanaka* chief Manuel "Flopping *Uhu*" Braga once said, his *malo* unraveling as he dug out from one fierce kine battle, "I will retreat to fight one noddah day.

Preferably not right away, but in da distant futcha with some moa guys and one really big machine gun. Aloooha and **PAACOCK!**"

I split. I neva like meet Haunani Freitas all shet-faced. Foa da firs time in my adult life I felt shame, you know. Cuz she was my dream.

I wen drive home like one ninety yea ol lady. I wen eat one can Vienna Sausage in my apartment while Rocky beat da patooties out of my souvenir shell lei. He was running around wid it in his liddle sharp teeth, and bus'ing um to pieces on da hard floor. When he was *pau* beef um, had only one single tiny, shell left. Dat pooah shell was dangling from da tread, like my las shining hope in one busted lei of failed relationships. I tought about it, about how I neva like foa her see me all *pilute*. Shet, I tought, maybe I can acktually try foa be one betta person and afta dat sawdus ting today, maybe I can try foa be one betta brokanic, too. I could be moa betta at a lotta stuff, now dat I was tinking about it.

My mind was spinning, and I was all confuse. I put on one old tape of Ed Kenney singing "Da Twelve Days of Christmas" and began singing along wid my favorite part (da 40 stinking peegs). Afta about 10 times tru, and trying foa remembah all da words —Ed nail um every time— we called it one night. Rocky drag one moa Vienna Sausage unda da bed. He roll ova on his back and snoa like one dam doofus. Me, I had neva eva snoa, even once. Despite da huffy testamony to da contrary insai da courtroom.

I closed my eyes and remembahd dat last day in court. Was like one nightmare. I gotta change my life. I really gotta change my life.

"Was he hostile?" Da judge wen acks.

"Ho judge!" Su Yen wen hiss tru her pouty lips. Steam was comin out of her eeah, like da funnel from da smoke stack of one small kine Lionel train. Da pooah ting was strugglin wid her mean tempa. She wen rake da hair from her forehead, an stan up quickly from da chair.

"Hostile, dogstyle, anykine style!" she yell out, pointing at me. "And den, right afta dat, all da time **ZZZZZZ, ZZZZZZZZZ**, like one chain saw, yoa honah. I res my case!"

Da sherif by my side was ready foa bus out laughing. His face was all red, an his eyes was buggin out, like da buggah was holding his breat unda da wata. Da judge, he get up and run insai his chamba. I tink dat bastad was laughing too, cuz could hea tru da doah. Ho, right dea I wanted foa turn into one small inseck and axcape into da alley.

Maybe das what was goin happen to me if I neva change my evil ways. I was goin stand up on judjement day, say "howzit" to St. Peeda, and feel someting funnie kine coming out from da top of my head. Den I was goin make one big carmic-cannonball into da public swimmin pool and come back in one noddah life as one crooked politician, one defrocked trustee or noddah kine ting wid "feelers." Holy Shet! At da rate I was going, St. Peeda not even goin give me one small kine "The Kamehameha Schools Est. 1887" bumpa sticka foa paste on my cockaroach *okole*.

Early da next morning, I made one cup coffee and wrote Haunani one letta. I told her I seen her dance, and was wondering if she would like to see da Willy Kay concert at da Shell next week. I wrote um all nice, too. Took me tree tries.

I showed up in da hockey unifoam I had jus get from da UPS guy, cuz da mainland Sports Authority lady on da telephone had come thru. In my hand I had one dozen pink carnation, long stem flowers, da ackspensive kine.

"I didn't know there was hockey in Hawai'i," she said sweetly looking at my unifoam.

"We just getting started. Me and Binky and da boys. Binky da goalie, cause he build like one brick sh... er... house. And no moa ice, so us guys use da in-line skates. Except for Binky, his feet too big.

He just wea slippas."

"How fun! Can I watch you play sometime?"

"Shoots. Next week we goin play Stan's Auto Body in Kakaʻako."

We had fun at da Willy Kay Concert. Ho Braddah could sing! He take da guita and he shred um. Nice you know! Willy sang "Oh Holy Night" and my Christmas Angel almost wen cry. Me too. Jus sittin dea wid her unda da stars, I was so happy, like was one dream come tru. Afta da show, I drop her off all gentleman like, and I even open da doah of da Camaro and walk her to da lobby.

Da week went by quick. Me an da boys wen practice couple times afta work in da parking lot. Ho, da hard foa teach mokes to skate, wid dakine, inline skates. Wid any kine skates, acktually. Wen came time foa da game, we neva play too good, but we had fun. Stan dem was pretty lousey. Shet, dey was just doing me one fava for fixing Stan's wife's tranny last yea.

I zipped around and bodychecked Martinez wid one shoulda in da chest. He went fly off into da hibiscus bushes. I guess Mexicans no can skate too good eeddah. "Way to go! Honey Boy!" Haunani shouted excitedly from da sidelines. Den I skated on da outside around Stan's fenda guy Leo, and crank da puck wid one sly backhand shot. Da buggah slip past dat big ape Eric Nakasone and went into da empty dumpster dat was da goal. Ho, I SCOA!

Haunani got togeda wid some of da odda girls and wifes and dey started making cheers li' dat. Dey wen yell;

"Float like one dragonfly, bang um in da yoys
Geef um, geef um, Honey Boy!"

Ho, I was so proud, I was skating like one lunatick. Binky was running around all happy. Instead of taking something, dat big bastad was acktually protecting something, even if it was jus one empty dumpsta, nocked ova on da side. Bein da goaly seemed to agree wid him. His boys an his ol lady was cheering foa him too. Haunani had teach dem some cheerleading stufts. Dey wen make dakine chearleada dance kine moves. Dey was yellin;

"Standing by da dumpsta, man of steel

Binky, Binky, he's unreal!"

We was all having so much fun, like we was all *ohana*, intead of jus a bunch of guys who no give one rat's ass. I wen skate pas Eric for one moa goal. "Gee Portagee," he said grudgingly. "You not too bad."

"Hurray for Honey Boy!" Haunani screamed. "Way to go, Rodrigues!" Ho, I was burnin da bearins in my in-line skates and looking at her sweet face, all happy an perspiring. I guess my liddle angel jus needed somebody foa cheer in her life.

I tink I can be dat guy. I goin work real hard foa show her dat I love her and I no goin let her down. Me: Honey Boy Rodrigues, Transmission Repair Specialist and, oh yeah, "Hockey Wing."

Afta da game, da boys wanted to make one game foa next week and drink beer foa celebrate, but I leaned ova and told Haunani,

"I no drink alcohol. You like Jasmine tea?"

"Do I!" She smile and touch my swety arm.

On Christmas day, she came ova to my place and watch Rocky beat da crap out of a ping-pong ball she wen give him for Xmas. Da Rock was so happy, he neva like beef, even once. I had a feelin tings was goin change soon in my life. Maybe I was beginin to learn some stuff dat I should have learnt long time ago.

"Wow," she said, looking across da street, "you can see my place from here!"

Whoops. No moa stalking Haunani foa me. From now on, I goin try learn stuff about her da regula way. By paying attention and caring. Oh, yeah and something else I was neva any good at. One ting called "listening."

I stood up ackin all surprise and look out da window across da street.

"Not. You mus be kidding. Whea stay?" I said laughing.

She opened her Christmas present, one light yellow neglahjay from Macy's dat was goin fit her dead solid perfeck. She excuse herself and was gone for liddle while, den came back insai da living room.

"Merry Christmas, Honey Boy," she said giggling.

Author's Note;

Once, I played a series of concerts for the University of Hawai'i. On the same bill was an excellent jazz guitarist by the name of Frank Vignola. Frank hailed from New York City and after playing a couple of shows together, we became friends. We were staying at the same high-rise hotel in Waikīkī and had a few hours free one afternoon, so I decided to play tour guide. Frank and I walked over to the Honolulu Zoo. When we got to the monkeys —the ones with the bald 'elemu; don't know the species— Frank's eyes lit up. He was so happy standing there watching their naked buns. In front of my own eyes, a studied and talented musician had turned into a little kid. That's what I love about my musician friends. Sooner or later a "quirk" appears and it is usually a pretty damn good one. Later, having a drink on the balcony, I accidentally noticed a lovely maiden, partially clothed in the window of an adjacent building. This was way better than the monkeys, I thought. The sweet scent of the zoo drifted in the air and "Stalking Haunani" was born. The Hawaiian words in this story are from the character's point of view and as such, are intentionally misspelled.

"Stalking Haunani" is also a tribute to my good friend, Lee Cataluna. Lee and I

worked together on the musical "You Somebody" which premiered at Diamond Head Theater in July 2002. While we were thinking about what to do, I kind of just hung around with her for a while, watching the stuff fall out of her head. I consider Lee to be the best Pidgin-English writer in Hawai'i. Her plays have a delicious local humor in them. It was so much fun reading her scripts that the songs came bursting out of my heart.

Glossary of Non-English Terms Used
by Kaliko Beamer-Trapp

Introduction:

Following is the glossary of italicized non-English terms used in the stories; most are Hawaiian, but there are some Japanese, Portuguese, French, and local English words listed as well. Please remember that in the interest of leaving this a story book and not a dictionary, the entries have been somewhat restricted to mentioning only the meanings of the words as they occur in the contexts of the stories.

Although I have done my best to be as accurate as possible, any errors or shortcomings are entirely my own.

Use of Terms and Layout:

To find a word, simply look it up in the left column. The words are arranged alphabetically (using the English alphabet), with the macron and glottal-stop falling after the letter "z." There are no articles before the words themselves, so for example, to find "*ke akua*" —where "*ke*" is the article "the"— you would merely look up "*akua*." Compound terms (like "*liko lehua*" for example), are found by reading the entry for the first word of the compound ("*liko*" in this case), where "*liko lehua*" would then be defined. All genus-species names are italicized. Cross reference and comparison words that may be found within this same glossary are included in parentheses after the each entry for your convenience. Finally, enclosed also in parentheses at the very end of each entry are the numbers (*n*) that indicate from which story the word comes, following the table below:

    The Shimmering - ka ʻolili ....(1)

    Pōhaku ....(2)

    Our Ticket to Cannes ....(3)

    It Swims When You Sleep ....(4)

    Nā Iwi ....(5)

    My Beautiful Puka ....(6)

    Hănau Hope..(7)

    Stalking Haunani ....(8)

'a'ā   some people remember what this word means by thinking "a! a! (ooh! ouch!)" which is the sound you make if you try to walk on it barefooted: it's the rough, jagged, usually light brown or rust-colored lava that Pele creates. It contrasts to the other kind of lava, *pāhoehoe*, which is relatively smooth. Noteworthy perhaps is the fact that *'a'ā*, when leaving the vent, is actually *pāhoehoe*, but as it cools and crumbles over a rough substrate in places, it becomes the broken *'a'ā*. (see also: *pāhoehoe*) (2)

'a'ali'i   the *'a'ali'i* is a native plant of the genus *Dodonaea* which is used frequently in *hula* (on the *kuahu* altar dedicated to the goddess Laka) and also in *lei* making. (see also: *hula*, *lei*) (2)

'a'ama   a tasty black crab, *Grapsus grapsus tenuicrustatus*, that is often seen running around the rocks on the Puna coastline. (3)

adieu   French, meaning "farewell!" or "goodbye!" (3)

ahi   fire. In the story, it is a reference to the goddess Pele. (1)

'ahi   belonging to the *Scrombridae* family of fishes, along with *aku*, *ono*, and *'ōpelu*, the large *'ahi*, a deep-water albacore or yellow-fin tuna, is one of the favorites of Hawaiian fare, being found raw in *poke* and cooked upon the plates of hungry gourmands the world over. *Ali'i* and warriors were sometimes likened to the *'ahi*, for it was respected as a strong and hard-fighting fish. (see also: *aku*, *ali'i*, *ono*, *'ōpelu*) (6)

āholehole   *Kuhlia sandvicensis*, a fairly small, light-colored, and very popular fish with local people. In the past, *ali'i* would sometimes go to great lengths to procure adequate amounts of this fish for themselves. It can be found in salty, brackish, and sometimes even fresh water (if acclimatized). A variant name for this fish, used when involved in Hawaiian sorcery, is "*'ōlapa*." (see also: *ali'i*) (8)

'ai ha'a   a style of *hula* in which the performers bend their knees in much the same way as the ancient gods' knees are shown bent when carved into wooden or stone images. This is a very ancient style of dance, having a close relationship to other traditional Polynesian forms by being a little faster, lower, and more bombastic than most other *kahiko* forms of *hula*. (see also: *hula*, *kahiko*) (1)

'ai kanaka	literally, "to eat people"; cannibalize. (see also: *kanaka*) (5)
aku	this is the bonito fish, *Katsuwonus pelamis*, which is very delicious when eaten raw (in *poke* perhaps), or dried and salted, or even cooked in any number of ways. Polynesians have traditionally enjoyed eating every part, including the eyeballs of this fish, and thus it was eaten from head to tail with nothing left to waste! It is still very popular in stores today, along with *'ahi*. (see also: *'ahi*) (2)
akua	the word for a "god" or other divine being or image; when capitalized, it is the Christian "God." (3,5,6)
'alaea	this is a red-brown clay-like earth that is found only in certain (usually secret) locations around the islands. It is often mixed with sea salt and eaten as a delicacy with raw fish and other foods. This combination of salt and *'alaea* clay is often mistakenly called "*alae* salt" or just "*alae*" (which actually means a "coot"), so watch what you say when you ask for "*alae*" with your fish! It has many other uses, one of which is for ceremonial purification and honor. (3)
ali'i	a chief; a ruler of a district or island; of chiefly rank. (2,7)
aloha	what single word could be more difficult of concise definition than "*aloha*"? It has been officially adopted into the English language, meaning simply "love"; but as anyone who has anything to do with Hawai'i knows, this gentle and simple word spans the range of emotions from affection to veneration; compassion to pity; mercy to grace; and everything in-between. It is used as a greeting when getting together or going to part. (1,6,7,8)
'ama'uma'u	these are the young *'ama'u* ferns, *Sadleria cyatheoides*, that grow in the forests of Hawai'i. The fully grown *'ama'u* is somewhat similar to the *hāpu'u*, and was used for many things in days past, including as an adornment for the thatching of the Hawaiian *hale pili* ("grass shack"). Most notable here is the fact that Kamapua'a himself is spiritually connected with the *'ama'u*, it being one of his possible *kino lau* body forms. The name of the crater where Pele resides is Halema'uma'u, which is a contraction of "*hale*" and "'*ama'uma'u*." (see also: *hale*, *hāpu'u*, *kino lau*, *pili*) (1)

'ami	used in *hula* mostly, it is that circular movement of the hips that we probably all have tried to practice at one time or another with a go at the "hula hoop." Of course, a true *hula* dancer has much finer and more controlled movements than anyone could possibly attain with a "hula hoop." (This word is intentionally misspelled in the story). (see also: *hula*) (8)
'apapane	a small commonly seen scarlet-crimson honey creeper, *Himatione sanguinea*, with black wings and tail, which feeds on the nectar of the *lehua* blossoms. Its wings make a particularly identifiable whirring sound when it flies, and it is noted for its song. (see also: *lehua*) (1)
arare	rice cracker snacks, often sold in little bags. Similar to Japanese "*osembei*." (3)
'au	to swim. (4)
'aumakua	an *'aumakua* is a guardian, often visible after taking the form of any number of natural objects or living things. Oftentimes, the *'aumakua* is a family ancestor who, through a reciprocal relationship with a living person, may provide aid or guidance in exchange for being remembered in prayer and being fed at an altar (*kuahu*) or other location frequented by that *'aumakua*. Certain families claim certain types of animals as their *'aumākua* (plural spelling), such as *pueo* (owls), sharks, lizard-like *mo'o*, and certain fishes such as the *'ōpelu* or the *'o'opu* (gobies). There are many fascinating stories of *'aumākua* in traditional Hawaiian literature and newspapers, as well as in the memories and collective *na'au* of modern day Hawaiian families. (see also: *hula* (*kuahu*), *na'au*, *'ōpelu*, *pueo*) (4)
'awa	this plant, a member of the black pepper family, has been used by Polynesians for countless generations, and was transported by them on their long ocean voyages to new lands. It is commonly called "kava" in English, taken from the more ancient Polynesian pronunciation. The *'awa*, *Piper methysticum*, was said to have been brought to Hawai'i by the god Kāne, and was used for all manner of things, perhaps most notably as a mild relaxing drink —often likened to "slightly muddy pond water," according to some— which was either pre-

pared by mastication or pounding, mixing with water, and then straining. (1)

'ehu before the arrival of Captain Cook in the late 1700s, certain Hawaiians living on Moloka'i were said to have had *'ehu*-colored hair. The *'ehu* color is a reddish tinge present in a normally brown-black head of hair, not at all like the "red" hair that one might see on an Irish girl for example. In the modern day, *'ehu* describes anyone with a light tint of blonde. (This word is intentionally misspelled in the story). (8)

'elemu buttocks; hind region of a mammal. This term is much more polite than the rather vulgar "*'ōkole*." (*'Elemu* is intentionally misspelled in the story). (see also: *'ōkole*) (8)

'ena makani a very strong and usually cold wind. The word "*'ena*" gives a feeling of anger to the wind (*makani*). It also lets us think back to Pele herself, as "*'ena*" refers both to the "heat" of her flames, and the "heat" of Kamapua'a's desires for her. (see also: *ahi*) (1)

foie gras French, an hors d'oeuvre, the name literally meaning "greasy liver" (feel hungry yet?). Actually, it's quite a delicacy, being a pâté made out of goose liver or other type of animal liver and spread on crackers, toast, or French bread. (2)

habut local slang (origin unknown) meaning sulky, pouty, upset, or bothered. A Hawaiian word for this is *nuha*. (6)

hālau a *hālau* is a place of learning. The *hālau hula*, traditionally considered a sacred site, is specifically used for learning and practicing *hula* and its associated arts and traditions. (see also: *hula*) (1)

hale a house or building. When used with the possessive "*o*" following, it means "the house belonging to [somebody]": *hale o Wackenhut*, the Wackenhut office [building]. (3,6)

hana to work, to do something. In our story, Butch yells "*HANA PA!*", which is a common misspelling and mispronunciation of the traditional fishermen's phrase "*hana pa'a!*", meaning variously "do it right!", "make it firm!", "pull!", or "hold on tight!", depending on the state of emotion and the size of the fish! (6)

hānai	to adopt, to feed. (3)
hānau	to give birth; offspring. The meaning of "*hānau hope*" is the last (*hope*) of the offspring (*hānau*). (7)
haole	this word is an ancient word which meant a "foreigner" or "foreign thing" in pre-contact times. Kamapua'a himself is called a *haole*, perhaps because he and his family came originally from Kahiki. Another meaning of "*haole*" is "white," when applied to a pig's hair color; thus Kamapua'a may have been "*haole*" because of his striped white coloration. Either way, linguistic and cultural evidence have debunked the often heard and popular modern myth that the word "*haole*" is referring to a person without the Hawaiian breath of life: "*hā*" (breath) + "'*ole*" (none). After the arrival of westerners to Hawaiian shores, the word *haole* came to mean any caucasian foreigner, as opposed to other people such as "*pākē*" (Chinese), "*pōpolo*" (Black), "*kāmoa*" (Samoan), and so on. In more modern times, the word "*haole*" has come to mean a caucasian American by default in local English, although Hawaiian speakers take its meaning from context. (see also: *pākē*) (1,2,6,8)
hāpai	used most commonly in Hawaiian to mean "to carry" or to "be pregnant," and still used that way in Pidgin. (This word is intentionally misspelled in our story). (8)
hāpu'u	a tree fern of the genus *Cibotium*, endemic to the Hawaiian islands. The ferns are sometimes thought of as the parents of the '*ōhi'a lehua*, because the latter often take initial root in the young ferns' soft trunks as they grow on cooled lava fields. Many parts of these ferns are useful, which almost caused their demise in the late 1800s and early 1900s when their soft "wool" was used for stuffing pillows and such, and their pith used for starch. The ferns are now mostly used as garden ornamentals when not left happily growing with their "friends" in the forests. (see also: '*ōhi'a lehua*) (1)
hau	a type of primitive Hibiscus tree, *Hibiscus tiliaceus*, with often complex and low interwoven branches, the wood of which being lightweight is often used for the outriggers of traditionally made Hawaiian

	canoes. The bark, stripped from the young branches, is used to make a strong cordage. *Hau* grows commonly near the shore on all the Hawaiian islands, but certain varieties live upland as well. (2)
hemahema	weak; unskillful, clumsy. (1)
hemo	there are many meanings for this word in Pidgin, but in Hawaiian, it is always a descriptive-type word meaning unfastened, removed, released, opened, and so on. In Pidgin, the meanings can also be made into active verbs, such as "to unfasten," "to remove," "to release," "to open," etc. (8)
hōʻiʻo	either of two separate types of edible fern: that of genus *Diplazium* or genus *Dryopteris*. From ancient days, the young green fronds have been picked from the uplands and eaten raw. They are easy to find in many stores today. Some Hawaiian speakers have made the reasonable suggestion that *hōʻiʻo* was a substitute for meat at times, as the name indicates (perhaps literally, "to make like meat"); this is unconfirmed however. (1)
honi	to kiss or to smell; a kiss. Interestingly enough, the "kiss" of the ancient Hawaiians was not so much the smacker that *haole* people think of as a kiss, but rather a gentle inhaling through the nose as one pressed against the other in greeting. (see also: *haole*) (3)
honohono	also called *honohono maoli* ("native *honohono*") or *honohono kukui*, it is a grass that grows in the shade of certain trees, most particularly the *kukui*. (see also: *kukui*) (1)
hūi	"*hūi!*" is the Hawaiian interjection often used to announce one's arrival at a house, with the idea that someone inside will answer with an invitation to enter. This practice of calling out arrival is, of course, not only Hawaiian, but is used in many cultures around the world. (This word is intentionally misspelled in the story). (6,8)
hula	the well-known traditional interpretive dance of Hawaiʻi, *hula*, as practiced in a *hālau*, encompasses not only the physical movement of the body or the sound of the instrument, but also the spiritual and cultural values of the Hawaiian people. It is related to the various dance styles of the other Polynesians, and as such, has an ancient lineage.

Despite having hundreds of styles, *hula* is often divided into two main categories: *hula kahiko* (also called *hula kuahu*), the ancient *hula* done to chanting and without modern instruments such as the guitar or *'ukulele* in accompaniment; and the *hula 'auana*, or modern *hula*, incorporating imported styles of movement and accompaniment from the time of King Kalākaua in the late 1800s to the present. More recently, a new term has been coined to refer to newly-created *hula* in the ancient (*kahiko*) style: *'aiakahiko*. (see also: *hālau, kahiko, 'ukulele*) (1)

huli in Hawaiian, this word means "to turn over," amongst other things, like a canoe might turn over in the sea (that's also how "*hulihuli* chicken" comes about, for as the chickens are cooked, they turn repeatedly on a spit). But in local Pidgin English, the word *huli* has a broadened meaning, including "to tip over," as the tree did in our story. In Hawaiian, that would be "*hina*." (8)

hūpē that slimy greenish stuff that runs out of one's nose, as that which is especially noticeable on the upper lips of little kids suffering from colds. Also called "*hanabata*" in Pidgin. (6)

'io the *'io* is a beautiful hawk, *Buteo solitarius*, that lives in various places on the island of Hawai'i. It is endemic and is now endangered. It holds a special spiritual place in many people's hearts today, as it has done for many centuries, and is an *'aumakua* for some families. (see also: *'aumakua*) (1)

irashaimase a Japanese welcoming greeting frequently heard when a person enters a restaurant or a store. (5)

iwi any bone of any animal is called an *iwi*, but when we think of humans, the *iwi* are very special. In Hawaiian thinking, the *iwi*, being repositories of *mana* and sometimes even emotions, are the symbols of family ancestry and progeny, as they remain for such a long time after a person is gone. The *iwi* of all people —and especially those of the *ali'i*— were secreted away in places where no other could molest or steal them: they would be carefully entrusted to either the land, the ocean, or caves for safekeeping. As the spirit of the person sometimes might remain with or be called back to the *iwi*, it is most important to show respect lest that spirit be insulted. Furthermore, a person's spirit might never be able to join its ancestors if the *iwi* are destroyed (by a bulldozer, for example). Note: *ka iwi* is singular; *nā iwi* is plural. (see also: *ali'i, kā'ai, mana*) (5)

kā'ai the *kā'ai* are the containers made by ancient Hawaiians for their departed chiefs' *iwi*, or bones. Usually made of strong finely interwoven plant roots such as those of the *'ie'ie* (*Freycinetia arborea*), they resemble wickerwork baskets, taking on the general form of a head and body the length of the skull and thighbones combined. Sometimes, the *kā'ai* were stored in religious temples, and at other times secreted away in caves forever; in either case, a guardian would be assigned to make sure that none of its *kapu* were broken. (see also: *iwi, kapu*) (5)

kāhea a call; in *hula*, to call out the first phrase of a chant or song to ensure communication between the dancer and the chanter, instrumentalist, or musician. (see also: *hula*) (1)

kahiko ancient, old. It is a relative —rather than absolute— term, meaning that the time period is understood by context. For example, *hula kahiko* would be "*hula* of the ancient style," which is generally understood to be in the style of the pre-Kalākaua era of the 1800s. But a car that you owned only two years ago (which has now been sold) could be your "*ka'a kahiko*" or "old car." In our story, it is frequently used by itself (as, "I learned *kahiko*...") meaning *hula kahiko* in all instances. (see also: *hula*) (1)

kala the Hawaiian name for the surgeonfish of the genus *Naso*. Furthermore, "*kala*" means "to forgive" or "to absolve"; it also refers to the rough, sandpaper-like skin of the shark. All of these things have direct relation to our story. (4)

kanaka the word "*kanaka*" means a grown-up person, either male or female of any race, although it has traditionally meant a Hawaiian male by "default," if you will. When further defined by the word "*maoli*" (native or true), it means a "true human" (*kanaka maoli*). Hawaiians

	today often use *kanaka maoli* like a proper noun; and with a little intrinsic political twist, "*Kanaka Maoli*" means a "native Hawaiian." Now, if the word "*peke*" (short or tiny) is added to "*kanaka,*" then you have a "dwarf" or "midget." (5,6,8)
kāne	this word means "man," "male," "masculine," or "husband," as well as many other meanings. It is often used in local English, as is its counterpart "*wahine*." In our story, it is intentionally lacking the macron, as the computer screen could not display the marking. (see also: *wahine*; *'ōhi'a lehua, kino lau,* and *'awa* for references to the god Kāne) (1)
kano	a word in need of a delicate translation, *kano* is a term used here to mean… a male erection. (1)
kapa	the word *kapa* originally meant just "bark-cloth," a finely textured "cloth" made of flattened *wauke* or *māmaki* tree bark, or any object made from it such as clothing, bedding, flags, and so on. It was brought into the English language as "tapa" by missionaries working in the Marquesas and Hawaiian islands in the early 1820s, for the ancient pronunciation in both places was "*tapa.*" The usage has now broadened to include any type of bed covering or quilt, and this is how it is used in our story. (see also: *māmaki*) (2)
kapakahi	crooked, bent. (8)
kapu	sacred; protected; taboo; rule; a power related to the *mana* of an *ali'i* or sacred object. The ancient pronunciation of this word, "*tapu,*" was heard by westerners as "taboo"; thus the English word was born. Sometimes, people place signs on their properties indicating "*kapu*": "stay out!" (see also: *ali'i, kā'ai, mana*) (5)
kā	(see *tī*)
kiawe	the *kiawe* is the thorny Algaroba tree (*Prosopis pallida*) which grows very well in dry areas and has found itself a place nearly everywhere it seems. Most annoying are the thorns which fall all over the ground and get stuck in bare feet and even go through "slippers"; it was said that the missionaries of the mid-1800s brought the tree to Hawai'i to make Hawaiians wear shoes, but this is most likely untrue. More plau-

sible is that the first seeds were planted in Honolulu in about 1827, after having been brought here by accident in the pockets of a French priest's clothing. (2,5)

kibidango a Japanese bun made of a millet grain (*kibi-*) that is pounded and shaped into sticky balls, like rice balls. (5)

kiʻi pōhaku found throughout the Hawaiian islands, the *kiʻi pōhaku*, or petroglyphs, are designs carved into the face of rocks to commemorate an event, or to represent a significant person or object, or even to use as a "board" upon which to play *kōnane* (like checkers). In certain locations, such as Puʻu Loa on Hawaiʻi, the circular *kiʻi pōkahu* in the *pāhoehoe* lava were used as placements for the umbilical cords of babies to signify longevity. (see also: *pāhoehoe*, *pōhaku*) (5)

kino lau any of the several forms that a being might take; the natural objects that are spiritually related to a being and under its control. For example, the well-known god, Kāne, had control over and assumed the form of taro, sugarcane, or bamboo, as well as many other things. Similarly, Kamapuaʻa called upon certain plants such as *kukui*, *ʻuhaloa*, and *ʻamaʻumaʻu* in times of need. (see also: *ʻamaʻumaʻu*, *kukui*, *ʻuhaloa*) (1)

koa this is a native tree, *Acacia koa*, that can be found growing in the dry upland forests of Hawaiʻi, with sickle-shaped leaves (when mature), and tall, stately trunks. Its wood is often made into bowls in the modern day, but in the past this was not the case for food bowls, as *koa* was said to impart a strange taste to the food within. Its main use was for making the hulls and paddles of Hawaiian canoes. Today, it is prized for its beautiful grain and is used in the manufacture of many things, such as Keola's guitars and *ʻukulele*. The symbolism of the *koa* is strength and bravery. (see also: *ʻukulele*) (2,6,7)

koa haole *koa haole* (lit., "foreign koa"), often mislabeled "*haole koa*" —which would mean "valiant white guy" by the way— is known to science as *Leucaena leucocephala*. It is a scrubby, shrubby, shabby-looking persistent foreign invader which can grow just about anywhere if given the chance. It originated somewhere in Central America, and was brought to Hawai'i around the time of Kamehameha the Great, perhaps as a food for cattle (although it is said to give even them stomach ache). Now just in case you might think this vexing weed has no saving grace, here's what may be its only one: the tiny seeds can be made into several styles of fairly nice looking *lei*. (see also: *haole*, *koa*, *lei*) (6)

kōkua   help; to help. (6)

kūkae   this word is definitely not to be used in polite circles. It means feces, excrement, dung, or even "ejectamenta" if you so please. (3,6)

"kūkapaila"   from the Hawaiian meaning "the pile stands," used in local English to mean "plenty." Intentionally misspelled in the story as "kookah pilah". (6)

kukui   the name of a tree, the candlenut *Aleurites moluccana*, which is most respected today for the beauty of its nuts which fall in great numbers and are collected to make both *lei*s and *'inamona*, a relish made with the roasted kernels and eaten with raw fish. In olden days, the nuts were broken open, and the expressed oil burned for lighting houses and such. The tree and its nuts have many other uses. (see also: *lei*) (3)

kumu   a *kumu* is a teacher, or source of knowledge. Therefore, a *kumu hula* would be a "teacher in the arts and traditions of *hula*." (see also: *hula*) (1)

kūmū   the goatfish, *Parupeneus porphyreus*, which was desired by both priests and *ali'i* (chiefs) in the past, due to the fact that its red color connected it with sacred events and objects. It was also sometimes used to signify that an apprentice had reached the stage of becoming a teacher ("*kumu*"). Besides all that, it has always been delicious to eat! Furthermore, a sweetheart girl or woman may be poetically spoken of by a man as being a "*kūmū*." (see also: *ali'i*, *kumu*, *mele*; compare: *ulua*) (8)

kupuna   ancestor; grandparent; also a respectful term sometimes used to refer to a person of advanced years who has been elevated to a position of "*kupuna* status" because of affection by an individual, family, or the

	community. (see also: *tūtū*) (2)
laho	technically, the scrotum of a male. (8)
laua'e	this is a fern of the genus *Microsorium* which, when crushed, often produces a wonderful fragrance. It is commonly seen planted as an ornamental throughout the Hawaiian islands, reaching about 18 inches in height. The *laua'e* is a favorite for use in *lei*-making of many different styles. (see also: *lei*) (1)
lehua	these are the red, golden, pink, or very rarely white blossoms that are found on the *'ōhi'a lehua* tree. Most common is the red, which is sacred to Pele. The *'apapane* birds feed commonly upon the *lehua* nectar. As the old people say, it is wise to pick *lehua* only on the return journey from the mountains, lest a heavy mist cover the pathways and cause one to become lost. (see also: *'apapane, lei, 'ōhi'a lehua*) (1,7)
lei	the word "*lei*" has been officially added to the English language; thus we all know what it means. There are many excellent books written about these Hawaiian-style adornments, so here are but a few points. The *lei* can be made in any of a great number of styles, perhaps the most common today being the *kui* style (*lei kui*), where items are strung on a thread and worn around the neck. Another style, the *haku* style (*lei haku*), is a braiding together of materials upon a flexible but strong foundation of *tī* or other dry plant leaves or stalks. The *lei haku* are most often worn on the head, and are commonly worn by *hula* practitioners. One of the most fragrant *lei*s is the *lei 'awapuhi*, made of ginger flowers strung or woven together in any of several styles. One cultural point to remember is that a pregnant woman should not wear a *lei* which completely encircles her neck, for this may indicate a possible strangling of her unborn child by the umbilical cord. (see also: *tī*) (1,5,7)
liko	the small young leaf or the leaf bud of the *'ōhi'a lehua* tree; the red bud of the *lehua* flower. The young green or reddish leaves are often covered with fine fuzzy hairs, and are used commonly in *lei haku*. They symbolize in part new growth and delicate beauty; and they

receive strength from the "parent" *'ōhi'a* tree. (see also: *lehua, lei, 'ōhi'a*) (1,7)

lepo   soil, dirt; dirty, muddy. Kamapua'a, as a true hog, has a strong connection with the earth upon which he runs and in which his *kino lau* grow. Thus, his liking of the soil, which is the foundation of his forest domain —as opposed to Pele's dry lava fields— is rooted deep within him. (see also: *kino lau*) (1)

lo'i   a depression, or paddy, made in the ground, the *lo'i* is often part of a terraced system of irrigated ponds which are constructed either in the uplands or lowlands and traditionally used for farming taro. (7)

lōlō   crazy; paralyzed; numb. (see also: *pakalōlō*) (6)

lū'au   a feast or party, usually with many people in attendance and an abundance of Hawaiian food. This word is now officially in the English language. (It is intentionally misspelled in the story). (8)

mahimahi   said by the old-timers to be found sometimes traveling with *ono*, the *mahimahi*, genus *Coryphaena*, is another of the fishes commonly cooked and eaten in Hawai'i and elsewhere, where it is known by its English name "dolphin-fish." (6)

māhū   a male who acts like a female or in a feminine way; more commonly, a homosexual (of either gender). (This word is intentionally misspelled in the story). (8)

makana   a gift, present; to give someone a gift. (3)

make   dead; death. When further defined by "*loa*" (completely), it means absolutely dead (*make loa*): therefore, in the story, the Hawaiian words *make loa* give us the feeling that the rock "actively" killed the sailors. (2)

mākoi   a fishing pole. (2)

malo   a Polynesian-style loincloth about one foot wide and twelve feet long made of *kapa* cloth, the *malo* was the article of clothing most commonly worn by Hawaiian men of ancient days. The commoners usually wore white *malo*, the red or yellow colored ones being reserved for the *ali'i* and their priests. The chiefly *malo* were made of dyed *kapa* or, very rarely, of bird feathers sewn onto a net matrix in much the same manner as the Hawaiian capes were made. You can imagine the fright that those poor missionary women had when they saw Hawaiian men in nothing but their *malo*; it wasn't long before they had Hawaiians all dressed up "nice and proper." *Malo* are rarely worn today except for during traditional ceremonies and *hula* performances. (see also: *ali'i*, *hula*, *kapa*) (6,8)

māmaki the leaves of the *māmaki* plant, a nettle of the genus *Pipturus*, are commonly used to make a tea which aids digestion. In the past, the bark of this plant was used for very high quality *kapa* cloth, and the fruits used as a laxative. Be sure not to make the common mistake of saying "*mamake*," as "*make*" means "*dead*." (see also: *kapa*, *make*) (1)

mana spiritual power; supernatural power emanating from within a being or a god or any special object; essence; life force; authority. (2,5)

manapua used in Pidgin, from a contracted combination of two Hawaiian terms: "*mea 'ono*" (cake or pastry) + "*pua'a*" (pork); it is the Chinese "*char siu bao*" (*char siu* bun). In English, it is called a "pork bun." Whatever you decide to call it, it is surely a tasty treat! (8)

manu the generic term for a bird. (see *'ō'ō*). (7)

ma uka contrasting with "*ma kai*" (towards the sea), this term means "towards the uplands" or "inland." Both of these terms are used frequently when describing the location of something, and are often seen written as one word (i.e. *mauka*, *makai*), although this is not grammatically correct in Hawaiian. (5)

mele this Hawaiian word means a "poem" or "song"; it can also mean "to sing" or even "to chant," although the word "*oli*" is usually used for the latter. Another meaning for "*mele*" is "merry," taken directly from English. This is how "*mele Kalikimaka*" ends up being a Hawaiianization of "merry Christmas." (see also: *oli*) (7,8)

menehune a small fellow somewhat like a pixie or elf or leprechaun perhaps, who often does wondrous things at night or whilst no-one is around to see. He works with all of his friends to accomplish tasks such as building fish ponds, platforms, canals, *lo'i*, and so on. (see also: *lo'i*) (6)

merde	a French exclamation meaning "hell!" or more literally, "shit!" (7)
moe	to sleep. (2)
moke	local slang (origin unknown) meaning a male who doesn't care about his looks or behavior; ugly, low class, good for nothing tough guy, like the kind of guy that would want to beat up a *haole*. (see also: *haole*; compare with: *tita*) (3)
mon ami	French for "my friend." (7)
"*mumu*"	the mispronounced Pidgin version of the Hawaiian "*muʻumuʻu*" (a reduplication of the word "*muʻu*," cut-off, maimed, and so on). Though not used this way in our story, the word "*muʻumuʻu*" refers to a popular type of long dress or gown with *muʻu* sleeves and yoke. (see also: *muʻu*) (8)
muʻu	cut off short; amputated; describing a lost limb. Almost the same as the Hawaiian word "*muku*." (see also: "*mumu*") (8)
naʻau	besides being the seat of emotions and being connected with the mind —in much the same way that the heart is thought of in western culture— the *naʻau* is also the intestine of a mammal. (5)
nēnē	the native wild mountain goose, *Branta sandvicensis*, is the largest native Hawaiian fowl that has survived into modern times; its habitat is now sadly restricted to Maui and Hawaiʻi islands. It is well-protected by various laws, and is increasing in numbers in places. In the past, it was considered a delicacy by the Hawaiians, who would hunt it on the open mountainsides at certain times of year. Its feathers, being a unique grey and white, were sometimes used in *kāhili* feather standards for the chiefs of old. (1)
ʻohana	this word is well known to almost everyone here in the islands, because it embodies one of the most important things in all of our lives: family. (3,8)
ʻōhiʻa	this is a well known type of Hawaiian endemic tree of the genus *Metrosideros*. It has beautiful wood that is used for house building, adornment making, and carving of images, amongst many other uses. This tree is sacred to the male *akua* Kāne and Kū, and thus has a connection to Kamapuaʻa; the red blossoms (*lehua*) are, however, associ-

ated with Pele. The *lehua* and leaves (*liko*) are used in making *lei*s because of the feeling of strength, expertise, honor and beauty that are brought forth when wearing them. The tree is often referred to as "*'ōhi'a lehua.*" (see also: *akua, lehua, lei, liko*) (1,7)

'ōkole a little rude to use (as opposed to the "nice" word *'elemu*), it means buttocks or their associated *puka*. In case you were interested, this latter fundament is sometimes called the "*puka kahiko,*" or "ancient hole," an old-time Hawaiian term. (see also: *'elemu, puka*) (3,6,8)

'ōlelo language; to speak. Thus, *'ōlelo Hawai'i* means either "Hawaiian language" or "to speak Hawaiian," depending on how it is used in the sentence. When referred to as "*'ōlelo makuahine*" —or simply "*'ōlelo makua*" in our story— it means "the mother tongue," the Hawaiian language. (1,7)

oli to chant; the chant itself (also called a *mele oli*). There are perhaps as many reasons to compose a chant as there are grains of sand on the shore, but here are some examples: to dedicate something newly built; to honor someone or something; to praise life or love; to beguile someone; to pray; to welcome; to cause things to grow; to complain about something; or to remember genealogies and stories. (see also: *mele*) (7)

'olili a shimmering, like the rising full-moon's reflection upon the surface of the sea, or the glassy shimmering mirage on flat black *pāhoehoe* lava on a hot day. (see also: *pāhoehoe*) (1)

'olo (same as *laho*) (5)

ono a type of fish, *Acanthocybium solandri*, related to the *'ōpelu, 'ahi,* and *aku*; Hawaiians knew the *ono* especially for its strong teeth and jaw muscles, and of course for its delicious taste too. Now, despite looking like the word "*'ono*" (tasty), the name is "*ono*" (pronounced without the glottal-stop); the meaning being completely different. They sometimes are found swimming with *mahimahi*. (see also: *'ahi, aku, mahimahi, 'ōpelu*) (6)

'ō'ō any of several endemic Hawaiian honey creepers of the genus *Moho*. They are thought to be extinct, except for the Kaua'i *'ō'ō 'ā'ā* (Moho braccatus), whose status is unknown. (7)

ʻōpelu	this is the mackerel fish, genus *Decapterus*, of which there are several Hawaiian named varieties. It is considered by some to be an *ʻaumakua* (family ancestor). They are plentiful on the Kona coast of Hawaiʻi, where our story takes place, and are eaten raw, dried, broiled, or steamed. (see also: *ʻaumakua*) (2)
ʻopihi	a little black limpet of the genus *Cellana* that clings very tightly to rocks by the shore, especially when a hungry human comes wandering along. (3)
ʻōpū	stomach. (6)
pāhoehoe	there are two distinct types of lava that are recognized around the world by their Hawaiian names: *ʻaʻā* and *pāhoehoe*. The latter is a smoother and usually darker type than the former. People often mispronounce this word, leaving out the macron of "*pā-*," and putting the emphasis on the first "*-hoe-*"; so please be sure to place the stress on "*pā-*" and let the rest of the word just "flow" out. (see also: *ʻaʻā*) (1,5)
pahu	a wooden standing drum, often made of coconut with a skin head and carvings at the base, used for *hula kahiko* performances. (see also: *hula*) (1)
pakalōlō	marijuana (*Cannabis sativa*). Literally meaning "crazy tobacco" or "numbing tobacco," the word *pakalōlō* is well known throughout the islands. "*Paka*" is from the English word "tobacco." (see also: *lōlō*) (5)
pākē	intentionally misspelled in our story as "*Pake*," this Pidgin and Hawaiian word means "Chinese." (8)
"*pan duce*"	correctly spelled "*pao doce*," this is a round Portuguese sweet bread roll, brought to Hawaiʻi by immigrant plantation workers. (It is intentionally misspelled in our story). (8)
pau	finished, done, completed. (3,8)
pilau	stinky, smelly; putrid, foul. (8)
pili	*pili* is a type of grass, *Heteropogon contortus*, that grows very well on the dry leeward slopes of the islands. It is a thick golden "spray" of grass blades all clumped together at the base, which makes pulling it out of the ground an easy task. In the past, bunches were pulled out, cut, and then added one after another to thatch traditional Hawaiian

	hale: thus the "grass shack" famous in song! The word "*pili*" also means to be close or attached to something (like sweethearts perhaps), and so the grass gets its name from the fact that it is clumped at the base. (see also: *hale*) (2)
pilikia	problem, trouble. (6,8)
pilute	local slang (origin unknown), meaning "drunk." (8)
pō	night; darkness; that realm from which we come before birth and to which we go after passing; it is also the realm of the *akua*, *'aumakua*, and spirits. (see also: *akua*, *'aumakua*) (4)
pōhaku	a *pōhaku* is a rock or a large, usually rough, stone (as opposed to smaller water-worn stones which have their own names). (see also: *ki'i pōhaku*) (2,5)
pōhuehue	this is the beach morning-glory, genus *Ipomoea*, which is associated with fishing, as the tough pliable vines could be easily found and woven into cordage or nets. Interestingly, the genus name *Ipomoea* can be translated as "the sweetheart who married," although this may or may not have anything to do with its given scientific name. (3)
poi	a somewhat glutinous and grey mass of cooked and pounded taro which, after being mixed with a quantity of water, achieves whatever consistency one desires for it. It is often referred to by *haole* people as "wallpaper paste," but this is doing this fine and very nutritious food a terrible injustice; not to mention the fact that we may very well wonder how they know what wallpaper paste tastes like in the first place. Indeed, *poi* has been a staple of the Hawaiian people for countless generations, and shows all signs of persistence. (see also: *haole*) (2,6)
pueo	any owl; specifically, the Hawaiian short-eared owl, *Asio flammeus sandwichensis*. The owl has been revered by countless generations of Hawaiians, and holds a special place in their hearts to this day. (As a fine example of this, please listen to Keola's song "Old Man Pueo"). The *pueo*, showing itself to only a few, is perhaps an *'aumakua* (ancestor) who is watching over, warning, or aiding those that see it, and may be telling a person to go back or find another way because of some danger that lies ahead. (see also: *'aumakua*) (1)

puhi	an eel of any type. One source indicates that in Hawaiian waters there are six types of conger eels, one snipe eel, eight snake eels, a *Moringuidae*, and thirty-five morays. Indeed, there may be more. In ancient days, some were eaten, some used in medicine, and some presumably left alone. (Only the saltwater *puhi* were eaten). (4)
puka	hole that goes completely through something (like a doorway in a house, or a hole punched in a paper); perforation; cavity, or entrance to a cavity. Note that in Pidgin, the word "*puka*" has also come to mean "pit" or "pothole" (like the kind one sees in a road), but in Hawaiian, the word for this kind of "hole" is "*lua*." (6,8)
pūpū	describing an hors d'oeuvre or appetizer of any kind, this Hawaiian word finds itself today not only used here in Hawai'i, but also in various places around the US and the world. (6)
pu'u	a lump or bump; a hill or pile, mound. (6)
tī	often pronounced "*kī*," this is the plant, *Cordyline terminalis*, that is so common around houses, parks, graveyards, and gardens throughout the islands, because of the feeling of spiritual protection (*mana*) that it gives. It has a great number of uses, ranging from food wrapping to *hula* skirts to shoe and moonshine-making. (see also: *mana*) (1,3)
tita	pronounced "tidah," this is a Pidgin word meaning a tomboy or tough girl, comparable to a *moke* on the male side. Actually, "*tita*" (pronounced as written) is the Hawaiian pronunciation of the word "sister." (see also: *moke*) (8)
très belle	French for "very beautiful" in reference to a girl or woman. (7)
tūtū	this is the affectionate term used for a grandparent. It is most likely a shortened and affected form of the word *kupuna* (old Hawaiian *tupuna*). Also can be said "*kūkū*." (see also: *kupuna*) (7)
ua li'ili'i	any light or very fine rain. (1)
'uhaloa	this is a plant that is still well known in Hawai'i for its medicinal property as a soother of sore throats, even in today's world of "modern medicines." Like the *'ama'uma'u*, this *Waltheria indica* is one of the forms that Kamapua'a could take in his journeys through his domains,

	wet or dry. (see also: *'ama'uma'u*) (1)
uhu	commonly called the "parrot fish," the *uhu*, genus *Scarus*, is a beautifully colored fish. It lives around the coral which, it is said, it eats and grinds in its beak-like mouth to create "sand." At night, it makes a cocoon for itself out of saliva and sleeps within it. It is a tasty fish to eat, with its soft, pale colored flesh and its very palatable liver and roe; it may be eaten raw or cooked. (4,8)
'ukulele	everyone knows that this is the little instrument that is "native" to Hawai'i; it has represented the islands for over a hundred years. The word *'ukulele* is made of two parts: "*'uku*," a flea, and "*lele*," to jump around. There are several stories of how this instrument, based on the imported Portuguese *braguinha*, came to be called an *'ukulele*, but perhaps the quaintest is the one about a spry musician in King Kalākaua's court who played one of these little things and jumped around like a flea as he did so. (3,6,8)
ulua	known by some as the "crevally" or "jack," this is the adult stage of the equally well-known "*pāpio*" fish, genus *Caranx*. Perhaps due to its strength, it is symbolic of a male, and most especially of a male sweetheart. So a woman might mention an *ulua*, when she actually means her "man." By the way, you may wish to know what to do with the *ulua*'s eyeballs when you cook the fish (for they become hard and distasteful after drying out in the oven): just stuff them into the belly cavity and the juice therein will keep them soft and delicious. A great Hawaiian trick! (compare: *kūmū*) (4)
weke	a *Mullidae* fish very similar to the *kūmū*, and often either the same red color, or at times, a whitish color. There are many varieties. (4)

About the Author

Keola Beamer is a recognized master of Hawaiian artistic expression. The fascinating history of his family can be traced back to the 15th century. In traditional Hawaiian society, *ali'i* (royalty) recognized that sounded words possess *mana* (spiritual power). They encouraged musical expression as a way to preserve information and communicate with one another and the gods.

Throughout the generations, the Beamers have been involved in the performing arts. In the 20th century, they have produced a number of influential performers, composers and teachers. Keola's great grandmother, Helen Kapuailohia Desha Beamer (1882–1952), was one of Hawai'i's most prolific and accomplished composers. She was also a skilled dancer whose grace left a lasting imprint on the *hula* (Hawaiian dance). Her granddaughter, Winona (Nona) Kapuailohia Desha Beamer, is Keola's mother. A noted chanter, composer, and teacher, Nona is revered for her scholarship and accomplishments in the education of Native Hawaiian children.

Keolamaikalani Breckenridge Desha Beamer carries the legacy into the 21st century. "My family is serious about music," Keola says. "We came from a history of oral tradition in which music and story telling was a central component. Our genealogies, land boundaries, and navigational information were all in the chant form. We are just beginning to realize the wealth of that knowledge and how so much of it has been lost. We are finally regaining some of these meanings and incorporating them in our own lives."

Keola has played guitar, piano and *'ohe hano ihu* (Hawaiian nose flute) since he was very young. He studied *hula* and sang in glee clubs while attending Kamehameha School, a school for children of Hawaiian ancestry. Keola attended Goddard College in Plainfield, Vermont. He was an active teacher of *kī hō'alu* (slack key guitar) in the 1970's and compiled the first comprehensive teaching manual on the subject, **Hawaiian Slack Key Guitar** (Oak Publications, New York). His contributions to slack key during the '70s began to spark public interest in *kī hō'alu*, launching a statewide revival of the tradition. His teaching continues today with extensive seminars on the Island of Hawai'i at which guitarists and dancers from all over the world gather in an "extended *'ohana*" format that the Beamers have called "The Aloha Music Camps." Keola views this immersion-style method as a way to responsibly share the traditions of music and dance within a cultural context.

Keola is especially noted for his ability to recontextualize ancient Hawaiian *mele* (songs) into contemporary settings in which he has created a style uniquely his own. His history has been a series of groundbreaking events, beginning in 1972 with the solo slack key album **Hawaiian Slack Key Guitar In The Real Old Style**. That LP is considered by many to be the catalyst for the revival of *kī hō'alu*. His 1978 release, **Honolulu City Lights** is the largest selling recording in the history of Hawaiian music. In 1994, **Wooden Boat**, Keola's first release on George Winston's Dancing Cat label, became the first Hawaiian music CD ever to reach the top 15 on the Billboard World Music Charts. All four of his subsequent releases for Dancing Cat, **Moe'uhane Kīkā -Tales From The Dream Guitar, Mauna Kea - White Mountain Journal, Kolonahe - From the Gentle Wind, and Soliloquy – Ka Leo O Loko (The Voice Within)** have also reached the Top 15. Keola's recent recording, **Island Born** released on his own 'Ohe Records label, is getting rave reviews and airplay nationwide.

Keola Beamer's live concert performances embody the magical "other worldliness" of this melodic language of dreams. His unique and polished style of musicianship skillfully accentuates the stories that his songs tell about the culture and the experience of being Hawaiian in a contemporary world. The repertoire he presents is often a three dimensional experience, combining the elements of *mele* (song), *hula* (dance), and *oli* (chant) with native percussion instruments and Hawaiian folklore.

Keola's contributions in performance art outside of his solo career include "Here is Hawai'i" at the former Maui Surf Hotel in Ka'anapali, "'Ulalena" at the Maui Myth and Magic Theatre in Lahaina, and "You

Somebody" at the Diamond Head Theatre.

Keola continues to expand on the slack key tradition as well as author books. He lives on the Island of Maui with his wife Moanalani.

Be sure to check out Keola's web page at **www.kbeamer.com** for on-line instruction, method books and CDs, information on "The Aloha Music Camps," and free downloads of music, videos, lyrics, and performance notes. You can also join Keola's mailing list to be informed of live concerts in your area.

Keola Beamer: selected works

Keola Beamer's body of recorded, print, and video work is matched by few in the field of Hawaiian music. Here are some favorites. You can order most of these items in his catalog directly from his website:

www.kbeamer.com

Soliloquy – Ka Leo O Loko
Ka Leo O Loko is Keola's fifth Dancing Cat album. "It's totally guitar focused," he says. "No singing, no other instruments. It all originates from a guitarist's point of view." Keola says that much of the inspiration comes from his teaching. This album features more of his solo guitar (eight songs) and more original compositions by Keola (nine) than any other he has previously done. Release date: January 8, 2002
Copyright 2002 Dancing Cat Records

Island Born
Island Born clearly demonstrates Keola's wealth of talent: its songs are musical landscapes that paint vivid pictures of growing up in the islands the Hawaiian way and as part of one of Hawai'i's most talented and celebrated families. His arrangements of five original compositions and nine classic Hawaiian songs display an elegant simplicity. Keola captivates you with his voice, his slack key guitar and carefully placed Hawaiian instrumentation and background vocals. Release date: February 20, 2001
Copyright 2001 'Ohe Records

Kolonahe - From The Gentle Wind
Keola's 1999 Dancing Cat Records release is his second consecutive all instrumental album for the label, and has allowed him to dig deep into the soul of his instruments and come up with music that captures the essence of the slack key tradition, yet is incredibly innovative.
Copyright 1999 Dancing Cat Records

Learn To Play Hawaiian Slack Key Guitar - (instructional book and CD)
Keola Beamer and Mark Nelson have put together this wonderful instruction book. Based on arrangements by Keola and Mark, it is another great means for preserving this most beautiful tradition.
Keola Beamer and Mark Nelson
Copyright 1999 Mel Bay Publications

Listen & Learn: Keola Beamer Hawaiian Slack Key Guitar - (instructional book and CD)
This instructional book/CD set is a marvelous addition to the collection of slack key players of all levels. Keola has chosen five traditional pieces and teaches them in depth. His tunes employ a variety of tunings and techniques that will help you create a distinctive guitar sound.
Copyright 1999 Homespun Tapes

The Art of Hawaiian Slack Key Guitar - (instructional video)
Here's an opportunity to learn the lovely and elegant guitar sounds of Hawai'i. Keola teaches seven traditional tunings and original compositions in the special tunings used in slack key playing.
Copyright 1998 Homespun Video

Mauna Kea - White Mountain Journal
Awarded a Nā Hoku Hanohano Award as the best instrumental release of 1997, it is an intimate portrait: a journal of Keola's memories from growing up at the foot of the most beautiful mountain in the world, Mauna Kea.
Copyright 1997 Dancing Cat Records (8022-38011-2)

The Golden Lehua Tree
Stories and Music from the heart of Hawaii's Beamer family. Narrated by Nona Beamer.
The art of storytelling is revived with these stories, passed down to Auntie Nona Beamer from her childhood days. Keola provides his guitar textures behind Auntie Nona's evocative voice.
Copyright 1996 Starscape Music (SM 96112)

Moe'uhane Kīkā - Tales From The Dream Guitar
This recording is a landmark in the rich recorded history of *kī hō'alu*. Keola explores deeply the intonation and resonances of his guitars in various tunings. Fortunately for slack key aficionados everywhere, his explorations have been recorded for posterity.
Copyright 1995 Dancing Cat Records (08022-38006-2)

Wooden Boat
Keola returns to his acoustic roots for his first Dancing Cat release. Instrumental classics like "No Ke Ano Ahiahi" feature his own arrangements and his flawless fretwork, and features Keola's vocals on several pieces.
Copyright 1994 Dancing Cat Records (08022-38024-2)

Sweet Maui Moon
This recording features Keola in a contemporary-pop format; he is joined by some incredible musicians, such as Ken Wild on bass (from the legendary Island band, "Seawind"), and Brazilian Percussionist Paulinho Da Costa, as well as Keola's all-time favorite singer, Kenny Rankin.
Copyright 1989 Paradise Productions (SCD980)

Honolulu City Lights
The best-selling Hawaiian album of all-time has been re-released with a special cover, celebrating the 20th anniversary of its initial release. Keola's composition "Honolulu City Lights" is one of the most instantly recognizable contemporary Hawaiian compositions.
Keola and Kapono Beamer
Copyright 1978 Paradise Productions (SLP808)

Hawaiian Slack Key Guitar In The Real Old Style
This album is one of the all-time great recordings in the history of Hawaiian music. It is the debut recording of a then 21 year-old Keola Beamer, and is a mixture of solo slack key guitar and vocals, all performed by Keola. He also composed four original songs for the album.
Copyright 1973 The Music of Polynesia (MOP 22000)

On-line Publications:

Slack Key Guitar Lessons With Keola Beamer
You've heard the music - did you ever think about creating it yourself? The Hawaiian Slack Key Guitar is a wonderful platform for expression. And guess what? It's not that hard to learn to play! It's a rewarding and relaxing hobby that could give you years of meaningful interaction with a whole world of rich, beautiful, and somehow still mysterious music. It can take you places that you never imagined. Are you ready for some seriously fun guitar playing? Come join our 'ohana (family)! Go online to www.kbeamer.com.

Intermediate Hawaiian Slack Key Guitar Pieces by Keola Beamer
Original Slack Key Pieces for Intermediate Level Guitarists, includes music, tablature, recordings and study notes.
Go online to www.kbeamer.com.

The following compilation CDs from Dancing Cat Records can be ordered directly from your music retailer.

Hawaiian Slack Key Guitar Masters Collection, Volume 2
Keola Beamer, selected Dancing Cat artists
Released July, 1999
Copyright 1999 Dancing Cat Records

A Winter Solstice Reunion
Keola Beamer, selected Windham Hill artists
Produced by William Coulter
Copyright1998 Windham Hill Records

On A Starry Night
Keola Beamer, selected Windham Hill artists
Produced by Tracy Silverman & Thea Suits-Silverman
Copyright 1997 Windham Hill Records

Summer Solstice
Keola Beamer, selected Windham Hill artists
Produced by Brian Keane
Copyright 1997 Windham Hill Records

Kī Hōʻalu Christmas
Keola Beamer, selected Dancing Cats artists
Copyright 1996 Dancing Cat Records (08022-38006-2)

Hawaiian Slack Key Guitar Masters
Keola Beamer, and releases by Ray Kāne, the late Sonny Chillingworth, Ledward Kaʻapana, Cyril Pahinui, the late Leonard Kwan, among others.
Copyright 1995 Dancing Cat Records

A Winter's Solstice V
Keola Beamer and George Winston, selected Windham Hill artists
Copyright 1995 Windham Hill Records (1934-11174-2)